Zwilling's Dream

Also by Ross Feld

Fiction

Only Shorter

Shapes Mistaken

Years Out

Poetry

Plum Poems

Criticism

Philip Guston

Zwilling's Dream

a novel

Ross Feld

COUNTERPOINT

Library of Congress Cataloging-in-Publication Data
Feld, Ross, 1947–
    Zwilling's dream : a novel / Ross Feld.
      p.   cm.
      ISBN 1-58243-021-7 (alk. paper)
      I. Title.
PS3556.E454Z44   1999
813'.54—dc21   99-34454
                                                     CIP

FIRST PRINTING

Jacket design by Wesley Tanner

Printed in the United States of America on acid-free
paper that meets the American National Standards
Institute Z39-48 Standard.

COUNTERPOINT
P.O. Box 65793
Washington, D.C. 20035-5793

Counterpoint is a member of the Perseus Books Group.

10   9   8   7   6   5   4   3   2   1

For my sons: Aaron and Zachary;

For the original boatmen:
Larry Merrill, Archie Rand, and Josh Rubins;

For Ellen.

Life has no memory.

—*Ralph Waldo Emerson, "Experience"*

Prague Spring

About three times a week right after my wife died, I would drive in the evening across the state line and go directly to one particular Ramada Inn. I would take a room, settle in, turn the air conditioner down, and sit on a short hard chair in front of the writing desk that bridged a pair of dressers beneath a wall mirror.

We all tell ourselves tales, and the story I then was telling myself was that I would use this room to try to write in.

I no longer could do any work at my office at the college, and writing at home was even more out of the question: Home had become historical, the place where the phone call from the hospice would (and did) find me. And even though I knew that there was going to be no such particular call again, still, whenever I stayed home I kept feeling there just might be. Unless it's our very own, we seem to stand bewildered in the shallows of death, which evenly approach us without introduction.

But all I ever really accomplished when I was by myself in the motel room was to square a ream of apricot-colored copy stock that I'd brought along with me as a kind of prop, taking it out of its wrapper and setting it on the desk, hitting and hitting at it with fingers and palms till the stack was long past perfect. This was my primary activity while I waited for one of the two women (here I should call them Alpha and Beta) who—unknown to each other and on different evenings—had arranged to visit me there.

These women were friends of my wife's, coworkers. We'd been together socially a number of times and we had gotten along easily in each other's company. Both of them were down-to-earth, experienced women—one divorced, the other never married—and in both of them sorrow seemed to have been decently managed. Neither one was particularly talky, and in that way they were much like my wife, who wasn't an expressive person either. In fact, my wife was someone from whom, after she'd say "the tape thing" or "that pointy kind" and I'd say back "cassette" or "Phillips-head," I'd get back a look of genuine pity for my immersion in a universe of pointlessly specific names. Sometimes this deeply irritated me—yet in her friends, from a distance, I found the same kind of thing attractive. From them it seemed to convey the suggestion that what we mostly bother to express are our temporary whimwhams anyway.

We had an unusual agreement, myself and these two discreet, mature women. Whenever one of them and I were alone together at the Ramada, I would stay wholly dressed, but she would be minus her blouse and/or her bra, sometimes her skirt or slacks too. The first time the suggestion came out of my mouth, it seemed like a kind of big strange exotic fruit—but in time, little by little, it became possible to explain myself better.

I was asking them to remove some of their clothing because otherwise I wouldn't be able to deal with their colossal sympathy. I somehow couldn't be the only one in the room at a severe disadvantage—and though now even as I write this it comes off as maudlin and self-pitying to me, at the time it was the plainest truth. Both women must have sensed it, too, because almost no negotiation ensued. Independently, they shed their clothes. The heart has its reasons—but Dostoevsky must have come much closer to the truth than Pascal when he concluded that most of the things we do are largely *to see if we in fact can do them.* Alpha and Beta were at the very least suspending their hard-won balances for me, I felt. Also suspending their tastes to some degree. It didn't much matter to them *how* I needed, only *that* I did. These were remarkable concessions, although the little they had to say about it pretty much amounted to the same thing: that it felt "good" to them to be with me like that, near-naked. As Alpha put it, undeterred by the corniness, the one-way exposure simply seemed "life-affirming" to her.

Of course this was the crux: life. Healthy flesh makes a strong argument for wanting to be seen, and their bodies belonged to *live,* hence *lively,* women, not to wasted, freshly dead ones. Alive enough to take the chance of sitting naked before a man they knew not very well as a token of their fellow feeling.

My body, from which all three of us weren't sure exactly what to expect, was a knottier issue. All of us seemed to be under the assumption that my body—like my heart—was shell-shocked, therefore better left hidden under clothes. I thought of myself as so small a sexual threat that, the first night one of the women undressed for me, what came to mind was the famous newspaper picture of the Czech student draping a ragged rope of flowers over the outstretched cannon of an invading Russian tank in the streets of Prague in 1968. Who would I have been in that picture? Not the tank's rigid steel prick. Not the brave, rebellious young Prague ironist with the flowers. Maybe I'd have been the unseen invading Russian gunner inside that tank—the helpless Ivan in no position to order himself forward or to retreat.

But I was never the whole focus anyway. I was merely their instrument, helping Alpha and Beta toward candor as together we enrolled in a ritual of service, in a whacked-out, desperately one-of-a-kind idea.

Yet, in my heart of hearts, I still do know what it was that *I* wanted to see. It wasn't only the women's nakedness, or their tender second skins, their self-consciousness. What I wanted to see was if these two women would *keep* coming to me—and then see how long I could keep my own self-disgust at bay. I wanted a repetitive, multiplying, prospective kind of seeing, something completely different from the defeated eye-resting I had done when looking down through my wife's hospice-room window at the little park below. No matter how flimsy and illusory it may have been, the women and what they had agreed to was the only taste of a future I had.

Beta, who of the two was the closer friend of my wife's, was certainly waiting for me to at least ask her to do something more than sit nearly nude for me. When I continued *not* to ask, the set of her mouth somehow betrayed her, a letdown born of vanity. Even the more casual Alpha seemed to have a framework for it worked out in her head. On one of the first nights (Alpha, interestingly, referred to them as "meetings" but Beta as "visits"), she told me that, even though I hadn't asked, she wanted me to know why it was that she'd *never* make love to me in the motel room. She'd gone to Costa Rica with a man about a year before, she said. But they hadn't had sex while they were there, which left the man very put out. Alpha had explained to him that for her to make love in Costa Rica would have been to render Costa Rica no more remarkable for her than his or her bedroom. From their first hours there, Costa Rica seemed to ask to be kept peculiar and special; Costa Rica didn't *want* them to bring their habitual needs into the middle of it. So no sex. And this motel room, Alpha explained to me, was like another Costa Rica to her.

What we did instead was watch *Jeopardy!* on TV. I would sit on the straight chair by the desk while Alpha or Beta reclined semi-undressed on one of the two beds. Once I recall shutting off the TV right after Beta called out a guess at the question, and before the program's host could verify. But the swagger felt so phony even to me that I quickly switched the set back on.

Jeopardy! soon palled and the TV stayed off. One evening, for something to talk about, Beta asked me if I ever bought individual stocks. She'd begun to buy mutual funds but wished they were more fascinating to her. Did I have a stockbroker? She gave a little laugh: It sounded to her like she was asking me for something illegal, like a bookie. I said it wasn't that far different.

(Money, numbers, the calculus of sex. What husband and wife haven't played john and hooker at least once? Is the term "scoring" at

4

all an accident? How much? How good? How bad? How deep? How amazing? How wonderful? Is it coincidental that the more symbolic or abstract math, algebra, geometry, is first taught to us as kids when we are in pubertal bloom? Is it done to blunt the growing knowledge of the big tally?)

Yet when I recommended to Beta that she stick with mutual funds—less risky, more diversified—she turned furious. It startled me. If being in a motel room with me with her clothes half off wasn't *risk*, she spat, what would I call it exactly? Was I saying that she couldn't be trusted to buy a lousy stock? If she removed her damn *panties* for me, would I then give her the name of a stock? She promptly hauled them off.

This turned out to be the moment that both of us simultaneously acknowledged the idea that Ivan the Gunner inside his armor-bound vehicle of loss could be something of a sneaky danger after all. I did go ahead and give her the name of a stock, something cheap that I myself owned a few hundred shares of but had no great hopes for, a steel company that made specialized trim for automakers, telling her that this stock was probably never going to throw a dividend and very likely had already run up about as high as it was going to go. But she probably would lose no money on it, or at worst very little. As I spoke, I had done my best to look mostly at the wall above her and not below her waist, where she had extraordinary hair.

Beta turned away to slip her panties back on, but she was unmollified. She reminded me in quick order that her teenage son owned a boa constrictor. That she lived divorced in a cavernous house with a too-long driveway on an unlighted street with a seventeen-year-old who usually wasn't there. To stay by herself in a house with a huge snake that occasionally got out of its cage . . . just how constitutionally fearful did I think she was? *You're not the only brave person in the world*, she said—words that were like ashes. Whatever it was that she'd come there for, it wasn't especially for knowledge, but knowledge—knowledge of *me*—was what she'd ended up with, more of it than she ever wanted. Knowledge, in particular, of my aloofness, my stinginess with chaos. *(How could anyone but me be worthy of it?)* And with this unasked-for, unedifying knowledge came the collapse of the whole project for her. Beta continued to dress and five minutes later left. She tried for my sake to at least look partly confused but couldn't quite bring it off, and she never came back after that night.

My other collaborator, Alpha, hung in a little longer. I could tell that it was wearing on her too, though, for she was especially quiet one night and then all of a sudden fell in with a run of self-accusations. What good was she as a friend, my dear dead wife's friend, if she went along with what I'd asked of her here? No friend at all, obviously. God knows what that then left her to be in relation to *me*.

A few moments later something else emerged. She'd had an unsettling experience since the last time we met. She'd been at a pro-choice counteraction, something she occasionally volunteered for on a Saturday, helping monitor the family-planning clinic's doors, ushering people safely in and out. At some point on this previous Saturday morning, she had suddenly found herself on the ground, and as her wits came back to her, her first thought was that she'd been pushed from behind by one of the pro-life pickets, despite the fact that the last time she looked they all seemed to be across the street in an orderly row with their signs, none of them even close to her at all. She hadn't seen or been warned of anyone breaking ranks to charge at her. She maybe just had turned her ankle on a stone. Although nothing hurt her.

She simply had fainted, she realized. She knew she wasn't pregnant (a zero likelihood of that anyway, she said) because she'd gone to see her doctor. It took her half the following week to figure out the faint. "A strong maybe," she said, was that she'd collapsed because she was helping to kill babies.

Telling this story to me was a complex sort of tribute. In our social circle, my wife and I were known to be dissenters about abortion. Our childlessness had something to do with it, although not everything. My wife took a nuanced offense at the fact that women—so much encouraged to feel deededness and entitlement over their otherwise humbling, on-the-fritz bodies—would choose to demonstrate their power upon a potential and helpless *other* body, exercising a right that required the destruction of someone else's rights. And not just any abstract someone's, either, but the rights of one's own fruit, however out-of-season, blemished, or bruised.

I, on the other hand, more blithely threw the onus onto God. (Men, good at blaming, generally aim high.) If a Dostoevsky could recognize that people do things most times just to see if they can do them, didn't God realize that too? Letting human animals bear interiorly, allowing the uterus to be so hidden, seemed to be one of His mess-ups. Secrecy was just too much of a temptation for us. A uterus probably would have been better designed as a transparent or at least semi-opaque sac, attached not inside but *out*. Clothing generally would hide it, but not always, and sometimes we'd have to see what was contained inside. How disastrous it was that we couldn't. In plain sight, who could suction out the fetus? The primacy of the visible is magnificent—and if I didn't think that, how could I have ever been a writer, an artist?

Despite all that, though, I still didn't go over to touch Alpha, to hold her. I stayed in my chair. The moment was charged enough. Instead, what I did was say something to her so thoughtlessly arrogant that it allowed me a glimpse of just how poor a shape I really was in. I said to Alpha that maybe the faint had marked the true beginning of her moral life—and in some beaten-up part of me I even may have meant this as a compliment.

Alpha began to gesture wildly around, at the motel room:

"So what's this then, Joel? *The end of yours?*"

In fact it wasn't, I could have told her. The Ramada ranked high among my moral lapses—but the most perverse and wrong-way foray I'd ever made had come much earlier in my life. I'd once paid a visit, back when I was in college, to a sick uncle of mine. This uncle—Sandor, Uncle Sandor—was a clever, soulful man who'd had enough gumption or luck to come to America well in advance of the rest of the family. Their hesitation had delivered them all to the camps where, except for just a few (like my own parents), they perished. But Sandor, safely over here, went on to lead a good, prosperous, gratefully philanthropic life. He was a metals trader. He had a bit of a lisp. He'd married an American woman who promptly died young, childless, and he had never remarried, though was unfailingly tender toward his house-keeper, a Latvian woman named Simsa whom the grown-ups in the family all appreciated as a de facto wife.

When Sandor's own life began to fail, squeezed shut by esophageal cancer, he tried—very much true to his cheerful character—to partici-pate in his own dying to a degree unheard of in such a clan of victims as mine. Three times a week he went to a sort of faith healer, a fellow émigré, sleek and wealthy like Sandor himself, a Dr. Kurnitzer. (Whose name my parents could only bring themselves to hiss, like that of the *moloch ha'moves,* the angel of death—thus getting it exactly wrong.)

Kurnitzer worked out of an office on Seventy-second Street. In pos-session of a prewar European medical degree he paid the barest attention to, he instead stressed positive thinking and the homeopathic powers of benevolence. His patients were encouraged to do good, simple, unpre-tentious deeds that would give themselves ease as well: reading to the blind, picking up stray paper in public parks, calling the lonely on the phone no matter how discomforting the conversation. He wanted his af-flicted flock to feel that death was a certainty, yes, but it wasn't without its carved-out resting places, platforms breaking up the descent.

In fact, Kurnitzer's idée fixe was that the path was not even all that steep but more like a falling off the end of a world that would stay flatly recognizable till the end. This apparently gave his patients solace. There also happened to be a tonic involved—un-FDA-approved—which was meted out in short green bottles, as well as a couple of group-healing rituals and the like.

Sandor attended Kurnitzer's therapy meticulously. Yet during this visit of mine, at a time when his disease clearly was getting the upper hand, I, his twenty-year-old snot-faced nephew, decided that I must engage my uncle in a decisive colloquy about Dr. Kurnitzer. Assum-ing some never-before-assumed "family responsibility," very full of myself and without much overture, there I was saying:

"Look, Uncle Sandy, you *know* this guy is a crock of shit, don't you?"

Of course it was all in *how* I said it. Even with the nonauthority of a twenty-year-old, I was able to say it in such a way as to insist on Sandor's complicity. *The only way he could prove to me that he really was well—that he had been aided—was for him to say that he was clear-sighted enough to doubt the reality of the help he claimed to have been given.* With directness plus a particular facial expression—the half smile that arises from the inhumane application of intelligence—I roped poor Sandor into weakly saying, "I guess, Joely."

Women of my mother's generation always were mailing recipes to each other. Not necessarily my own mother (who to my knowledge never once shared a recipe; who, being a child of the camps, in fact had to be humiliatingly walked through how to set a formal table by a neighbor in the building), but other mothers. My mother, however, did *receive* plenty of these recipes in the mail, which she would leave on the kitchen counter for a day or two as if needing to ponder what to do with them.

I would glance at them there. Invariably, they ended with the same hopeful exhortation: *Enjoy!* Like so much of life itself, the recipes were dreams—dishes you might never get around to making unless you were desperate for a new idea—but their essential worth never had been the food that could be reconstructed from them. It was all in that final reminder: *Enjoy!*

Enjoy! was something that I, for some reason, because of some fissure in my soul, would not let Sandor append even to his own dwindling life. I refused to let him give it away in a style pleasing to him. It had to be in a style pleasing to *me*.

So it's been a fantasy of mine that on the evening Alpha told me about her faint I in turn would have told her about Uncle Sandor and what I'd done to him, a story I had kept back even from my wife during our marriage. But, as it turned out, even if I was going to, I never would have had the chance to tell it to Alpha that night. As we were talking, I thought I heard the room's doorknob being jiggled, then a voice out in the hallway calling "Maintenance," but unusually quietly.

Hearing it too, Alpha grabbed for her clothes and ran to the bathroom while I went to the peephole in the door.

I saw nothing. But to be safe I rechecked the door's lock and chain. A few seconds later there was the sound and vibration of footsteps running in the hallway outside. By then Alpha had come out of the bathroom fully dressed, shoes and all. Once more there was the clear sound of someone running down the corridor outside. A minute or so later, the phone rang: the front desk, telling us to please stay in our room because apparently there'd been a robbery.

"There is no way in hell . . ." Alpha announced.

And so the great experiment ended in comedy: both of us stepping nervously out into the corridor and hurrying through the exit door to our respective cars. Only later did it occur to me that, had we been seen, *we* might have been taken for the burglars.

I haven't met either woman again since. To this day I haven't run into them even casually. Sometimes I like to imagine that one or both of them will get back in touch with me, though I know better—which is probably why I've written this at all. Writers, when they receive no messages, tend to compose, send, and accept back ones of their own making. The writing of this has been one of those ghost correspondences, no more real a form of communication than is yelling over a cliff to fetch back an echo.

Ivan that I am, I'm left to accept that the most likely reason I wrote this—or anything else, ever—was just so that it could be published.

—◦◦◦—

It took about six weeks in the mid-1970s for a New York writer named Joel Zwilling to write all this. In the end, it bore some resemblance to a story, he felt, he hoped.

At the time he wrote it his wife was not dead. Instead she was in her vital thirties, the mother of a young family, a set of twins, a boy and a girl, with life for all the Zwillings being outwardly good. Joel held two acceptable part-time jobs involved with writing, and the family lived in a roomy apartment in Chelsea. That winter, he had even rented a country house upstate for the whole coming month of August.

At the deepest of levels, though, the story (or whatever Zwilling finally thought of it as: fake essay, seventiesish nonfiction-fiction experiment, hypothetical I'm-so-bad confession, whatever), even if allegorical, was also absolutely true. It expressed a dread and a growing desperation. At twenty-two Zwilling had published a precocious autobiographical first novel, *Less Him*, about growing up in a Holocaust survivor family, a book he'd written when he was just barely nineteen. It had received a lot of attention. But then the two more he impatiently produced and published after that barely were noticed at all. Zwilling came to learn, as many had before him, that neglect doesn't spritz the self into a mist of oblivion. Instead, it makes for a bottleneck in which doing and being are intolerably squeezed.

Harper's quickly and surprisingly bought this story he wrote. And as a summer publication date neared, Zwilling's mind worked overtime, trying to imagine what it was going to be like for his wife actually to read the thing, which up till then he'd held back from her. What could she think?

But just a week before it did run in the magazine, in early August, his wife was killed while driving on an upstate New York country road near the family's rented cottage. A small tractor came loose from its moorings, slipping off the back of a trailer being towed by a pickup truck; in the car immediately behind, Zwilling's wife Rebecca and daughter Alissa—the girl twin, seven—instantly were killed.

For going on twenty years since that day, Zwilling essentially wrote nothing more. Fate's message he took as clear enough. Other than a small piece of pseudonymous criticism, an experiment he regretted, whatever Zwilling did write in a moment of weakness he threw away in shame. He had packed up his surviving child, the boy, and left New York for a teaching job in a small Indiana college. A few years after that, he moved to Cincinnati for an equally undistinguished teaching job. And in Cincinnati, once enough years of not writing had established an impression of control over his life, he finally felt he had been given reentry to the unghastly part of the world. He even married again.

And, ironically, his son started to write—at first comic books, then diaries. The boy dropped out of his Cincinnati high school in the senior year and moved back to New York, where he developed a small fame for himself, living on the Lower East Side and appearing in small self-published broadsheets and then finally larger ones, high-paying music and youth-culture magazines. The boy, Nate, felt securely enough in demand that when he wanted to beat back a drug problem, he left New York and returned to Cincinnati without worry.

And it was back in Cincinnati, out of the blue, that a call came to Nate from a movie producer, telling him that she and her partners were interested in Nate helping them do something with some of his father's old work.

Part One

1

Waiting to hear the weather, Selva made a pot of coffee in the kitch-
enette's Mr. Coffee machine, inserting a sealed packet of coffee
grounds just about the size and shape of a diaphragm. The morning
shore light flooding the room made even the color on the TV thin and
dilute. All the standard luxury updatings were here—the minifridge,
the honor bar, the wall hair dryer—yet there was a sense of half-will-
ingness to them, a sense of concession. The resort was very old-line.
Selva, checking in late last night, observed formally dressed old
women with wooden Florida bags being squired in and out of the
lobby bar by even older men wearing pastel sport jackets, ties, and
white bucks. The few younger women she'd seen this morning from
her balcony had on WASPy sunflower-colored float dresses, or cotton
shorts sets, color-block shirts, stock-color Keds.

She took her china cup of coffee back out through the screen door
to the balcony again. The beach, even from two stories up, had a raw,

placid smell. Brian had insisted they take separate flights here, as though they were equal partners with something irreplaceable to survive each other for. From San Francisco, Selva had gone directly to Miami, in Miami had changed for a plane to Jacksonville, and in Jacksonville boarded one of the resort's jitneys that brought her directly to the island. When she checked in at the desk and asked if Mr. Horkow had arrived, she was told he had. But even up till this very moment he hadn't yet called her room.

Not that she expected him or anyone else to remember—but it was her birthday today.

The ocean's wide thrum following her like noise from someone else's party, Selva went back inside and lay down on the king-sized bed. But she wasn't weary enough to lie still for very long and got up and went into the bathroom to shower.

She questioned whether or not she had heard a knock at the room's front door through the shower's spatter. "Brian?" She turned off the water.

"Room service, ma'am."

Selva had ordered nothing. But it turned out to be a fruit basket: bananas, softball-sized navel oranges, red pears with vinylish coatings, a couple of heavily cellophaned bricks of water biscuits. The card attached read: *This is going to be fun again, I hope.*

She got on the phone. "Yes, this is Ms. Tashjian—in it's I think Seventeen. Can you connect me to Mr. Horkow's room?"

"I certainly can. I'm the concierge, Mark. Everything all right with your room? Need anything?"

"The room's very nice. I'm fine. Thank you for asking."

"I think I did see Mr. Horkow go out onto the beach before. At least towards it. But he may have come back in by now. If you need anything, do call me. Again, my name is Mark."

Who, Selva wondered as Brian's room phone rang and rang, became a concierge at a place like this? Gay? Married? She allowed Brian's phone to go on ringing, since in time it would fetch Mark back, or else the switchboard operator, and she'd be able to leave a message. Yet suddenly the phone in Brian's room was snatched up.

"You're *there?*" she said.

"Who . . . *Sel! Hi!* The sink water was on. I was clipping nose hairs. I don't have a phone in the bathroom—do you? The trip all right?"

"Fruit wasn't required, Brian, but thank you nevertheless. What number room are you in?"

After a moment's hesitation he said, "Thirty-six . . . but I'm in a whole other building!"

"I'm going to walk over, anyway. I want to give you at least half of this fruit. It's much too much for me."

"No no, eat all of it by yourself! Don't you get constipated on planes? Besides, there won't be time—we're meeting in twenty-five minutes downstairs in the main dining room."

"We're meeting when?"

"We have seven-thirty reservations for breakfast."

"Seven-thirty? In twenty-five minutes? I don't believe you! When were you planning to tell me this, exactly? To let me know?"

"Can't you be ready? Oh, sure you can. As soon as I was finished with my nose I was going to call you, I swear. You've been up a while already this morning, haven't you? I know I have. So we'll see each down there. Otherwise it might look . . . "

"Look what?" she said, simply to annoy. "All right, I'll meet you in the dining room."

This long sexual pantomime of theirs. Long ago, they had slept together a single awful time, an incident they'd found so immediately embarrassing that the pains they took not to repeat it established something like the footings of a loyal friendship. The seducer/seduced roles had never snapped down tightly enough. She had been his student, yes, but even back then she was already more than that for them both. Brian didn't know it, but Selva had been expressly asked by his wife to accompany him on this trip and keep a watchful eye. ("He'll be fine," Selva had reassured Shelley Horkow. "Aug'll be there too.") "Big help. I love Aug dearly, but he's a dodo and these are slick operators. They already use him." Shelley then had begun to cry over the phone in frustration: "Brian won't take the medication, that's what bothers me most. If he just was taking what he needs to. When he doesn't, the enthusiasms aren't trustworthy. Someone will take advantage." "Well, I'll be there," Selva had said.)

"Brian?" she said to him now. "This is all going to go well. Only normal nervousness is required. Don't bother getting all lathered up if all you're doing it for is the exercise."

"You are good to me, Sel. I love you."

"And you to me."

Professionally, Brian's staircase had turned into a slide when his last film tanked, his third flop in a row. Selva had been the line producer on *If Means When,* yet had walked away relatively uninjured, able to get subsequent European production work, two English films, one Hungarian-French. Either the industry wasn't yet fully comfortable associating a woman with a certain kind of profound miscalculation or else she'd been just too small a fish.

Brian, on the other hand, had been left seriously stranded. His phone never rang anymore. Even Phil Dreyer, his friend from the old days, who now could have helped him without effort, stayed uncommunicative. Even more than a modest success, Brian needed just plain paying work. His oldest child, a girl of eleven, suffered from cystic fibrosis (though lately she was doing nicely), and there were two additional children as well, a set of three-year-old twins he and Shelley had adopted from Romania a few years back: Jesse and Jeremy, nicknamed Bim and Bom. There was the forever-in-flux house he'd foolishly bought years before in Sonoma, à la Coppola and Lucas, then spent far too much redoing. At the moment, the family subsisted solely on the earnings from the practical books Shelley compiled and wrote, handbooks filled with specific do-this do-that information about cystic fibrosis and foreign adoptions. Her next one, she once told Selva, would probably be about bipolar disorders, the diagnosis pinned on Brian but strenuously resisted by him. The medicines he was given for manic depression were ignored, mocked, tossed away.

Brian and the others were already seated at a pink-clothed round table by the time Selva got down to the dining room. She and everyone else was dressed in resort wear, but Brian had on a crisply pressed suit, out the sleeves of which he shot his cuffs over and over. Jay Loftspring, the attorney for the Warshaw Foundation, an extremely tall thin squinting man, sat to the left of Aug Jimmerson. Aug, as usual, looked splendid, almost godly. To his right was his wife, Paulette.

As Selva took her seat at the table, Brian was in the midst of rhapsodizing about a well-mannered old Southern grandee he'd stood next to at the urinals in the men's room off the lobby. While zipping up, the gent had asked Brian how he was doing. When Brian asked back the same, the old man had replied: "*Think I am in fact just going to about make it. With some help.*"

"Now I wish," Brian marveled, "you all could have seen the *quality* of his smile. Why can't *everyone* think so optimistically? Of course, the question always remains whether or not a smart person *can* be an optimist, which I still don't know. I mean, if you have any kind of imagination, is it possible *to be* happy? On the other hand, you have to account for this old Georgia gent in the can, walking around with a completely and perfectly serviceable philosophy. Makes you want to be just like him, doesn't it?"

Loftspring the lawyer was holding his spoon filled with fruit salad higher up into the light. "What do you suppose this red color is? It's hard to tell. If it's raspberry, that's minimally okay, but if it's strawberry . . . I can be allergic." He pushed the whole bowl away, rescuing one single last cube of honeydew and popping it into his mouth.

Paulette Jimmerson began to laugh. "Okay, tell them. Oh, go ahead," she permitted her husband. "You know you want to. Just tell them."

Aug announced with solemn pleasure: "'Lette here's discovered she's allergic to her darlin'."

"To *you?*" Brian cackled.

"To her cat. To Richard."

"To my *baby!* Named after Richard Pryor, and I ain't *never* giving *him* up. August here maybe, but Richard I die with, with my nose in his coat!"

"Love's what kills you," Brian said. "My motto as well."

"Since when?" Selva said, fearful for the moment that everything might dissolve right here before them at the table. Brian's nervousness had started to enervate her, and jet lag pushed down at her shoulders like a weight. Selva sat up straighter in her chair.

"From this moment on. From now on it is."

Waffles, omelets, muffins, and cereals were being brought to the table. Brian had ordered only juice and toast, and for him the food's arrival seemed to be a signal to get serious. Out came the contents of his twenty-five-year-old briefcase. He scanned his notes once and twice and then came bursting forth from the unprepared-for middle of his thoughts, as if he'd already begun his pitch privately to himself:

"Memories that become genetic, for instance. I'm not into high concept," he assured a confused-looking Loftspring, "nor would we necessarily want to do a *Marathon Man Meets Sophie's Choice* here. But there *could* be a slight cyber-angle. You know, camp experimentation, primitive attempts at implantation."

Selva was all ready to step in and put things back aright when another guest in the dining room, a prematurely white-haired man with a forehead like a reddened wall, fortunately appeared at their table, dispatched by his own party, he explained, to determine "whether or not this *really* is Aug Jimmerson." Aug provided the necessary autographs; Brian caught both the table's mood and Selva's pointed look and quietly put away his notes.

Saved by Aug once more. In a sense, Brian's career had originated with Aug Jimmerson. Back when he was still a New York college instructor, Brian had written a magazine article about Aug. He then expanded it into an indiscreet book about celebrity, about hanging out with such a celestial football and baseball figure in a fast drugs/gambling/hipster circle. Brian next had fashioned a screenplay from that book, which in turn brought him more script work, which ultimately allowed him a chance to act and direct. In Los Angeles in the late seventies, he had even shared an apartment with Phil Dreyer, before the actor had become a worldwide name. Directing in turn landed Brian a part-time faculty job at Cal Arts, where Selva had been in one of his classes.

Of course, Aug himself had something of a genuine talent for being saved. Gates Warshaw, a corporate buccaneer, a wily old crook, had been forced some years back to leave Fort Lauderdale for Tel Aviv just ahead of the SEC. But before he fled, he had more or less adopted Aug, pulling him out from under a mound of paternity suits and failed restaurants and bad product-endorsement-partnerships. Aug's face, in his role as local-markets vice-president for a Warshaw-owned soft-drink manufacturer, grinned down with faked pleasure over a can of F3 sports drink from the billboards in every southeastern and Sunbelt ghetto. About a month ago, after noticing a corporate memo touting the newly established Warshaw Holocaust Studies Foundation and its planned arts tie-in with novels and TV and film, Aug had immediately called Brian. Brian, sounding hysterical and redeemed at the same time, in turn had called Selva, locating her in London.

"Sel! This lawyer wants to know if I have any ideas. Do I? Do I have any ideas?"

Because she had lucky access to the Lexis-Nexis database, she was able to fax over a large load of trolled-for stuff to Brian in Sebastapol. Under the category of *Holocaust Fiction,* he had rediscovered Joel Zwilling, someone he'd known casually when both of them were abortive medical students decades ago. Zwilling's out-of-print first novel had shown up leading a surprisingly short sublist: *Fiction: Holocaust: Survivor's Children.*

This poor Joel Zwilling, Selva more than once subsequently thought. It wasn't so easy to drop yourself in a trash can and then try to hurry away. People like us may come along even years later and fish you out. Rebuffing Brian's initial call inquiring after the rights, Zwilling had said he had no interest in his old book or anything else he'd ever written being turned into a movie. Brian, who was easily checked, had next turned to Selva, who'd had the idea of trying to go through Zwilling's son instead. The son was a writer too, she had discovered from a small amount of legwork. When on the phone she'd asked him when he himself began to write, Nate Zwilling had responded: "I don't know, maybe at about fifteen"—then adding with a startling grimness: "It was in self-defense."

The reason she'd been in London (and this was something Brian still didn't know about, that she'd been putting off telling him) was in order for Peter Swainten, the Channel Four guy over there, to take her out to lunch, Mumm and sevruga, and tell her that he'd been given a go-ahead to offer her free rein on multiple documentaries, films that could be shot in America and that Channel Four hoped would be different, personal, quirky. While in London, Selva had also gone to see one last-shot doctor, a Harley Street gynecologist, the best in the field, she understood, and a very lovely doctor at that: Dr. Coffman. To her great embarrassment, it was a fourth opinion she was seeking. Yet Coffman, a peppy young grandfather, had been wonderful and made her feel like anything but a hysteric. She had provided him her list: the two ablative surgeries, the medications, the no-dairy diet, the castor-oil packs, the acupuncture with Chinese herbs. "Intercourse painful?" he had asked. When she replied, "Not physically," he had smiled. Well, he said gently, surely she knew that her body was telling her, by such frequent pain and bleeding, that these overgrowths must soon be made to go. Regrettably, endometriosis as severe and disseminated as hers "cried out," he said, for hysterectomy and hysterectomy only. Her HMO doctors in California had legitimately gentled her along, but now they were right to recommend surgery. "And this, mind you, is a Brit talking—we're less knife-happy as a rule." Were he the one doing the surgery, Coffman said, he would at least consider a vaginal hysterectomy, although he wouldn't be able to make any promises. Never having birthed a child, she might not be wide enough. Yet it remained his first choice of approach. The hormonal blitzkrieg after surgical menopause was somewhat softened when the vaginal route was taken. "Until then, Ms. Tashjian, I want you to devise ways not to hurt quite as *much*. Stress is your number-one enemy. Easier cursed than vanquished, I realize, but still." Selva, in love with his calm and fatherly ways, swore to Coffman and to herself that she'd call back within the week to schedule the surgery with him. Instead, she flew home to California never having called.

After breakfast, Selva and Paulette Jimmerson had nine-thirty reservations at the spa. In the sauna, Selva admired the frank shelf of

Paulette's big behind. Selva's late father, Varak, a sculptor and restorer of public monuments, would have swooned with pleasure to behold Paulette's light-coffee bulk. Afterward, in the locker room once they'd showered, Paulette opened her workout bag to offer Selva any of six different wrapped chocolate bars and as many kinds of packaged cookies. All of it came from what she called her glove-compartment stock: "I *do* love my car!"

But Selva had to leave for the morning's golf. Never intending to play herself, she had promised to drive Brian's cart for him, to root him on during the part of the trip he'd been dreading most of all. He had even desperately practiced at home in California for it. Yet for Selva the morning was nothing but pleasant. The cart path of the golf course at one point led to a stone heap of a ruined embattlement set right in the middle of one fairway. There were small creeks veining their way down to the sea and forming small estuaries next to some of the greens. Polyp-like marshes were everywhere.

Brian wasn't even remotely able to appreciate any of it. All his hacking shots were tending right; eventually, he even seemed to walk with a rightward list, the effect probably of the whiter-than-white spiked golf shoes he was wearing for the first time. He began to overcompensate by shooting too far left, trying to get his foul-ups to balance each other. In the end, he basically was shoelacing the course. "Shit!" he screamed on the sixth hole. At the eleventh, he ditched Selva as bad luck and demanded to ride instead with Aug.

So Loftspring the lawyer and Selva bumped down a slope together toward the twelfth hole's tee. Where in San Francisco did she live? After Selva told him, the lawyer said he thought that was "truly neat. A houseboat docked in Sausalito—my wife would love that."

"Then come visit me sometime, the two of you." It was a relief for Selva not to have to bear any flirting. These intensely mothered-and-wived men rarely strayed, for fear of being lost. When his hyper phases weren't upon him, Brian was largely the same way, something his wife Shelley knew deep down.

Peter Swainten, in London, transparently *not* a mothered man, was married too—though Selva surely would sleep with him eventually, resigned as she was to a life of married lovers, a knowledge that took up next to no room in her mind. She had never truly or deeply or finally wanted a man of her exclusive own. Or hardly ever. What she wanted perhaps was a man to wholly have *her,* somewhat in the manner that her father had had her—as a cherishment, a responsibility, a worry. Married men were thus for her by now a decided taste. Their hesitancies and compunctions, their contexts around them like a suit of mail. No sudden surprising lurches or blows.

"Brian's very excited by this Zwilling project," she told Loftspring the lawyer.

"That's good, isn't it?" he smiled. "The PGA tour doesn't look like the way he'll go." Immediately he was unsure of the propriety of his joke. "Let me ask you this, though. That cyberpunk implantation thing he was talking about over breakfast. I'm afraid there he lost me."

Selva was easily airy. "Oh, that's just Brian. He makes a wild film in his head first, then filters it out, and finally discards it completely. What's left is the real movie. In the beginning he's going to say a lot of things that sound strange."

"You'll be the producer, I'm assuming, Ms. Tashjian? I'm right about that, aren't I?"

"Selva, please."

"Selva. Hi. I'm Jay." He gave an uncomfortable laugh: "But you knew that."

They'd been sitting at a fork in the path for what seemed like an age and finally Loftspring directed Selva to angle the cart up and right toward the next tee. Walking to the post that held the ball washer, the lawyer inserted his ball and worked the brush-and-canister mechanism vigorously up and down. Flecks of soap foam fell to the grass. "Actually, to tell you the truth, Mr. Horkow's being flexible and relaxed is great with us. We're in no rush on our end."

"What kind of frame is it that you're looking at? Till rough cut, I mean."

Loftspring teed up his ball, banged his drive, and walked back to the cart. "Your first check should be there already, at the address you gave us in California. When you go back I'm sure you'll find it. And I want you yourself to let us always know if we've underestimated at all. Please remember that. We have to know *all* your needs. It's great for Brian Horkow *and* for us that you'll be the contact person."

"Well, I'm delighted to be involved."

"I'm going to have to catch a flight out of Savannah before dinner unfortunately—a meeting in Dallas tomorrow morning, something that just came up—so it's fantastic that we can do some of our first talking now. For instance, I want to leave knowing you're completely up to speed and comfortable with how we see our support structured. So, for instance, you ask about time. The Foundation sees your film in a frame of twelve to eighteen months minimum. Remember, of course, we're new to this—if two years, give or take, isn't enough to get you ready for production, we can go longer, however long it takes."

"*Pre*production two years?"

"Too little?"

"We'd be a lot *more* than ready! Two years, we'd have a film in the can. Why are you envisioning such an extended setup period? Is it to bring in other backing?"

Loftspring looked at her blankly. "No, it'll be all us. The money's wholly earmarked already. I think yesterday a first check was cut and sent, about four hundred thousand, give or take."

Selva hoped that her voice was going to sound at least minimally controlled and even. "Well, that's great, that's wonderful."

They had not even submitted a treatment, a script!

"We'd like you to see that our support is understood as a *continuing* thing. We're proud to be helping this to be developed slowly. We'll talk it up as such, too. Which reminds me: We'd be who's always doing that, the talking it up. Publicity would always come from us, not from your end. No publicists."

It was a done deal, Selva realized—even if one that was cradled within an agenda she didn't completely appreciate yet. There had been no reason to fly out here in the first place.

"Well, that's hardly a producer's favorite part of the job anyway, Jay."

"Then good."

Suddenly Selva was afraid she might accidentally knock something over, something fragile. "You know, I'm wondering if even though he fired me as his caddy I shouldn't maybe show my face back there for a minute and see how Brian's doing."

"Do you want to guess?" said the attorney.

Selva gave a phony's laugh. "Do you mind driving yourself a little while?"

The lawyer looked at his watch. "I should finish up anyway and go back and make some calls from my room before the afternoon. I'm delighted we had a chance to talk."

Aug was standing beside the green of the previous hole. He'd already finished his own putting and now just was waiting for Brian to work his way there. "Our friend has had better days."

"I would disagree." Selva affectionately squeezed his massive upper arm. "I just had a terrific talk with Jay."

"All's cool?"

"We love you, Aug," and she hugged him. "It's cool because of you. Go ahead and catch up with Jay and play some actual golf. I'll stay here."

Anxious despair had sealed Brian's face, for he had lost his ball in deep rough beneath a stand of pines. Even four hundred thousand dollars would not gentle his panic right now. Selva stood near, self-consciously silent, the thought occurring to her—a guardian thought that stretched out from her like a pair of hands left and right—to not tell Brian at all yet. At home he'd get the check, which would be reality enough for now. Did he really need to know about a two-year setup? Brian, finally spotting his ball, yanked it from a tangle of moss and low ivy. "Shit!"—and he promptly dropped the ball at his feet in overgrowth almost as bad.

"Can't you hit it from someplace better?"

"That's cheating!"

Selva said, "Can I maybe try to hit one? No one's watching. Just one swing?"

To her surprise, Brian handed her the club. Yet two seconds later he was shrieking at her: "Grip! Grip! Look at your grip!"

"I am gripping it. What's this club called? What number?"

"That's not a grip! That's no grip. That's just *holding* it."

"Hush. This way's comfortable for me."

Selva hauled the club back across her shoulders and brought it down so confidently that it came as a literal shock to her when the club head hit the ground before touching the ball. A muddy thunking impact squeegeed through her body.

"See? Give it to me! You see? *Give it back to me.*"

Aug and Loftspring would not have cared if he'd skipped the second eighteen holes for the afternoon (if the lawyer even would still be around), yet none of Selva's attempts to convince Brian came to anything. His hurt pride left him deaf. He even chose to skip lunch in favor of repairing to his room for a nap before his additional hours on the cross of golf.

Selva herself wasn't especially hungry and decided to try out the beach.

It was empty for a hundred yards in each direction. As soon as she chose a spot on which to lay her towel, a young black man in a wallah-like uniform was before her, offering a beach chair and umbrella.

Selva looked at the sea, the shoreline, tasted the dry heated wind. A pale blond woman with two school-age children, a boy and a girl, eventually came and set up camp twenty yards away. The young mother wore a tunic swimsuit complete with little skirt. Yet there was nothing modest about the way she sprawled backward on her beach blanket as soon as the kids were off to dig in wetter sand. With the sort of surrender Selva wished she herself could make, the woman absolutely flung herself open to the sun.

Unobserved, Selva studied the woman, whose top half was neatly nipped, waist and breasts, tiny face, pertly bobbed hair, but whose bottom half was a Maillol sculpture, solid thighs that looked as though they'd be capable of reabsorbing those children if called on. Selva glanced down at her own thighs. Aesthetically finer, they were infinitely more useless; architectural detail, not structural support. In any sphere that truly mattered, Selva's body was never going to be *enough*.

She packed up and left the beach.

With Loftspring gone and the golf only a bad memory, dinner was merry, just the four of them. Selva even briefly considered ordering a birthday dessert for the table but at the last moment vetoed the idea, not wanting the attendant fuss. Brian decompressed by drinking too much wine, with Aug happily along for the ride. Selva and Paulette finally left the men to their jokes and nostalgia and Hennessy.

In her room, Selva changed into her shortie nightgown. She said a silent prayer of thanks for a whole day—such an important if oddly hollow one—without any cramps or bleeding. She thought about phoning Shelley Horkow but decided not to. Finally she watched television for a while and dozed, only to startle awake an hour later and shut off the set.

Later in the night she awoke once more, but this time into a darkness so deep that the strange room seemed to hold a kind of transient intelligence inside it, frank and voluptuous and beckoning. It stirred her. She found herself stretching into it, holding one bare arm straight out and allowing the fingers of her other hand to explore downward along the forearm hairs, into the crook of the elbow, her finger pads slowly rolling left and right, making deeper and lesser channels, varying the pressure but never going any lower than her arm.

She would get on with the more focused business of making love to herself in a moment, but for right now this was enough. To be smoothing herself out like this in the dark, with the surf sounds outside, made her feel as though she was slowly, minutely describing herself to herself, as if in anticipation of something . . .

Of Dr. Coffman?

Selva dropped her hands, flipping onto her belly, horrified, stuffing her face down into the pillow.

But she didn't cry. Crying would not soothe the raw patch of need and lack that her arm and fingers had been exploring, her fantasy of a rich, replete body. Getting onto her back again, she switched on the bedside light and opened one of the books she'd brought with her, a fat scholarly edition of the essays of Montaigne. In her girlhood house, her father kept shelved only European classics; his daughter, in homage, still was catching up.

So for an hour, inside her life as it was and as it was going to remain (minus an internal organ or two), she grimly read Montaigne, that old realist-of-all-realists, and tried not to have a single hope.

2

Over the Rockies, in Seat 22A, with his son five rows up on the aisle,
Joel Zwilling was bound from Cincinnati to San Francisco. Nate was
used to traveling and was more savvy about flight arrangements, so he
had been the one who booked the tickets and approved the seats. Because the plane was full, single seats perhaps were all that was left. But
Zwilling remained slightly curious to see what kind of seating arrangements Nate had made for the trip back.

Separation probably was for the best now anyway, he felt. Father
and son needed the time to settle and prepare themselves. The trip was
heavily fraught.

So far Nate had done the bulk of the dealings with Brian Horkow,
or more exactly with his collaborator, a woman with an odd name. It
had been explained to Nate that the movie they had in mind would
be "built around" his father's work, particularly that old first novel.
But anything else Nate thought might be appropriate would be welcomed too. That it was wholly a ruse was something their vagueness

only proved—Nate was the one they really wanted, Nate who was young and in the know, whom you read in the youthful magazines.

Such a different breed of cat, his son. When Zwilling compared how he and Nate approached being a writer, the two different styles of unsatisfiableness were so striking. Zwilling's own approach (back when he still considered himself a writer, before he had taken some measure of control of himself and banished the pointless ordeal of it all) was the classical one: the constant need to shave distinctions down ever more finely, to fasten the unfastenable, the attendant botheration, the hunger to fiddle forever, to blahblahblah. To "postmodern" Nate, on the other hand, all this twitzkering with words, turning them up here and down there, right and left—all of it amounted to nothing more than neurotic behavior, an overselling, a cloud of dust raised to hide the real story. Zwilling was accustomed to being left perpetually hollow by his own productions, while Nate found it impossible to be engaged in the whole process, period, even before it yielded. Instead, he pretended to egolessness: His first small fame had come from second-person, androgynous diaries he wrote jointly with his girlfriend, Polly. Published in their own low-rent sheet, a "zine" with a very limited circulation, the diaries were signed with the cutesy pen name Iff-Udair, the gimmick being that you had to guess whether Nate in fact had written Polly's entries or vice versa.

Polly, Nate's live-in girlfriend still, did *not* seem to be a hot property anymore, at least not as far as the film was concerned. Horkow hadn't asked her out to California. In pique, she hadn't seen Nate off at the airport this morning, and Nate had implied to his father that for some weeks now he'd been given the cold shoulder by her. It was genuinely too bad that Polly was being left behind in Cincinnati. She could have served as a deflector at the very least, a spellbreaker. The clothes she wore were difficult for the eye to get around. Her shirts, buttoned to the collar's limit, could make her look as though she had no breasts at all; then, if you caught her from a slightly different angle, she seemed buxom enough to burst the material. She favored tight black pants worn too short, above her ankle bones, and high-topped black sneakers, sometimes bomber boots. She kept her reddish-brown hair alarmingly short and sometimes highlighted it with lurid tints. Despite this, she rarely looked punky or snarly—but essentialized, like a nun who'd recently shed her habit. The look was just different enough to be appealing. Sometimes the editors of the slicker alternate-scene magazines she and Nate eventually came to write for liked to have pictures of them both on the contributors page.

Zwilling couldn't imagine—and certainly he couldn't ask—how their *you be me and I be you* collaborations worked exactly. Nate and Polly had fled together from Cincinnati's Walnut Hills High School to New York. ("Back *home*," Nathan used to call it.) There, on the Lower East Side, they and another Walnut Hills alumnus managed to make a small mark for themselves as a reverse-cool Ohio contingent. Nate for a time was in an underground rock band, The Tha, which was about when he also unfortunately embarked upon a first romance with amphetamines. But what Zwilling came away with mostly from the Iff-Udair diaries and their whole downtown *demimonde*—musicians, artists, stand-up comics, computer-aided-design geniuses, second-generation quasifeminists, cokeheads, saintly boys from Alabama seeking stardom with new wave country music, chefs, jugglers—was a sense of boys and girls touchingly and sadly wanting to be each other more than themselves.

Inside Zwilling's carry-on bag in the airplane bin above his head was a manila envelope containing his own set of clips taken from the Nate-and-Polly diaries; how good Nate would be at blowing his own horn for the movie folk his father wasn't sure. But last night, assembling the clips, Zwilling had managed to stumble over a few exquisitely painful ones in which he himself figured:

> Big fight, much anger, so fly home to Cincy because you don't want to undo all the work in beating back the crystal. (Yet doing Stoli, hard, instead.) Pops you find in one of his self-pity periods. Took you for a drive over to Newport, to a garage building near Monmouth Street that was for rent. Parks the car. What kind of driving school did you think that would make? Seventy-five dollars a month. Room for two

compact cars in back. A room large enough to show the required training movie on, plus enough space for a few driving
simulators. When they drop out of high school, they drop
out of Driver's Ed too, remember.

As if these Jethros, you said, half bombed, really think they
need a license in the first place.

Which made him nod, say that was true, and well, okay, forget it.

Zwilling knew, sickeningly, that Nate had written that particular one
himself. A father passed down to his son no legacy worse than a lack of
initiative.

"Spoke with that movie director today, the guy you blew off." This
was how Nate had first reported to his father his initial conversation
with Horkow. Actually, a few hours before, Zwilling had heard the
same news from his wife, Barbara, whom Nate had called first. "Isn't
it wonderful?" Barbara had said to her husband.

It had put Zwilling in a bad spot. He'd never mentioned to his wife
his own phone conversation with Brian Horkow, someone who
claimed to know Zwilling from way back long ago, med-school days.
Yet of course it was Barbara whom Nate would have told first. He relaxed around Barbara, who for him was a kind of demilitarized zone,
a Switzerland, a Cincinnati of stepmotherly domesticity. They had
lunch together downtown near her office every few weeks.

So Zwilling, never much of a moviegoer, had dutifully gone down
to the main library in order to read in old *Times* and *Newsweek*s about
Brian Horkow, who'd made a small Hollywood name for himself with
writing and directing but seemed to be known as much for his sports-
star and famous-actor friends like Phil Dreyer as for his own original
work. "He loves your work, Pops," Nate had told his father on the
phone. "Really is into it. He says he misses the sort of New York that
was in your books."

"Does he?" Zwilling half waited for his son to ask what kind of New
York that had been, especially since Bohemians, at least as Zwilling
and perhaps this Horkow fellow had known them—or even had

been—were creatures passed and gone. Bohemia had metamorphosed into something else. How else to explain the equable way in which Nate and Polly had returned from New York to Cincinnati? Of course, Zwilling was relieved that it might mean Nate was done with the methedrine. But still he found the kids' return dispiriting. You could take the boy out of Cincinnati . . . but apparently you also *couldn't* take the boy out of Cincinnati.

Why really *had* they returned? Certainly it wasn't to be near him. Zwilling and Barbara lived childless in an overly large old house on the Kentucky side, in Fort Thomas, a house that looked down over the Ohio like a piece of bourgeois privet. Barbara was an intellectual-property attorney and Zwilling was . . . was a what? What example of freedom did he provide his son?

Admittedly, it was a different Lower East Side that Nate had originally fled to and then run from. Chic had been introduced (even to some degree by Nate and Polly themselves, and their broadside sheet, *Hick Hoc*), but when Zwilling was seventeen and leaving Brooklyn and the apartment of his quaking fearful survivor parents to live on East Eleventh Street, chic was not yet in evidence. Zwilling had camped in an apartment containing an upright piano, a bed, a kitchen table, and no chairs. The slum building was owned and managed by a Hasidic property company that with a straight face called itself Phantom Realty. From eight to nine o'clock each evening, heat was provided by a whisper of the radiator, and of those days Zwilling chiefly recalled tea: hot tea, tea against the unforgiving cold of the winter, tea in homage to the very good bread baked in almost every Italian or Ukrainian bakery along Avenue A. Tea as an antidote to the bourbon of the bars, the very good bars. Bohemian booze, Bohemian bread, Bohemian tea.

Did Nate drink tea? Zwilling couldn't say he'd ever noticed, who now himself only drank coffee, needing at this time in his life an opponent more than an ally. Writing used to be his opponent, but now it was only coffee, which made him so jumpy and sick that he couldn't do without it. Whenever he crossed the river to use the university's library, he liked to head first for an arch little neighborhood place that made a powerful, druggy cup.

It was there, at a table of the coffee place, that Zwilling was accustomed to seeing one particular couple. Sometimes he saw them out on the streets as well, where they showed off a great grizzly vigor to their walking. The man, potbellied and bearded, was nightmarishly intense; the wife or girlfriend, a blonde with rosaceous patches on her cheeks and brow, was mousy. Usually they were dressed in catalogue gear: ragg hats for the autumn, sometimes even knickers, large visored sun hats for the hot months. And every single time Zwilling saw this pair, only the man seemed to be talking.

Talking didn't quite capture it. *Haranguing* was closer. Yet the woman didn't look strained by this at all. Her man's self-absorbed nattering may have been the most solid substance of her day, which she received and received until he was tripped into sleep. Even *then* he probably was still talking for her, his very thoughts making a noise. In their perfectly aligned madnesses, Zwilling was sure they were the very happiest couple he knew of.

In the past few days, preparing for this trip, whenever Zwilling thought about Brian Horkow, he pictured just this striding couple—half expecting Horkow to be just like the bearded man: one of these rapacious mental Huns, spewing and vacuuming, spouting at the same time he slurped.

Zwilling had been staring at the same ad for a sales communication course in the in-flight magazine for ten minutes now.

What kind of foolishness were they flying into, truly? Was Horkow going to be one of those storied sadistic types who'd haul their midwestern asses out there in order to dismiss them empty-handed? According to Nate, Horkow had made mention of his father's long literary silence: "Said he thought it was interesting. You start writing, stop writing, and who can know if you've started again?" So did he maybe also then wonder if Zwilling hadn't fabricated a writer-son, written all Iff-Udair's stuff himself? Maybe he just wanted to see Nate, to see what his nose looked like compared to his father's. The whole trip might be Horkow's own expensive prank.

Yet here on the plane they were. Within a week of the first overtures, Zwilling knew that he'd have no real choice but to go along, that he certainly would let Horkow have an option on anything he wanted, however personally disgusting, as long as he agreed that Nate somehow would be involved in writing the screenplay, the treatment, the outline, the memo, whatever the hell. Let him ship me home but keep Nate there a day or two more, treat him like an independent agent, kick around an idea or two, and only then pack him off for home after his ego had been stuffed-up enough so that he didn't immediately feel the razor.

Mainly, mainly, let Nate be paid a frivolously large amount of money.

> Pops loves hipness in any kind of package, overvalues it. It's got to be particularly esoteric, too—of no interest to the unwashed, only to "the circumcised," as he calls it.
>
> Is called Pops by you, by request, since you're two years old. Louis Armstrong (Louisss, not Louie) therefore was honored at the same time.

Zwilling's seatmate had already been in his seat when the plane, flying originally from New York, took on its Cincinnati passengers. Once the death-defying part of the takeoff was over and they were again leveled out, the man made an unusually formal introduction. He told Zwilling his name was Vovoda and that he was a consular official with the Polish legation at the UN. (The ex-writer already had half guessed the man to be a Pole: the same kind of brutal eyebrows as the poet Milosz's, and skin the color of veal.) When asked by the Pole where he was going, Zwilling—feeling surprisingly expansive—provided a sketch of his mission to the coast. Maybe it had to do with the man being a European, thus experienced in compromise.

Vovoda, hearing the outline of the tale, immediately seemed to find the ex-writer adorable, the half-dismayed, half-delighted look in his eyes saying, *Oh, you will be fucked over good!* "I would like to be there with you. Too bad there is not some way." As if some Old World assistance might be required in the matter, he urged upon Zwilling the Palo Alto number of a friend through whom a message at least could be left for him. "My situation is also quite delicate. As a writer, you will be interested. I am going to see a woman in Reno. From San Francisco I will be renting a car."

"Can't you fly directly there, to Reno?"—Zwilling only then, an instant too late, picking up on the intrigue that mention of the two separate places, Reno and San Francisco, implied. "This woman's married?" Zwilling ventured.

The Pole shook his head with the weight of it all. "From Chicago originally. A cousin. The husband's a very fine chef, and he was offered a half partnership in the best restaurant in Nevada. She, though, is totally lost there."

"And now something's coming to a head between you two?" The idiom here was too rich for the Pole and he looked at Zwilling blankly. "It's getting serious?"

Zwilling, who had himself so long depended on luck (or the total absence of it) for romance, felt unworthy sitting beside a man who would possibly risk his diplomatic status by dallying with a married cousin. If nothing else, maybe there'd be a woman on Horkow's moviemaking staff who'd take Zwilling back to the airport, pull the car off the road, and take his cheeks in her hands to kiss his mouth, his eyes, his chin, the old joke about the Hollywood ingenue so dumb she fucked the writer.

"*Always* it's been serious," said Vovoda. "I only meet her this last Christmas—in Chicago." The burr of the man's accent, its slow porous edge, seemed designed for secrets half revealed, gestured to. "It's . . . he's . . . you understand—a *distant* cousin. You are married— I see your ring . . ."

Yet soon the conversation stalled, for where to go from there? Zwilling looked unseeing through his in-flight magazine, while out of a blue canvas briefcase the Pole removed a square black case not immediately identifiable. Then a thin medallion of dazzling silver appeared—and the man slipped the compact disk into the portable player. He started to settle wire-thin earphones atop the crown of his head.

"That's, over there, my son," Zwilling pointed. "His name's Nathan."

The Pole only nodded. Under the earphones, he was within his music already, and for all he knew Zwilling could have been commenting on how the other side of the aisle was getting the worst of the corrosive high-altitude sunlight. He was hearing not a word Zwilling said. For all his lust and drive, he was yet another of those commonly bound souls who couldn't manage to do two things at a time. Ditching the insipid in-flight magazine, Zwilling found himself straining to hear what ghost sounds were leaking from the man's button earphones.

3

Couldn't all this wait, Brian pleaded to his scolding wife, until he'd gotten himself halfway ready here, his briefcase, all the notes that he needed in it, the copies of the Zwillings' writings, the father's as well as the son's, while at the same time he made sure that Tess was properly set up with *her* paraphernalia? Her tote bag, for instance—was it at all ready? Or her Alf doll? Book? Markers? Change of clothes in the event (though he always prayed not) . . . ?

Things had to be *done,* in other words.

"When'll Marta be here?" Brian asked the air—as though he were the only one dependent on the too-casual housekeeper; as though he were accusing Shelley (which he was) of bringing up this whole sugar business now only so that she could be exempted from helping him and Tess get out the door to their onerous destination in time.

Yet Shelley, with the patience given the queen of a house, simply continued on: "When I was picking Tessa up the other day at their house, Sari's mother told me that until age five—*five!*—she and her brothers thought crackers were cookies."

"Oh, that I doubt," said Brian. "I don't believe it. I smell myth. They were raised in airtight bubbles?"

"No one ever said or demonstrated the contrary to them. Despite the fact that their father even worked in the Sunshine plant."

"Don't ever invite this woman over here."

"By the time they *did* catch on, and she and her brothers had figured out that what was salty was not in fact sweet, at least then they'd had a good five years of no sugar. No metabolic insults. Teeth okay."

Shelley's palms, placed upon the back posts of one of the Shaker chairs, pressed down hard. "Think, Brian. *Think* for a moment. You can spare just one thought. You cannot be so cavalier with these kids. You can hate the trappings that go with health foods and health consciousness, but you cannot just stand there and deny that eating crap is simply terrible for children. Even if you *can* deny it"—on the fly she'd caught the beginnings of a smirk from him—"you'll never never make *me* believe that crap-eating is good for our kids."

Out of the corner of his eye, Brian had noticed something his wife hadn't. "Bimmy, no, stop that! Shelley, will you please look what he's doing! We're having a nice *theoretical* discussion here while he's seeing if he can break the refrigerator door. Don't do that, sweet boy!"

He picked Bim up and handed him to Shelley, just at the moment when Bommy, too, slid into the room on his vinyl pajama feet—sleepy but hardly about to miss out on any trouble his brother had been lucky enough to cause.

"I have to be out of here in ten minutes tops—and you're off on, to say the least, the epiphenomenal."

"Big words don't change matters, Brian. They don't protect you. When have they ever?"

"Marta!" Brian cried joyously at the sight of the housekeeper coming in the back door. The young woman lived close by, right in town, and usually she arrived at the Horkow house in the morning with hair so limply wet it made you wonder if she hadn't managed to shower in her car on the way over. The children never seemed to mind her shiny sopping head, but more than once Brian had been forced to change a shirt after brushing against her too early in the day.

"You're not all *that* late, Marta," Shelley said, punishing Marta for the happy relief in her husband's voice. "But would you please listen to what this man believes? He's defending the stuff that rots his own children's teeth. He thinks lousy teeth don't matter . . . except, that is, when his periodontist calls and reminds him that his appointment's due. Then for a few days it matters and he's Mr. Responsible. Yet the kids will have the same teeth and we all know it—just because he doesn't approve of what the women look like behind the counter at the Great Green Earth."

Brian's index finger had found a colorless area of stickiness on the kitchen's prep island. Old food perhaps, maybe Scotch tape residue— his fingernail rooted around in it luxuriously. Two things only do I wish for in this life, he thought. That the children not die too soon (meaning not before me, meaning not *ever*) and that I myself be tapped in somehow to authenticity. Not originality, not novelty—just a good center-cut portion of the real. With one sabotaged child plus two adopted ones, do I want to pass down *anything* that is intrinsic to myself and my crummy genes? So why is Shelley bringing up my gums?

No, all that he wished for his children was what he wished for himself: to not be so goddamned pure! Let them *blunder* onto reality. And the real, in this instance, would be that an Oreo now and then—*even every afternoon, with milk!*—was not going to peel the enamel off their little teeth. If it did, at least it would happen much later, and first would have come deep pleasure, plus a simultaneous introduction to the manifold ambiguity of the world. Wasn't pleasure *usually* dangerous? Wasn't everything? *Life* was dangerous. In fact it was a *sugar:* brittle, lacy, quickly surging, only later doing its damage.

Nor did Shelley have to tell him he was ridiculous, as if this were some late-breaking news. In this his long season of failure as a man, one of the few and last things he *liked* being was ridiculous!

Lifting his finger from the sticky spot—*could it be snot?*—Brian announced to his wife that he couldn't continue the discussion right now. "Tessa's still upstairs and we need to seriously hurry her up. I should have been out of here a half hour ago. Marta, you probably wouldn't mind having the kitchen to yourself to give these boyos breakfast, either."

Shelley's head trembled faintly, as though a minor chill had just then passed through it. "The way you won't deal with things, Brian."

"My wicked wicked ways, I know, I know. But what can I do, guys—all I'm saying is that time isn't endless."

Shelley turned to start leaving the kitchen. "Go, goodbye. You don't have *time* for a speech, remember?"

Marta, the poor klutz, giggled. This unfortunate constant urge of Shelley's to cope with, to anticipate reality! Why couldn't people be married long enough to finally convince each other of anything? He loved Shelley, and he loved loving her, but rarely nowadays could he locate the love exactly. It must be around here *somewhere*—as they seemed to be saying in this house of chaos every minute about one thing or another—but maybe, at best, love sat like a troll under the bridge over which the marriage rumbled back and forth, year after year. And in that case, what did the love troll look like by now?

Shelley returned to the kitchen to ask which car Brian would be taking. He told her the Jag: "I need the backseat room for later."

He would be delivering Tessa this morning down to UCSF Hospital for her regular checkup and evaluation. Her visits now were scheduled for every three months, down from monthly, but there was a new wrinkle to them. The medical center was participating in a clinical trial of a new genetically engineered spray drug specifically for cystic fibrosis. Yet whether or not Tess actually could be enrolled formally into the study was still not clear. It depended on her baseline levels over a number of checkups. So far, insanely, they had been too *good*.

His daughter was considered too *well*. To be rescued in the most scientific manner, they wanted her to be *sicker*. Up to her neck was not enough, the water had to be at her nostrils. It made Brian want to kill somebody.

And here now finally was Tessa herself, dragging herself into the kitchen, boneless, languid, and unhappy. Her bag in hand, she went to the back door as though to the executioner's block. "Ready to roll, Countess?" Brian asked her. Shelley planned to meet them later in the morning at the hospital and take Tess back home. Brian would go from there to meet the Zwillings' flight at SFO.

"You comfortable?" he asked Tess, seated beside him in the car. "Scoot forward—I've got the button depressed. You're too far back."

Tess stared out her window but didn't move. "Who exactly is it you're getting at the airport?—and I hope you're not taking them back to *our* house."

"They'll be staying at a hotel in the city, I think."

"You're going to stay there with them?"

"Maybe only for one night, if that." On hospital-visit days, Tess could be undecided about whether or not she wanted anyone but Shelley near her. Brian tried not to take it personally, for, on those days, her war with the how-it-is was fought on many fronts. "Maybe not at all."

On 101 they hit traffic. It wasn't anecdotal here-and-there traffic but a thickened wad of it, unusual for this far north of the city at this hour. When it forced Brian to slow way down, Tessa seemed distinctly encouraged. Her posture changed. Maybe by the time they finally got to the hospital it would be too late; it would be the clinic's lunch hour; the right technicians wouldn't be around; through some harmony of bureaucracy and laziness she'd be dismissed. Brian easily could imagine her hopes. He too sometimes felt that her illness had become, through long use, mostly a matter of appointments and scheduling. Sometimes she'd say, "I wish they'd just forget about me!" as though her lungs might finally uncloud if only people would cease to recall she was imperiled. His brilliant and deep girl. (Although the sick would do better to be more obtuse, less registering.) What keeps us netted more than half of the time is the *idea* of the trap, which was exactly what bothered Brian about Shelley's guidebooks to misfortune. *Don't forget,* they drummed, *don't forget, don't forget.* Yet a person could keep himself alert for only so long before he needed rest. Or the illusion of it.

The car now crawled down to seven, five, three miles an hour. The freeway was a welded sculpture before them. On sick-kid time, no other kind of time cut it, was pedigreed enough—and yet how tiring and tiresome it was to live in a state of constant perspective, in the fucking vanishing point! Right now, someone in one of these cars might not be minding this stall at all. But not Brian—he was starting to panic. The traffic was going to screw him. He rode the brake, nickel-and-diming the yardage offered to the Jaguar's nose. Because there was no alternate route to take, the radio was of no use, and he began repeatedly looking in the rearview mirror, as though he might figure a way to back-and-forth the car enough to drill downward, to free them that way, given enough clearance.

Tessa, from her tote bag, which up till now had been resting on the floor mat, pulled out one of her faithful stuffed Alfs, outgrown but still beloved, as well as a book about African plains animals. Nesting in, she was now the one to give her father a little smile that urged patience.

Could Shelley have been aware of some road construction before they set out? Such a paranoid thought puckered Brian's mouth like a lemon. No, of course not. Yet his wife did hope, and not so secretly, that he never made another movie. They'd get along on the proceeds from her guides to woe and the "available resources" to share them in.

Had she ever really thought this through, though? What if her books stopped selling? They would lose the house. Have to go into Chapter 11. From where could help then be expected to come? That time, not so long ago, when *If Means When* had tanked and Brian was at wit's end, when he had run out of other contacts and was desperately sending Phil Dreyer scripts—what then had happened? Did she not recall? What had happened was that Brian never heard a word back from Phil, other than a lousy card that never even mentioned the scripts. All the old days were just that: *old*. Barney's Beanery. LA hipsters. The two of them in bed with the same girl one time. The softball jackets with *Team Actor* on them—all gone, all churned away to foam in the wake.

Whereas the Warshaw Foundation project moneys would water the Horkows, would water the Zwillings—wasn't that some kind of boon? And, Phil Dreyer to the contrary, it went some way in proving that the

past *could* be important. Someone reappears, takes on large, unex-
pected, unprovided-for dimensions. Twenty plus years ago, Brian and
Zwilling had been in the same entering medical school class at Flower
Fifth Avenue, a school Brian's father had figured a way to buy his son
into but not prevent him from chuting out of. As med schools went,
Flower was a piece of cake for everyone, it seemed, except for Brian,
for whom it had been Annapurna. Even the physical place had been
daunting: the big old double-breasted power building near Harlem, its
staff of elderly attendings drifting in about midnight to make daily
rounds, calling from the imperium of booze for residents and students
to enter with them into rooms containing patients whose illnesses they
barely recalled at that hour, or in that state.

Brian would have stuck it out, though, had he been able to. Zwilling
certainly could and should have stayed, despite the fact that he was already a published writer, the author of a single precocious novel. Had
he been in Zwilling's shoes, Brian would not have dropped out for that
reason alone. He would have tried to see himself farther down the road,
as one of those blessed doctor-scribes, Rabelais and Walker Percy and
William Carlos Williams and Chekhov.

Glancing over at his daughter, Brian said, "Ah, Alf," which immediately prompted Tess to ditch the snouted stuffed thing out of sight.
"Alf's essential, isn't he? We don't go many places without Alfie."

"Can I call Mommy on the phone?"

Even before Brian could reach down to pick up the handset, Tessa
already had it: "I know how. Marta? Is my Mom there? Mommy?"
Bravery-busting tears rushed out of her. "Call the hospital and tell
them that we're stuck in bad bad bad traffic. That we can't get there"—
Tess now was racing—"and that we'll come next time. Promise, okay?
He's here. No, he can't, he's driving. Goodbye!"

"Ah, Tess, honey." Pressing the redial button, Brian held the phone
above the steering wheel, fearing that she'd fight him for it— hoping
maybe that she would. Shelley answered with a half-amused "Hmnnn,"
but Brian assured her, "We're going. This'll break up soon."

These depressing parent games, the maybe-you-can't-handle-it-but-
I-can sort of thing. Yet it wasn't always so. Once, when Tess was little,

they had taken a family driving trip to Taos. At a point when Brian couldn't physically drive any longer, they had stopped at a Burger King, inside of which Brian had fallen in love: the Burger King's safety, the smiles given the baby, the indulgence shown by all around them when Shelley was forced to lay Tessie down on the table to change her wet diaper, no appropriate surface having been available in the ladies room. America, he saw, was good to those who had babies. But he had no idea how it would react to those who then also lost them.

The traffic now was moving not at all, at a complete standstill. Brian bellowed to the windshield: "What the fuck!"

"Turn off, Daddy," Tess calmly advised. "Just go back home. It's okay."

"No one is going back!"

Tess, stung from having been shouted at, climbed into the backseat and curled up. "I hate you for not just going home. We're going to be so late that you should forget it. But you won't listen! You only do what *you* want to do, never what *we* want!"

Brian turned to her in apology. "Honey, this is a traffic problem. I'm sorry I raised my voice."

"I want," Tessie murmured in a tone of pious defeat, "to go *home*."

"I do, too, Cakes. But first we'll get this over with." Ah, she wasn't very pretty, was she? Too thin, and the clubbing of some of her fingers (which Alf hid, his primary purpose) never did go fully away as the doctors had promised it would. The twins, their Transylvanian looks and fabulous eyes, outshone her easily. They would grow up to be dangerously beautiful men. Brian and Shelley had both come to acknowledge that these had been show adoptions; as semicelebrities in the first wave of Romanian placements, they had been spared the skin-and-bone cases, the head-batterers and the shit-in-the-beds shrieking madly through the night in the countryside orphanages. Instead they had received a lush pair of romantic buds of Bucharest.

Yet right now, just at this moment, Tess too was starting to look better. Lovely, even. Apologized to, thinking that perhaps the forces of accident had for a change gone her way, her dignity was inherently gorgeous. If only she had more access to it. When it was time for her daily postural drainage; when her mother pummeled her back and her chest with slams and slaps (the part Brian never could ever bear to do and that Shelley never let him forget he shirked)—during all this Tess would cry with insult from the hard kneading, mucus flying from her mouth and nose. She was utterly without dignity then. Shelley was without dignity. And Brian himself—no matter where in the house he'd fled to—he was without dignity too. Once, watching a black Baptist immersion ceremony on TV, he distinctly remembered thinking: *That's* what we need: To all wear white robes during Tess's sessions, some outward sign or vestment of good intentions.

It was 9:35 according to the clock in the dash. Seriously late for the clinic, therefore late to meet the Zwillings' plane. Again Brian got on the phone, this time to his office.

"Cynth, it's me, Brian. I'm stuck in traffic. The people who are coming in today at the airport—".

"The Zwillings." It always annoyed Cynthia if he held back names from her. She'd even told him so once: that she found it capricious and condescending. Which it was, Brian privately agreed. A bad habit. But something to waste an emotion over? What about other emotions? Had she yet shown him the relief he knew she must feel that they were in business again and that he had hired her back? With five jillion production assistants in California mooning around, waiting for a break, he easily could have had a fresh face, not someone from the disastrous old days.

"Send a limo for them. I'm not going to make it myself."

"I'm also glad you called, Brian, for another reason. I keep on forgetting to ask you if you want me to call in for food. They'll be ready for lunch their time, won't they? What do you think they'd like?"

"Food? I don't know. Terrangelo's? One giant po'boy, his best—that would be good. Or Yee's. Tommy can use his discretion, anything dim sum. But remember, nothing organic, nothing from Leaves."

"You're so prejudiced. It gets consistently great reviews. The food's delicious."

"How are we doing on wine?"

"Let me look." In a minute she returned. "Three bottles from that case of the Carr-Mokler cabernet you bought, the reserve '85."

"But do they drink or not? The three bottles *should* be enough—no, changed my mind—better to be safe: have another case delivered. All's cool otherwise?"

"And Tess? Should I call the clinic for you and let them know you'll be late, or have you done that already?"

Tess, especially from the back seat, couldn't possibly have heard what Cynthia asked. Yet Brian found himself whispering: "Yes, do that. That's why I called." Just now he could see faint movement up ahead. The traffic must have finally unplugged; soon a forward impulse would reach back to them and pull them onward like the musculature of a snake. "Please do that for me, thanks."

After hanging up, he looked back at Tessa and found her asleep. Genuinely asleep, as though gassed by what she interpreted as the greeny luck of missing her appointment. Yet the sight of her innocent sleep destroyed her father. Speed and gained ground were suddenly hollow to him; given a choice, he would have jumped the divider and turned the car back toward home, just as she had wanted him to do in the first place.

4

As they stepped free of the jetway, they were met in the terminal by a young guy holding a sign at the height of his navel: "ZWILLING."

"I love it," Nathan said. "Like it's assumed."

Zwilling's legs, wobbly from all the hours of sitting on the airplane, made him feel as though he were lurching across the terminal floor. "What is?"

"'Zwilling'—the quote marks, like it's an assumed name."

The kid holding the sign wore a tie over a denim shirt, and the car he led them out to was a more or less informal black Chrysler New Yorker, not the Mercedes or stretch Cadillac Zwilling feared it might have been. Yet he needed to examine his feelings here. Part of him still wanted to protect Nate from buying into all this, and that part probably should have preferred a white monstrosity car after all, since exaggeration invited parody.

The driver began to do tentative things with his lips while he was setting the bags down into the trunk. There was a glint in his eye, and as soon as he got behind the wheel he turned around to speak to Nate:

"You do writing? You once had those things in *Daze*? The name was a little familiar. Then like when I saw you . . . "

Nate nodded, yet said all but nothing back.

"You out here much?"

When Nate provided no answer, Zwilling told the driver that he himself wasn't, no.

The driver, however, kept at Nate. "You?" Nate's grudging negative seemed to give the kid enough charter, and in a spirit of information he then began to tell Nate what clubs to avoid in San Francisco. "Worst, man—forget it totally—is The Knock. Real snobbish. No one's admitted unless . . ." And just then he must have thought *What trash am I talking? This guy is sure to be let in,* because he suddenly let the rest of his sentence go.

Zwilling looked at his son. Nate wasn't skittish of embarrassment, not nearly the way his father was. Either other people's embarrassment or his own. No bad trait really, though it also did smack of a dreadful uninterestedness. After Nate started publishing his and Polly's diaries, Zwilling once even broached the subject with him, this lack of curiosity about others. Nate had evaded him airily—yet just last night, in one of the diary entries Zwilling discovered another facet to it:

> You decide that you are after all going to answer the letter from Deborah Cowtrer, Assistant Professor of English, University of Wisconsin, Eau Claire (What's she look like? Nice tits?), who wants to interview both of you about midwestern postmodernism and the resurgence of the journal form. You know exactly what you're going to tell her during the interview too. You're going to say that as far as you're concerned, the diary is the only justifiable literary form because it uses no one else for fodder. It's only you using yourself.

The great bright endless yolk of the California sunlight seemed aimed straight down through the core of Zwilling's tiredness. Otherwise he himself would have engaged the driver in chat about the clubs. So far, though, frozen as fathers are when sons disappoint them, he'd said nothing. Now he bent forward in the car and asked the driver, "Where are we heading?"

"This is roughly South San Francisco. We're coming up the peninsula."

Nate hadn't been able to get Horkow to be any more specific on the phone than to say that they'd either be staying at his own house or else at one of the local inns up near him in Sonoma. Or possibly in the city. Even Barbara, herself a business traveler, understanding of flexible arrangements, was less than crazy about such an indefinite destination—and Zwilling could only guess how Polly had accepted such vagueness.

"And where are you driving us *to*?"

"The address is south of Market, SoMa. Probably a loft building. Never been there before. I got this run last minute, so I'm not too sure." Trying to speak to Nate, the kid had turned back every few seconds, not very safely, but to Zwilling he spoke only into the rearview mirror.

The phone up near his right knee began to let out irritated chirps. After the kid answered, he put the phone down and said: "Your party? Mr. Horkow? He's delayed. His office called my dispatcher. You gentlemen want a tour of the city for about a half hour? The price'll be exactly the same for you. Free."

He shut off the motor but stayed in the car as the Zwillings left the limo to walk around Union Square. Zwilling made a beeline toward Gumps for a present for Barbara, but Nate held him back, a hand on his arm. "Not *now*. Not right away."

"Why not? We have the time."

"We'll have more later. Let's do all this other stuff first."

Zwilling, by this sudden eruption of responsibility and priority, was reminded that his son was nervous. "Just remember to buy Polly something too while you're out here. Don't forget."

Horkow's office, when they finally arrived there, turned out not to be impressive, merely a shell-colored four-story building spined by a minuscule, noisy elevator. A small, inexpensively wood-paneled outer office stood watch over equally tiny rooms beyond, and along the floors snaked ill-hidden extension cords and computer cables. There was a smell of fresh paint.

The receptionist was a thin girl with slicks of coarse dark hair on her forearms. She told them that Horkow still was delayed. And to Nate: "There's been a call for you? A Polly?"

The Zwillings sat alone on not especially luxurious or comfortable chairs in what appeared to be Horkow's inner office. The film posters Zwilling had expected to see on the walls weren't there. In fact, nothing was. Any view and most of the light from the windows was blocked by the corner of an adjacent building. A filing cabinet; a desk covered with papers; to one side of the room, under the windows, a long folding table on which sat a spread of food that could have fed twenty-five: Chinese dim sum in bamboo steamers, plus a six-foot-long sandwich on a parchmented plank. The receptionist came in to uncork not one but two bottles of wine. She made small talk, but when she left Zwilling was pleased. Their bags were outside, next to her desk, and he worried about them parked out there unattended.

She drifted back in a few minutes later. "This is for *you,* gentlemen—as much or as little."

"Isn't . . . uh . . ." Nate said. "Aren't other people expected?"

"Brian is all, I think. Start, don't wait for him. Please eat. What is it your time—four o'clock? That's a lot past lunch."

Nate approached the spread after she left. Zwilling stayed seated, not yet feeling securely arrived, not emplaced enough to eat. His son, taking a plate, dug right into the array. With a quickly filled mouth he said: "This food is extremely *excellent.* You should have some, Pops."

But Zwilling didn't know at what moment the director would come in upon them, a moment when he didn't wish to have his mouth—his only weapon of defense—stuffed full, disabled. Already he felt far too flushed-out. The wish to play possum right now, to not be in motion at all, not even to have his jaws moving, was overwhelming.

5

While Brian was explaining to him that there'd never been gross pancreatic symptoms, no need for dietary supplementation (though Shelley still worried about that and kept an eagle eye on what everyone ate), Zwilling had nodded, seeming to agree that that was to the good. Brian liked that. "The only thing we do is in hot weather we make a point of giving her more salt. But otherwise it's been pretty well localized as pulmonary."

"Isn't there a genetic determinant," Zwilling asked, "to which spectrum of the disease develops? I seem to remember something from way back. Northern Europe and southern?"

Brian nodded eagerly. "But there weren't any of the classical infantile signs. The meconium ileus, the steatorrhea. You're right, though. There was a hot spot in Shelley's family, a carrier we paid no attention to. I had no idea there was a chance I would carry too."

And Brian shook his head, still chilled by the fact after all the years. "Here Tessa was, at two, getting monster colds, thick secretions, paroxysmal cough, very pertussis-y. The pediatrician and I put our heads together after much too long. I don't know what it is with a lot of docs—*they* don't want to discover anyone's sick either? The whole thing's been bad juju. In the beginning she was not sick enough to diagnose, now she's not sick enough to cure. But finally, down at UCLA, they permitted themselves to do a sweat test on her."

This Joel Zwilling, he was having the effect of making Brian feel like a fourth-year student presenting a case to the senior resident. He enjoyed it. Ten to one, so did the writer.

However, Brian through all of this had been unjustly ignoring the son. And having spoken to him on the phone enough times, he now wanted to have a good, square look at him. Taller than his father, skinnier, the kid owned dark straight hair that probably issued from his mom. But also had his father's long bony fiddling fingers, troublemaking fingers, which the kid seemed to try to keep willfully still, shoving them under his thighs occasionally, bouncing on them a little as he sat and listened.

The elder Zwilling was wearing a pair of loden green Clark's chukka boots the likes of which Brian hadn't seen in twenty years. The boots were new, too, for he could distinctly make out the bright crinkly pillings of the foam soles. (The chukkas especially made Brian recall their original connection; only really in school did you ever notice someone else's brand-new shoes.) Zwilling also had on a brown tweed jacket, a checked shirt, a narrow solid blue tie, chino pants—the whole old-style arty uniform. Pouchy mouth and lips, although his face was more steely around the eyes. Most of his hair still was on him, ginger gone grayish, a color like patchy rust yet very fully textured. What he looked like to Brian, in fact—all this undertapped virility— was a goddamn sculptor and not a writer at all.

Yet both the Zwillings had been looking baggy by the time Brian had rushed in. Cynthia had let him know that they'd been waiting almost two hours already. They'd nibbled ridiculously little considering all that time, and the wine was opened but untouched. "Nate," Brian said, gesturing over to the sideboard, "did you have any of the dim sum here? What did you think?"

"Those buns with the meat in them?"

"Pork."

"They were very good."

"Say on a scale of ten?"

"Well, I never had one before." His face stayed appealingly open.

To the father Brian said, "Never a *shu mai*? Don't they have those in Cleveland?"

"Cincinnati," Zwilling said. He said it without any spin. Brian very much approved of him for this as well. Clearing brush before a child's path is what fathers were supposed to do. Somehow he himself never managed it for his own children, unhealthy excitement—theirs *and* his—never letting him reach that point. Case in point: his rumble this morning with one of clinical fellows at the hospital.

Tess had sat there on the examining table with her shirt off, trying to be brave, while Brian and the doctor sparred with increasingly poisoned darts. A bit too churned-up, Brian ultimately touched the doctor, the touch becoming a shake, a pull, and the guy hadn't cared for it and said so. Then Tess started crying. Since crying tended to make her cough, and coughing increased her secretions, Brian in his crazed state actually felt for a moment that a mucusy spell right about then might not have been such a bad thing. Let the asshole see just how robustly well this little girl was whom he was excluding from his study! It had been a hundred percent awful.

"I eat dim sum in New York all the time," the son corrected Zwilling. "Just not this exactly, those buns."

"So tell me about what you're working on now?" Brian said to Joel Zwilling. He knew full well that the man hadn't published in years. When Zwilling's sensualist's mouth bunched to one side and his palm started turning up powerlessly, Brian put a finger to his own lips and headed him off: "I hate that question also." (Along with the copious middle-aged hair and his reddish complexion, there were odd backlights in Zwilling's face, Brian noticed. Blood-pressure problems maybe? Fatigue from the flight? Or could he have been blushing?) "Don't you hate it, too, Nate? What are *you* working on now?"

"Well," the kid began, "I'm—"

"No no no—a joke: me asking you right away what *you're* working on. Stupid joke. You guys have had next to none of my wine!"

Brian lusted after that Carr-Mokler himself, though he would have to tailor his intake to the Zwillings', who weren't indulging. Cabernet on a day like today could act as a sanctuary for him, a cotter pin. The upshot of the stink he'd made with the clinical fellow at the hospital was that Brian was thrown a sop: Guiamaraes said he'd work Tess up "as though" she'd be enrolled in the study. Out of spite? Grudgingly? Was she going to get the placebo spray? Brian might conceivably have even said these suspicious things aloud to the doctor; he wasn't quite sure. Then, though, unimaginably, it got even worse; twenty minutes later, Tess barfed all over the EKG suite. The sight of an EKG strip being taken on an obese old woman right beside her had unhinged her.

Who could blame the child? The never-quite-fully-closing curtains on ceiling tracks, the too-easy-opening doors of hospitals. Once she'd been cleaned up and calmed down, the EKG postponed for now, the poor baby was completely staved in. "I'm sorry!" she sobbed over and over. "I'm sorry!"

"I think I *am* going to take a little of that wine." Brian was getting up for it when Cynthia buzzed in to say that there was a call for Mr. Zwilling. "Which one, Cyn?"

"For Nate Zwilling."

Father and son gave each other quick looks. "Nate," Brian told him, "take it through that door. We're in the middle of remodeling, so you may have to hunt for it a second, but it should be there. It's going to be the new screening room. You should see a telephone on a table. Hit buttons."

Zwilling and Brian now were alone. "I guess you're only rarely sorry you left Flower Fifth," said Zwilling.

"Do you remember me at all from back then? I was in such a fog, but I do remember you."

"My bet is that you're not, you're not sorry," Zwilling said. "You'd have been just another doctor."

"Yeah, but maybe I'd have been more alert to the family history, or Tessie would have gotten better initial care. Genetic testing—something. But overall, no, I don't think I'd want to be needed in the way a doctor is needed. Desperately. Desperately—then discarded like a bad memory. *You* ever sorry?"

Good-humoredly, Zwilling said, "A person finds ways to regret just about everything. About not being a doc, though, not that much."

"All the lying you would have had to do."

This seemed to genuinely amuse the writer. But Brian held his ground. "You lie to your own purposes as an artist. It's different. You know it. You don't lie to shield someone else."

"Sad to say. Can I change the subject a little and ask you something—while he's out of the room?"

"Nate? About all this? Oh, we'll bat it around plenty, don't you worry. We'll have all the time we need. Anyway, what I'll have in mind will have a lot to do with what you tell me I *should* have in mind."

"Maybe just a capsule now."

"I'll give it a shot." Brian got up, pouring wine for his guest and for himself. "*Less Him.* Fine book, right? Filmically—can you excuse such a pretentious expression?—filmically, a writer's work is usually interpreted in one basic way. A text gets transferred into a script, then with luck into a film. That's the absolutely classical procedure—every different step of which I've done up the wazoo."

Zwilling's tension was catching; Brian stretched and yawned like a dog. "I option one of your books—which is what I'm doing, which is why you're here, so that's step number one. My enthusiasm for your work is the *agency* for getting the film made. But what if it was *more* than that? I have qualms, for instance, about Spielberg-type Holocaust movies. I'm sure you have them too. Who am I to make such a thing? But what if, in a manner of speaking, we instead made a film *about* those qualms? Think of all the things that would get pulled in that way. Your life, my life, why I even *needed* to get involved with this."

Dicey territory, Brian knew—yet Zwilling seemed immune. He was sneaking looks over at the food now. Brian had either lost or bored him, either of which was satisfactory.

The writer, half-attentive but compelled to say at least something, asked, "Like cinema verité?" At long last, he was getting up from his chair to approach the food. After opening a few of the bamboo steamers, he finally chose a single small dumpling, which he took back on a plate to his chair before even tasting it.

"More like, say, fiction verité! An honesty that lets you make yourself up. To be realer than you are."

Done chewing and swallowing, Zwilling said, "Someone once pointed out that honesty's just another literary genre."

Brian rose to fill his glass again. "So true. Honesty isn't always *important* enough for certain situations. Something better's needed sometimes."

"Well, I wouldn't know anything about all of this, of course—but does a studio throw money at something this vague?"

"Who cares what a studio does! I don't. I have better money than studio money. Independent money, very forthcoming. I'll write you both a check before you leave to go home."

Looking neither pleased nor even impressed, Zwilling leaned forward and pointed toward the closed door of the screening room. Quietly he said, "Again, though, about Nate . . . "

The photocopies Selva had made for Brian were in his briefcase. He checked his desk phone once to see that an extension button remained red. "These diaries he writes, they're pretty, you know, remarkable. One here, a dream about being in a department store and making it with his doctor under a rack of dresses—"

"Yes, I recall the one"—quickly, uncomfortably—"I've read it."

"Strong. It's so strong! Where is it? Yes, this one here, starts, 'You're going up the escalator, you step off, you're about to make the turn to the next escalator up, you see your substance-abuse shrink, Dr. Tamara Halmon-Swed, who's saved your life . . . '" If that isn't a name straight out of S. J. Perelman! Is it the real name of his doctor?"

Zwilling could hardly look him in the eye. "That was her name, yes."

"So just imagine . . . Guy who takes chances like that . . . For instance, seeing the differences in a screenplay that *he'd* write based on *Less Him,* how different it would be from what *you* wrote in the actual book—*that* really would be interesting. Little father/son discrepancy.

You film that and you might have something! It would be a little like filming negative space. Negative capability."

Brian, hungry himself now, went to the sideboard. "I also sometimes think about the notion of the 'secret author.' We'll sit down and talk about it maybe." Brian began to assemble a plate for himself. "Dreams are good examples—like your boy's here. You're dreaming, but while you're dreaming you're also sensing that you dream. Lucid dreaming, isn't that what it's called? Sensing that maybe someone else in the dream may have wanted you to dream it, wanted you to cast them in it. A woman doctor, trying to help save his life . . . while he's dreaming about this caring, helpful person in a completely animal way. It's terrific."

Turning around to go back to his desk, Brian saw that Nate Zwilling had quietly re-entered the room. His father was looking up at him expectantly. The kid said, "Nothing important." But Zwilling's look lingered.

"Nate, I was telling your dad how much I admire your diaries. Maybe you heard me in there reading." But then Cynthia buzzed in once more, a call from Shelley, and Brian's heart slipped away into a puddle of doom. "I have to get this, sorry"—and took the call in front of them.

After hanging up he ordered the Zwilling pair, "Stay right where you are," and went out to Cynthia, closing the door behind him.

"I'm going to have to go home. Get two rooms for them at the Fairmont or the Four Seasons. I don't care which, either one. Get them for the next three or four nights. Don't let Reservations shit you. You *must* have rooms, tell them."

Brian stood there while she phoned, the Fairmont first. But her best pleading charm wasn't good enough and she shook her head at him. She called The Four Seasons and it was the same. "Nothing, Brian. Conventions in both."

He reached across her for the Rolodex. Benita's apartment in Russian Hill usually was free. He gestured for Cynthia to give him the phone. But Benita herself answered, saying it was funny that he should call, she was just going to call him, invite him and Shelley to a dinner party next Friday night. . . .

Next Brian phoned Piero in Mill Valley, but he, the yutz, was back in town too. All the dependable pilgrims had returned to their nests in a clump?

"There are plenty of other hotels in the city, Brian," Cynthia said.

No, he knew what he did and didn't want for these men. Plus, he had no easy elasticity of mind; the morning had destroyed that in him: Tess and the traffic and the clinic and now Shelley yanking him home. He literally could not imagine the Zwillings staying in a place he was not familiar with. Maybe the best thing would be for them to go home and then come back out later. Go home to Cleveland or Cincinnati or wherever and return another time. Or else he could travel out there to them.

"What about the Portman, Brian?"

"Too too ugly."

"All they need are just beds, right? They were going to spend the days at your house, I thought, right?" Cynthia screwed her eyes down narrowly. "What about my place? I can stay at my sister's."

"I've been to your house. You don't dust."

"Brian!"

"Well, do you?"

He went into the screening room to call Shelley back privately from in there. At first the phone was busy (the doctor? 911?), but after dialing again he got through and reached Marta, who told him, first thing, that Tessa seemed better just knowing he was coming home, that he was on his way.

"I am? Who said I am?" A promise someone else made. Brian was feeling like *he* had an author, and not such a secret one. His life didn't let him live! And what exactly was he supposed to do now with the two poor souls sitting out there in his brand-new office?

6

No one else entered the room for a noticeable time after Horkow left for good. The receptionist, Cynthia, may have been just as embarrassed as they were for them to have been left behind.

Zwilling looked to his son. "Any thoughts?"

Nate's brows rose unduly, as though he was trying to blink his eyes free of tears, and Zwilling realized that the boy thought he was being solicited for a definitive opinion of Horkow. "Stay over? Leave?"

Nate's face relaxed all at once. "I guess go. Polly is *so* bummed . . . "

"She all right? I figured that was who called."

Nate wasn't happy. "She just *does* this."

"Then let's go back. There's got to be at least one flight tonight. She's that upset . . . Listen, we had a short talk, he and I. The impression he left was that things are okay. Preliminary but solid."

"What did he say, exactly? What does 'preliminary' mean? What are 'things'? Tell me what he said."

"We'll talk about it later."

"Why not now?"

"Not here. He said we'd have a check. Really, Natey, later."

"He actually gave you a check?"

"Not now, Nate, please?"

Before flying from the office altogether, Horkow had gone through a series of phone calls in front of the Zwillings, each one of which seemed to upset him progressively. And his face wasn't well designed for stress. Open and square, with light-colored shallow Chinese-y eyes, a mischievous and sculpted mouth, they all gave Horkow the look of a man in suspension, a man who'd put his hand out and not had it shaken by another person.

During the last of the phone calls, he had turned positively bossy, half hysterical. "Where are you? Has the situation been explained to you? That you're needed and what you're needed for? Well get that fat butt of yours over here before everyone's gone and the need gone with it!" He offered his caller an unpleasant laugh of apology. "*Be here now*—isn't that what we used to blissfully say?"

Off the phone, he then reassured the Zwillings. "Between the both of them, Cynthia and Selva, you're going to be in absolutely great hands. My dynamic duo. Especially the Tash." Hauling up the brief-case that had held Nate's diaries, Horkow opened it—and then unexpectedly began taking things *out*. Papers and photocopies and finally books, Zwilling's own novels, two of which, without their dust jackets, looked dishearteningly archaeological to their author.

Then, as soon as Horkow seemed to have everything out of his bag, he began slotting it all back in again. Finally, he stood up and hitched at his pantwaist. "Guys, we will be in touch, yes? Call me if you need to. Any time, day or night. Let me know what you've decided to do."

Is he leaving, Zwilling wondered, to spare us the difficulty of first leaving him with so little accomplished? Zwilling had known a lunatic or two in whom untamed impulse could act as a kind of courtesy.

"Do about what?" Nate asked.

Horkow was busy thinking, though. "A little inn I know down the coast in Carm . . . No, forget that, not right for you, too far away. I'm blanking on other places, though. Suddenly I'm unable to *think*. In the meantime, lean all you have to on Cynthia and Sel for anything you need, a place to stay, anything. Promise, too, that you'll call me. Call me a lot. We'll talk and talk. Or I'll call and get back to you." He stood up, taking hold of his briefcase, thrusting out his right hand: "Nate, terrific to meet you. It was a pleasure, truly. Guys, call me! The Tash'll be here shortly." Then he turned to Zwilling and rested the briefcase between his ankles. "And you, compadre!"—a hug—"again after so long! This is going to be first-rate!"

The office door had opened.

"Hello? Very sorry it took me so long. I'm Selva Tashjian."

"I'm Joel Zwilling." He got to his feet.

The woman smilingly took Zwilling's hand. "Things would be in an even sorrier state than they are if I didn't know that by now."

"This is my son, Nate Zwilling."

"We're old phone pals, Nate and I. Hi, Nate!"—shaking his shy hand. "Brian, I see, is completely split?" She went behind Horkow's desk, setting her bag on the floor beside her before dropping down into the chair. "I really did rush. I'm just lucky I had my phone with me. Sometimes I don't, I forget it or don't turn it on. Luckily I was in the neighborhood." A stage whisper: "*Shopping.*"

She was perhaps in her mid-thirties. The defining feature of her face was a strong hooking nose that gave her a nomadic look. Olive-skinned yet blond, and her shortish hair was swept off to the side in a gelled curve. Irony was in her looks elsewhere too: scimitar brows, long lashes that gave her gray eyes a hoodedness. She wore clear lip gloss that showed off evenly healthy teeth. Her hips were small, and her breasts. She was beautiful in that initially three-quarters way that filled out its last fourth the longer you looked at her. How could Horkow—to her, of all people—have said "*Get your fat butt over here!*"?

"Brian—*Mr. Horkow*, I mean—wanted to wait," Nate told her. "But he couldn't. Finally, he had to leave."

Her eyes were grazing over some papers lying on the desk, two of which she without hesitation picked up and stashed away into a drawer. Zwilling was sure his wife Barbara would approve of Selva Tashjian's expensive, slightly offbeat clothes: an Eisenhower-like jacket over a port-wine blouse, tan slacks, a mischievously staid single string of pearls. She punched a number into the phone from memory.

"I know," she said to Nate. "Cynthia filled me in just now—Marta? It's Sel."

After hanging up, she told the Zwillings: "The housekeeper says things are not so very bad up there. Maybe not 'ipsy-pipsy,' as Brian likes to say, but also not disastrous. Tessie's all right. That's his little girl. I assume Brian filled you in. Brian himself is probably more the issue at home right now. He had an argument with a doctor this morning. Tess now is afraid that she won't be allowed back into the hospital again."

She went over to the long folding table near the window, where she sniffed at an open bottle of wine. In the afternoon window light, her hair appeared almost solid, a cap woven to her on an express angle. "Sometimes when you expect things to be a disaster, they oblige," she said quietly, almost to herself.

She returned empty-handed to the desk. "I guess you can't do that with kids. Confuse their authority figures." She sat herself down on one end of the desk. "Well, as much as this concerns you both . . . It is possible he'll come back down to the city, because I know it upset him to leave you. The only question would be when. And he may not be able to at all. I just want you to know the possibilities. I realize you haven't had much time to think about it, but how are *you* guys leaning right now?"

Nate, as though rendered speechless by everything that had gone on, simply pulled out an inch of ticket folder from his inside jacket pocket. Selva nodded. "I sort of figured. On my way here, in fact, I called Cynthia and asked her to call the airlines. She was able to get you on the eleven P.M. Delta tonight and maybe also I think on the seven-thirty American tomorrow. That one, though, goes through Chicago, she said."

She was Horkow's associate. His protector, his organizer—but also his lover? His ex-lover? She hadn't asked to speak to Horkow's wife on the phone. Yet that command, "get your fat butt," rolled around like a marble in Zwilling's mind. He had grown up in a family where cousins worked in the garment district, and he himself had written PR part-time for the ILGWU years back—he was completely familiar with the art of the fond insult: pulling at fabric that was expected to stretch. This lovely *un*fatbutted woman Selva Tashjian was obviously known to stretch.

She was looking at her watch. "If you *don't* have other plans, let's at least have dinner at my boat, the three of us. It's going on five now. That still gives us plenty of time. If Brian comes back down to join us, that'll be great, that'll be gravy."

Nate looked as though he might be thinking of declining, so Zwilling quickly asked, "Your boat?" The idea of a sullen father-son airport restaurant dinner before being shipped back so empty-handed was too dreary to consider.

But Selva already was on the phone. "Get a limo back, okay, Cynthia? Tell them that the driver's going to take the gentlemen here to my place in Sausalito, and then he'll wait so he can get them back to SFO tonight in time to make a ten-fifteen check-in. Thank you, Cyn."

She straightened up to stand. "Boat, yes," she said to him. "Houseboat. I would drive you up myself but I want to stop first and get a salmon. You like salmon?"

"Will only one feed us all?"

Nate, shocked, looked at his father. In truth, Zwilling couldn't have said why he'd made such a ridiculous remark.

But Selva Tashjian smiled. "I can get two."

The limo was a Chrysler New Yorker again, this time dark blue, and the driver now a small swarthy man about Zwilling's own age dressed in an open blue goosedown vest and hearty plaid shirt. "Sausalito, the marina, right? I picked you up a little early because of that. Golden Gate traffic's supposed to be awful today. They're working on the tollbooths again."

The parking area for the marina in Sausalito was topped with a pulverization of white shells that made coarse clicks of welcome when stepped across. The driver, zipping up his vest, said, "I learned my lesson down here once. I found out how chilly it gets after sundown. Watch your steps on those walkways. And don't worry about your bags. They're locked in the trunk here, perfectly safe. I don't leave the car. Some do. See you later. Have a good time."

"He's really going to *wait?*" Nate whispered to his father as they walked away.

The houseboat colony looked clumsy and almost penal to Zwilling in the weakening daylight. There was very little mood of shore. Traversing the pier that served as the colony's central entrance, Zwilling noticed an empty Fritos bag bobbing in the water against a piling. It rose and fell, its mylar still shiny, and the bag struck him as being closer to home, to rest, to security than he himself was at the moment.

Yet Nate seemed deeply impressed by the whole setup. When he saw Selva Tashjian descend the ramp of her houseboat—she must have kept watch for them—he called out to her: "This is fantastic! This is great!"

She led them up the gangway to her boat. "We're the riffraff. The humdingers are docked at the other end. They're the ones who pay. We, you see, don't. We just squat. Lots of old hippies here, nonconformist retirees, marginals. We're known as the 'anchor-outs.' We're either legal or illegal, depending on which court case you want to pay attention to. One year yes, one year no. But we're an endangered species for sure."

The boat's interior, with light fixtures only here and there, and a few candles going in sturdy holders on tables, pulsed with a narrow gloom. The few portholes and window slits, set up high, were covered by a burlap fabric that reappeared on the cabin's ceiling in large knottings, a kind of unaccountable accent. The low ceiling was ribbed thickly with beams; you didn't want to stand up without seeing where the top of your head would go first. Zwilling would have expected her to live in a place more clarified. Less like a dungeon on the water.

Selva had changed out of her daytime clothes and into white jeans and a plain black tee shirt. Her pearls had been retained but now her

feet were bare. "The town wants the dockage for pleasure boats be-
longing to yuppies. They've been pressuring for years. It'll happen,
too, of course. We'll go."

She served stingers in chilled balloon glasses. Nate let everyone know
that this was a drink he'd never had before; Zwilling, for that matter,
couldn't himself remember the last time he'd had a stinger. And it was
the potent charge of just one of the cocktails that must have been what
hurtled him smoothly through an hour, because suddenly the salmon
was ready and Zwilling was getting up to help Selva serve.

"The boat hasn't always looked like this, you should know," she explained. She'd been away a lot lately, in London most recently but before that on the Continent. Thus she had taken in a renter.
"Unfortunate decorating was perpetrated."

"Pleasure or business? Your trip?" Nate asked. His speech was a bit
sloppy.

"I'm going to make some documentaries for British TV, it looks
like."

"With Brian Horkow?" Zwilling asked.

"On my own."

Somehow he'd guessed this. Was it why she had seemed less than
comfortable back at the office?

"That's great!" Nate had slipped off his shoes in order to drink and
eat sockfooted.

"Well, I'll wait," said Selva, seeming to want to catch Nate's eyes
straight-on, and failing that, looking at Zwilling. "There's a lot of dan-
gle in this business. You have to be careful."

"As in the heartwarming comedy: You Never Get It If You Want It
Too Much," Zwilling said paternally.

"Until they—the big They at any particular moment—until they
get wrapped up in it beyond escape, I think you're better off assuming
the lure isn't even really tied to the line."

Zwilling's single stinger had left him in no shape for the wine Selva
was pouring to accompany the salmon. But he was drinking it anyway.
In place of saying very much, he was conscious of bestowing an iden-
tically wobbly smile at everything Selva said.

She was a good hostess, talking about the houseboat colony, about New York, about Cincinnati (where she'd never been, she said, but where her father had worked for a period of time), about books. In England she'd been reading the Martin Buber compilation of Hasidic tales, as well as some Montaigne. Also Max Frisch's wonderful *Sketchbooks*. The most impressive reader she'd ever known, she said, had been her own father, Varak, a fountain and public-sculpture restorer, a man who'd devoted his life's talent to fixing and refurbishing other artists' grandiosities.

Zwilling then said, or thought he said, or certainly intended to say: "A painter friend of mine back in New York used to say that if you came up short for anything else to paint, at least have the wisdom to paint a picture of your mother or father." Finally, he was less than convinced that he had actually said this, though.

Selva was thoughtfully choosing small forkfuls of her salmon and the risotto she'd served along with it. "My papa did something so immobile. I, on the other hand, have been so determined to do something that *moves*. I think about that a lot."

Raising his glass, Zwilling made a short toast to the Immutable Law, children defining themselves in opposition to their parents.

It clearly annoyed Nate. "What kind of name is Selva?" he asked her. "Armenian?"

Drunkenly, to himself, Zwilling murmured, " *'Oscura.'* "

"Excuse me?" Selva said.

Zwilling looked at her moronically. "Nothing. Talking to myself."

"What you just said," she insisted.

" *'Una selva oscura.'* Dante finds himself there in the beginning of *Inferno:* A dark woods."

"Oh boy," said Nate. "Here we go. Foreign languages now."

"You maybe are only the second person in my entire life who ever guessed it," Selva said, looking hard at Zwilling. "My immigrant father was classics-crazy. I think it might have been his and my mother's little joke, too. She died before I was two, so I never found out if the name was something private between them or just his own whim."

Nate worked doggedly to change the subject, asking how she'd teamed up with Brian Horkow originally.

"I was his student." She looked down into her glass. "You know, it's interesting—"

"Pops here met *his* wife, my stepmother, that way too," Nate interrupted. "She was his student in a writing class, though she actually was in the law school then. She became a lawyer." He pressed a finger down onto his plate and brought a rice grain up to his mouth. "You knew, right, that Mr. Horkow went to med school with him?"

Zwilling hoped his son would drink no more wine. He asked Selva if she planned to make her films in England.

"It's going to be funny," she mused. "My mother was English. I was actually even *born* in London, though I think we only stayed there for about ten minutes. The idea that I could do my own first independent things there . . ." She laughed slightly chaotically. Zwilling was happy to see that she wasn't totally immune to the wine and the stingers either.

Fresh raspberries followed the fish. Zwilling pressed Nate into helping him with a rudimentary clearing of the table. Then, hardly minutes later, with time passing on alcoholic clouds, the limo driver was honking his horn from the parking lot on shore.

"Forgot about him!" Nate yipped.

She was sorry, Selva said, that it had worked out the way it did. "Going home after just arriving. Missing Brian all but totally. But at least *I* got to spend some time with you both."

Handshakes accompanied the good-byes. The clear night sky was starry. The bay air smelled of oil overruled by wind. With a dishcloth in her hand, Selva stood on the dock, waving. Zwilling was less than pleased at having her watch him drop into the limo's backseat alongside Nate, drop like the stunned cargo he truly was.

Nate leaned on his father's shoulder and loudly said, "Hey, the checks! Weren't there supposed to be checks?"

Part Two

7

Zwilling could see that his wife was eating hardly any of the food she had cooked. Barbara seemed happier keeping herself free for conversation, which at the moment had to do with niceness, with being nice. In her role as guest at the Zwillings' table, Selva Tashjian had mentioned what seemed to her to be the kindness of almost every single stranger she'd had anything to do with since arriving alone in Cincinnati to start preproduction on Horkow's movie.

Zwilling, in half-serious response to this, had said that maybe Cincinnatians were so nice because they were so indescribably bored.

"No," Barbara took exception. "Being nice even when you don't especially feel like being it: there's something more complicated to that, it's more like an inheritance. And in that case, if it's a subconscious code of behavior passed down, you're going to feel subconsciously responsible to it, too. You *won't* be short if you can help it at all. You *won't* be curt." Her normally low voice was spangled with brightish colors. "You go the extra inch."

Usually Barbara was not this declarative. "Well, you'd better," Zwilling said with a smile. "The town is stocked with Bavarians." He felt good, relaxed, lightened. "There's an overflow of superego."

"Where are *you* from originally?" Selva asked Barbara.

"Belleville, Illinois."

"That's also Midwestern. Are people there as nice?"

"Belleville mostly defines itself as being *not* St. Louis." Barbara looked over at her husband. "You just think I'm being a Pollyanna. Naïve."

The writer put up two palms of disengagement.

"So, yes, they're nice," she answered Selva, "It happens to be an efficient way to keep lives livable, that's what I think, finally. And you can't condescend to that. Well, maybe you can—but you shouldn't."

Selva seemed to mull it over as she ate, a certain transparency to her face. "You wonder—at least *I* do—how much motive counts for, anyway. For anything. Most of the time it's gone without a trace, that quickly. But I will tell you that, whether it's something on the surface or deep down, to me this universal *being nice* is just very nice itself. Somehow it soothes me."

Barbara nodded appreciatively, then glanced checkingly again at her husband.

"Me again?" Zwilling said. "Did you hear me disagreeing?"

"Of course you are," Selva said neutrally, stating a simple fact. "'Bavarians. Superegos'—it's obvious that you disagree."

"That's why he doesn't even come close to cutting it as a Cincinnatian," Barbara said. "He's hopeless at hiding from people what he really thinks."

The front door could be heard opening. The antique patterned-glass insets of the door were so fragile that its hinges were almost never oiled; better a slow swing and a mournful groan than a smart sudden shatter. At the sound, Zwilling muttered: "Finally."

First into the dining room was Polly. She was a surprise. Nate had remained typically mum toward his father, but Zwilling understood from Barbara that Polly still was moody and resentful at being shut out of the film project. So Selva Tashjian's arrival could only have been salt in her wound. (Yet why hadn't Nate quickly cobbled together some way *to* involve Polly in the film? Couldn't they throw something together in tandem, as they had the old diaries? Horkow himself didn't seem to know exactly what he wanted from Nate—that much had been clear back in San Francisco. Free rein was there for the having, at least for a while.) Recently, though, Polly had found a job cooking in a group home for mentally retarded adults—an occupation Zwilling viewed as almost inquisitional in its virtue, a reproach to movie frivolity.

Yet here Polly was, tonight even wearing a dress. Right behind her came Nate, dressed in sweats, since this had been his night to play league basketball at the Jewish Community Center. He had warned Barbara earlier in the day that he'd probably be a little late. "Sorry all."

In deference to Barbara's meal already on the table, Selva kept her seat, but pushed herself up halfway up to shake hands, first with Nate, then with Polly: "We haven't met before. I'm Selva."

"That I kind of figured. I'm Polly Doecklein." As she pulled back her chair, Polly seemed honestly surprised she'd been saved one.

"Did you win?" Selva asked Nate.

"The more important question you want to ask him," said his father, "is did he shower."

"We lost." Barbara quickly had filled plates for Polly and for Nate, who leaned down to sniff his. "This looks and smells great, Barb."

"And Selva brought a wonderful present with her," Barbara said. "A whole case of fantastic wine. Chardonnay. Wait till you taste it."

Polly covered her glass, but Nate raised his for filling. Selva, reaching familiarly across much of the table to grab the opened bottle, did the honors. "I'm at the Kuyper," she said as she poured. "The Hotel Kuyper, the Kuyper Manor—whatever it is. I'm there for a couple of days more and then I'm going downtown into an apartment hotel for a short-term lease."

"How long is short?" Nate asked—for which his father blessed him silently.

"Six months, although I'll be in and out a lot. But the reason I mention it at all is that I was starting to tell your father the story of my drapes. The men can tell you," Selva said to Polly, "that I'm coming off an unfortunate sublet. My house had been made very dark by the tenant. So that's the background for my nuttiness."

Polly's eyes had narrowed. "I thought you lived on a *boat*."

"A small houseboat, right, which can be mucked up worse than any apartment, believe me. So I'm oversensitive lately to bad decoration. When I mentioned to Barbara the ugly drapes that I saw hanging in the apartment hotel, she gave me the name of a place to go to in the downtown district and told me how to get there. She lent me her sewing machine too."

Zwilling thought: Six months. Through the summer and into part of the fall. A movie took that long? Zwilling so far hadn't signed his name to a single piece of paper, and didn't think Nate had, either. Perhaps Nate was here tonight hoping to sign that something, hoping to get paid.

Yet Selva had moved into town, a will-o'-the-wisp. Wisp of the will. Father and son were sharing a puzzle. A puzzle was at least something.

"In Barbara's fabric store the woman helping me hears me and my crazy problem out," Selva was going on, mostly it seemed for Polly's sake. "And my crazy solution. Temporary drapes that I could put on the same valance the apartment hotel's using, hiding the ugly things they had up." Selva scowled down privately at her plate: "Silly, huh?"

Zwilling saw that Nate was scowling too, unconsciously mirroring Selva. Barbara already wore a face of being completely won over, a compact grin of shy pride as Selva nattered on—this reader of Max Frisch and Buber who was willing to seem ditzy simply in order to make people feel at ease with her. Usually Barbara found it safer to dislike things and people at first. The risk she ran was that every so often one of her snap aversions lodged in her life so deeply that she couldn't cough it up; she'd grow sick and weak from it, losing touch with the world. With Selva she'd taken a flyer and had been safely caught.

In the presence of his wife's pleasure, Zwilling enjoyed Selva even more as well. At a certain age, he had stopped knowing why he liked what he liked, anyway. He liked more and more things hollowly, lightly, experiencing them less in his brain than in his lungs. But with Selva there seemed to be mysteriously more weight. She was here expressly to prosecute Horkow's design, yet Zwilling liked her differently in Cincinnati than he had in San Francisco and Sausalito. In his own cage, she seemed less mythological and more like a songbird.

"Sort of a piggyback idea," Barbara added about the drapes, despite a faint arc of *Do we really care?* developing around Polly's mouth.

"And semi-sturdy," said Selva, "so that the maid won't rip them down. At the store, the salesgirl and I found a fabric. She worked out the yardage I'd need, and we sat down and devised a sewing plan." She looked to Nate now as well as to Polly. "So I pay. I've got the bag in hand, I'm ready to go. Suddenly the salesgirl gives me a piece of paper. Not the receipt—I already had that—"

"Her phone number," Nate guessed.

"And name: Maureen Keeney. Her *home* phone number, mind you, and she tells me that she's always up until at least midnight because she loves *Cheers* reruns and I should give her a call if I run into trouble while I'm sewing. And to also call her after the drapes were finished to tell her how they worked out."

"How did they?" Zwilling asked.

"I got the building guy to let me in so I could see. I couldn't quite fit the curtains on the valance, as much as I tried. I'll just live with the originals. But I did call my Maureen and tell her how good the curtains looked."

"Little white lie, huh?" Polly broke in.

Selva was unfazed. "Yes, there's that: niceness and dishonesty sometimes getting mixed up. Another one of life's messy recipes." She looked over at Zwilling. "But all I had to do was say hello and who I was and she knew me, she *remembered*. I might have thought she was faking, except that she then said: 'The seafoam, four yards.' And that already was about *a week and a half* after I was in there."

"Must have a really great life," said Polly sourly.

Polly's attitude sat Nate straighter in his chair. He suddenly seemed to stop attending to Selva so closely. The boy was so easily redirected by women. Any woman he saw as a finality, an unarguable endpoint. The first few years after they'd moved to the Midwest, following the accident, Zwilling had hauled the kid back to the cemetery in New York too many times, long excruciating car rides that spilled them out finally at a pair of graves before which they spent too much time at a complete loss. That rigorous embrace of the dead family females all but imploded them both.

Now Nate was drinking off the rest of his glass of wine in an unmannerly glug. "I'm Jewish," he declared to Selva, completely out of left field. "Pops and I. And Barbara, who converted." Where this left Polly wasn't clear; Zwilling didn't dare glance over at her. Selva, seeming to be the only one unsurprised at the swerve, looked merely intrigued. "This whole niceness business, therefore," Nate went on, "has only a little to do with us in the first place."

"You aren't nice?" Selva asked.

Polly looked up from her plate. "Of course he is."

"What I am isn't the point," Nate said. "Even if I were—"

"Let's not force him," said his father, "into a hasty admission of anything."

"—then it's accidental." Nate glared at Zwilling. "Not something I consciously buy into very much at all."

Barbara gestured for Zwilling's attention. "What's that thing you call it, everyone being polite?" When Zwilling fumphed for a second, she prompted him: "'Civil religion'?"

"Hardly my original idea. Lots of people—"

But Barbara already was letting Selva know that "Joel says that not making waves is America's civil religion."

Zwilling knew to sit quietly. To say now that nearly anything he ever said was cribbed from reading would not be advisable. His highly accomplished but childless wife felt diminished when he was humble. Bad enough that he no longer wrote. What to Zwilling was modest, Barbara saw—as if through the world's eyes—as enfeebled. She didn't believe in self-criticism, period. Every cross to bear was a weight hung on someone else's neck, too—she'd once come across this in a book and liked to repeat it. Though not that much younger than Zwilling, she had been his student, a law student clearing her mind with a writing course. Her own meekness had been a stumbling block for them both at first (other than in bed, where somehow she let it disappear). She'd shudder at the sound of her own will. Early on there had been a memorable walk together, a summer weekend together in steaming Chicago, going up Michigan Avenue heading away from the Art Institute:

"Don't do that." "Do what?" "Look at other women." "I just was—" "Look only at me, not at other women on the street. Even if they're wearing tee shirts. Don't look at them. Only look at me." Then quickly: "I'm sorry, Joel," with actual tears in her eyes.

But marriage had helped. She'd made progress and knew it—and the last thing she desired was to be lessened by her mate's frowzy habits of renunciation.

Nate explained, "I mean like it's obviously better to be nice than to be not nice. But just shelve the thought for a second. Put it away."

"Shelved," Barbara said.

Nate's neck started to mottle. "Being nice is something that's socially agreed to. That's why it's called *civil*ity, right?"

It took Zwilling a moment to realize that Nate was asking this directly of him. His son suddenly was sixteen all over again, a sharp pain in the intellectual ass, goading his father while simultaneously asking for his framework of approval. Zwilling made sure to say nothing now, to not respond at all.

"*Civil* necessarily means conforming. *That's* the part I take exception to."

"You're forced to think of someone else before you think of yourself," Polly said.

Selva asked with a smile: "That so bad?"

"Only," Nate pounced, "if you never give yourself the chance and opportunity to be good *to yourself*. And that may mean being not quite so civil. Then, yes, it's bad, it's very bad. Removing opportunities, finally, is bad."

"You're very High Romantic about this," Selva said benignly.

Nate's blush was an all-out flower. "I don't see it as romantic. I see it as just recognizing that to be automatically nice is to be *enrolled*. To be enrolled in something before you even have a choice of whether you want to be or not is not the greatest thing in the world. You yourself," he challenged Selva, "haven't enrolled. That's why you can be generous to people who had to be, who weren't given the choice *not* to be."

Barbara had gotten up and started taking plates away, though not everyone had finished. But Nate's lecture wasn't done yet. "When you praise niceness, you're in fact being condescending. Unconsciously. *You* do something out of the ordinary, you *are* special. That's why I brought up the business of being Jewish."

"Wait, and everything shall be revealed," said Zwilling.

But he was becoming disturbed. He had a bad feeling about where the talk would go. Returning this last time to Cincinnati, hungry for the non-druggy and non-Bohemian life, Nate had spent the winter playing indoor basketball at a few different places around town, mostly Ys and school gyms. At the Jewish Community Center, which hosted a militant Wednesday-night league, he'd met up with Larry Gersh, Rabbi Leib Gersh. Gersh had played point guard to Nate's small forward and soon was inviting Nate to learn Torah with him, one-on-one. A late-thirtyish transplant from Philadelphia, the rabbi had revitalized a moribund local synagogue, and Nate adored Gersh's dynamism, how he managed to be uncompromising and intelligent in his strict observance yet still a regular guy: the Mishnah, Rav Soleveitchek, *and* Earl the Pearl.

"Whether I want to be or not," Nate said, "being Jewish makes me special."

Returning from the kitchen, Barbara said, "Chosen?" but carefully kept her eyes away from Zwilling, who felt that Polly's being at his side encouraged the boy enough.

Anyway, to pick on Selva, this blamelessly smart cookie, made no sense. She only served as an available stand-in for Nate's frustration with Horkow about the screenplay. Barbara had reported to Zwilling in bed the other night on how badly Nate was floundering, how on the phone the director was giving him no direction whatsoever, even sending him down blind, unexplained alleys. But if Selva so chose, she could take Nate down in the wink of an eye.

"Well, yes, *chosen*," Nate acknowledged his stepmother. "And since you brought it up—chosen for what?"

"To suffer, it seems like," Selva said levelly.

It pulled Nate up short. "Yes, that, always that. But also chosen to be *better*. That's what I was going to say."

This seemed to embarrass even Barbara. "You're better than better, honey. You're like your father—you're *best*."

Zwilling felt he should step in. His distance soon would be read by everyone as unfair. "I remember reading once about some Talmudic opinion. The reason the Jews were offered the covenant, it said, was because no one else *wanted* the thing. A little modesty, I think, goes nicely about here," he addressed Nate directly. "If you know you're better, where's the need to let your inferiors know it too?"

Nate's eyes became fiery. "Speaks one of the greater lights of the Northern Kentucky Jewish community? Formerly of Muncie, Indiana, and as far away from his clan in New York as he can get?"

Polly put a visible hand of warning on Nate's arm and he began to stuff food wildly into his mouth. Quickly the room had gone grayer and grainier. Zwilling screwed his stare down into the table where his plate had been. "The clan's in the ground, Natey. Recall?"

"*I* do. Do you?"

"Dessert!" Barbara called. "Joel made a coconut flan."

Zwilling's glass of wine seemed to pour down past his taste buds as he drank more of it, more quickly, than he wanted to. Luckily, the women, even Polly, had started to pick up the frayed end. Selva related the funny details of her afternoon arranging for the rental of a Range Rover to be used by Horkow when he arrived in town for location scouting. Polly said, "That's *definitely* a snob's car," but Selva—with this talent she had for finding and returning a missing piece of another person that should-n't be misplaced—fully agreed: "Although Brian's no snob. You'll see."

"Will I?"

Barbara served the flan along with strong coffee. Talk soon expired, and when in no more than a half hour's time it was finally judged to be time enough, everyone who was able to leave began doing that, in a doughy knot.

Once they were alone, Barbara said, "That was sufficiently atrocious."

"Necessary maybe. Unavoidable."

"I wish he would have stayed home. Not come expressly to make a scene."

"If that's what he even had in mind. But Selva can take it," Zwilling said. "She's good. She *did* take it."

"Yes she did, but it wasn't Selva I was worried about."

8

The Queen City Hotel, where Selva had set Brian up, was elegant inside, though the room had no view to speak of (there she'd messed up), only the dull brick facade of an office building across the street, windowless until the sixth or seventh floor. But there was outstanding quail served downstairs at the restaurant, plus a fine vegetable medley for Brian's kosher-keeping dinner companion. Even a Styrofoam dinner plate for Baruch Steyne, as requested, strenuously decorated around its edges with colors of radicchio and mâche.

Anyway, in an effort to exercise spiritual peaceableness, Brian had made a vow in the taxi from the airport to like everything about Cincinnati. Absolutely everything.

Steyne, he already knew, wore a lot of hats. An Orthodox Jew, a musician, a potter, even a polygamist. And as a poet he'd been the subject of the oddest appreciation by Joel Zwilling years before, a rave review but published under a pseudonym. Yet Zwilling was supposed to be Steyne's old childhood pal. Zwilling's son Nate had brought the strange article to Brian's attention originally.

While they ate their dinners, Brian asked Baruch how many children he had. He was told seven, at which he said to Baruch that it was beyond him how any parent could manage to take a deep breath under the load of concern for that many kids. "Because, pal, you are looking," said Brian, "at the embodiment of that fine old joke, the Jewish Telegram."

"Don't know it," Steyne said.

"Oh, you do. You know it even if you don't know it. The Jewish Telegram: START WORRYING. DETAILS TO FOLLOW."

Baruch smiled politely but assured Brian that, to begin with, seven wasn't that many children. And that, no, he never worried even close to enough about them. Charmingly and without a cudgel of superiority or religious vanity, he said that he didn't really *have* to worry a great deal about them since he had considerable help with that. The children were watched over by far better eyes than his own.

"Well, God's been of little help with mine," Brian said, telling Steyne about Tess's CF.

But Baruch turned out to have a great woe of his own, a child with Down's syndrome; and Brian said incredulously, "And yet you still believe that God is your copilot?" This so genuinely impressed him that he loathed Steyne for a minute, until the quail and the wine uncoiled him again.

For dessert Baruch ordered fruit, uncut and unadorned, while Brian was a patsy for the glitz, a boysenberry tart. Zwilling's use of a pseudonym to write about this childhood chum Steyne was what had interested Brian the most, confirming a sense he had that this Joel Zwilling was a slippery character. When the library at Berkeley was able to track down and fax the article over to him at an outrageous fee, Brian became further intrigued, enough to go looking for Baruch Steyne by phone. Steyne's first question over the phone had been: "He told you himself that he wrote it? That he was Dan Fine?"

"You didn't know? That's wild! You didn't, did you? I feel like Ralph Edwards in *This Is Your Life.*"

"Oh, I was ninety-nine percent sure," Baruch had said, "because he was the only person from the neighborhood who'd become a writer. He knew too much about the feel of where I was coming from. But when I sent him a card about what he'd written, figuring it was him, he never answered."

"That's the way he is, I think," Brian said. And before hanging up, Brian offered Steyne a $750 per diem for a possible soundtrack for the movie.

Brian hadn't read any of it yet, but according to Zwilling's essay Baruch's poetry was very autobiographical, funded by an unusual life. Back before he was Baruch, when he was still Barry, Steyne had been a teenage bluegrass musician, a high-IQ New York Jewish borough kid of the sixties who in the summer bussed it down to North Carolina to place more than creditably in the instrumental competitions. In the article, Fine/Zwilling wondered if maybe there wasn't a musical resemblance in terms of melisma between Bill Monroe's high-lonesome yodel and Cantor Yossele Rosenblatt's. But then Barry chucked the banjo completely, went to Dartmouth, and there had some kind of breakdown—after which he packed himself up for Israel and returned to the religious fold, a *baal tshuvah*. He studied in a born-again yeshiva, became Baruch, married a girl (another *baal,* originally from Chagrin Falls, Ohio) and then, as chronicled in his poems, fell in love with yet another *baal.* Rather than discard wives, he decided to stack them. Polygamy finished him off in the observant community, and he had to return to the States, where he organized a semi-Hasidic band. At a college gig he even picked up one additional wife, this one a Gentile. Eventually, Baruch and all three wives and numerous kids moved to Tennessee, south of Knoxville. Apparently all this— baldly, unaffectedly—was in the guy's poems.

Steyne had called Brian back in two days' time. He'd been thinking of maybe touring again with his old band anyway, he said. So if he was able to line up a gig or two in Detroit or Cleveland—sure, he could probably work Cincinnati in . . .

Twice Baruch and Brian were interrupted as they ate their desserts and had their coffee. First was by a pert young hostess, buttoned into a bellboyish uniform she probably wouldn't have chosen on her own. "Mr. Horkow, a lady's here to see you. She says you might have been expecting her. If you want, I can show her to your table."

"The Tash—Selva Tashjian," Brian confidently said to Baruch after the girl left. "My producer, my protégée, a first-rate mind, although moody—health problems. You have to catch her at the right time. She's great, though. You'll love her. *Extremely* smart."

Yet it turned out not to be Selva and instead a chubby brunette, a breathless-looking woman wearing a dark blue party dress and big bangle earrings. She was bearing down upon them with a sheaf of manila folders that seemed to tilt dangerously in the crook of one arm.

"Mr. Horkow, what a pleasure. I'm Gwen Filler. Hello," she shook Baruch's hand too, "I'm Gwen Filler. Tri-State Arts Liaison Board."

The woman's name struck a very muffled bell with Brian, some perfunctory bureaucratic legwork with Cynthia or Selva. The sight of her, on him like a shot his first day here, was distressing, but he asked the waiter to bring another wineglass nevertheless.

"Oh, just a little sip. I don't plan to stay. I'm not even going to sit."

"Sit," Brian told her.

She sat. "I didn't know your exact flight or I would have been at the airport to meet you. Do you both get very messed up when you fly east? I sure do." Her slightly Southern accent didn't seem to mesh precisely with a sense of career-gal hurry expressed in her shoulders. She leaned forward in her chair like someone who once had been thinner, and not all that long ago. She wore no wedding ring. "Lately I've been going to LA about once a year. So I wasn't completely sure you might not just want to turn in early, fall apart for the night."

She uncradled the folders. "I was going to fax this extra material to you while you still were in California, but I wanted it in slightly better shape. Especially the dimensions of certain buildings that were lacking in previous versions we provided to other production companies. I thought that if you did maybe want to look at it tonight, this way you'd have it." To Baruch, who was absently training a strand of his scraggly beard, she specified: "Location possibilities."

Brian said, "Thanks very much."

True to her word, Gwen Filler stood up and was beginning to back away. "The whole arts community is delighted at the prospect of being your hosts. In fact, the city in general is." She pointed at the stack of folders on the table. "My phone numbers are all on the cover sheet in there and I'm at your disposal round the clock for anything. So nice to meet you," she said to Baruch. "I'm sure we'll see lots of each other. Oh, and Mr. Horkow . . . ?"

"Brian, please, Gwen, Brian."

"The tab markings on those folders: 'Horkow Film'? Just pay no attention to them. I know it makes it sound so generic, but since you're still in development . . . *Is* there a title yet? I know it's terrible of me to admit, but I hadn't even been aware that we had this man, this novelist, Joel Zwilling, living here in the city. I guess he keeps a real low profile."

Brian stood as well. "Thanks for these, Gwen. I'm sure we'll be back to you in a day or two."

"Well, you better be"—mock-sternly, and as she started away she blew kisses in semi-Hollywood style. The taper of her ankles below rounded solid calves was attractive in the high thin precarious heels she was wearing.

Baruch was doing some kind of musicianly fingerwork on the side of his plate as Brian sat back down. Out of the corner of his eye, Brian then noticed someone truly out of place in the formal dining room— a hippie, an actual God's-own-truth unreconstructed hippie. Hawaiian shirt, chinos, Vietcong tire sandals, long hair, Brian's age or so, the whole throwback package—looking about as plunked-down on a different plane of time as did Charlton Heston in *Planet of the Apes*.

And he was selling flowers. And, with an outthrust bouquet, he was coming toward their table. Brian shook his head at him, not interested.

"Brian? *Khakhpajivietya!* Herb Dichteroff, Department of Theatre Arts, College Conservatory."

A petal of an iris nearly dropped into Brian's wineglass as the bouquet was set crosswise on the narrow table between the plates. The man took the empty seat Gwen Filler had vacated.

"Just back from the Ukraine," he said, pointing at the flowers. "Great trip. We have a sister city there, Kharkiv—you know, Kharkov?—so we do cultural delegations back and forth. Fantastic trip. A great group, great time. We got to see a local writer's funeral. No one I ever heard of, but it was heartening and extraordinary. All these passionate *intellectuals* positively rushing the grave with flowers! Masses of bouquets were also brought to any amateur concert or theater production. I was so fantastically moved! Flowers are nothing *but* gesture—and if they, who have so little, could consider gesture so paramount, you realize we certainly could try to do the same. I came back with that conviction *very strongly.*"

"I'm sorry," Brian said. "Do we know each other? We've met? Spoken on the phone?"

"Have we met or spoken on the phone," the man purred meditatively. "Have we met or spoken on the phone. Actually, we really haven't. Certainly we *should* have! When your assistant called and spoke to the Dean about the resources around here, about casting and such, I'm the one the Dean actually should have consulted with right away before dealing with her. Which, as it turned out, he did *so* unhelpfully."

His face was now so close to the side of Brian's that garlic on the man's breath was evident. "*I'm* the improvisation teacher. I'm the one who's trained in Chicago. If I *had* been consulted, of course I'd have urged the Dean to get us as involved as you'd possibly let us be. What an opportunity! Just think of the experience for these kids! But you'll find them very provincial here in Cincinnati, very provincial."

"Ms. Tashjian, you mean? That's who you mean by 'she'? You've been in touch with her?"

"*Selva* Tashjian, yes! Hard name—I did a memorization exercise on that one. Well, no, as I say, the Dean spoke to her when she inquired about the acting pool around here. It could have been taken care of so easily if he'd just turned it over to me. Which is why I'm here, to let you know, to assure you, that *both* my sections are at your disposal. We've discussed it among ourselves. The kids would be doing whatever they could for your film as their Senior Practicum. And *that* is wholly under my direction, not the administration's."

Selva had mentioned nothing about all this to Brian, but what else was new? Maybe it was important after all. "How many students are there?"

"How many students are there," the teacher mused. "How many students are there—I'm going to say fifteen, maybe give or take three. Fifteen hard-core, *and* of course myself—if that's okay with you both." He included Baruch with his eyes. Brian belatedly made introductions. "Nice to know you, Brook."

The professor's hair was a little bit like Brian's own, banks of graying untamable curls. But recession had shoved the hairline farther back, where it had fashioned a sort of hair amphitheater around the naked pate circle. "I felt I ought to go directly to you, to put your mind to rest in person. Gwen Filler told me that her information was that you'd be arriving today or tomorrow."

"She's just been here," Baruch put in two cents.

"I took my chances it would be today. If not, I would have come back tomorrow and the next day. They wouldn't give me any information at the desk, so I've been sitting in the bar, but I did have to go to the bathroom once."

He stood up. "I'm not going to keep you from your dinners any longer. I'm in the book: Meiko and Herbert Dichteroff. We're over in an absolutely terrific and diverse urban neighborhood called Northside. We'd love to have you over some time for dinner. And of course you can get me through school too. I understand you're adapting a Joel Zwilling novel. Which one? Gwen wasn't sure."

"You know him?" Brian asked.

"Joel? Never met him. Isn't that strange? Two artists—despite the fact that he lives right here?"

Baruch had judged it safe to move the bouquet off the table and rest it down near his own feet. He asked the drama teacher: "How many people live in Cincinnati?"

"How many people. I'd venture a million, give or take."

"Wouldn't that make for quite a big *right here*, then?"

Brian told Baruch that he obviously didn't understand the relativity of actors. Yet Steyne was adamant on this point. "It just seems to me that, with a million people, there are going to be those you'll *never* run across in an entire lifetime. That's just basic probability theory. To me."

When Brian got back to the suite after dinner, the message button on his phone was blinking. Shelley perhaps, in a spirit of forgiveness? Even maybe missing him?

Hopes like these were irresponsible, he knew. *Responsible* hope was supposed to be the new theme of his reformed domestic life. Clearly he had violated the theme and therefore become a pariah at home because of his fight with the doctor at the CF clinic. Shelley hadn't kept her views on this a secret. "You have this need to disturb whatever's been made quiet. You must have the spotlight on you at any cost. That's what the childish acting out with Dr. Guiamaraes was really about." Last week, unable to think up another defense for himself, Brian finally had been driven to the point of saying the irretrievable to her: "Don't you *want* Tessie to live?" And after that his exile was guaranteed.

But the message on the phone was merely that Brian's rental Range Rover had been delivered and valet parked, and the keys were available to be brought up to him at his convenience.

It was a disappointment, and as the minutes ticked on, Shelley's might-have-been call cored out the room. Brian put his shoes back on. Coming in from the airport in the cab, Brian and Baruch had passed a barn-sized liquor store near the bridge on the Kentucky side. That large a store stood a good chance of stocking more than only cheap bourbon and kiddy schnapps. He dialed the inter-room phone number. "Baruch, it's Brian, man. You settled in yet? Still dressed? Come with me to try out the Rover I rented."

Baruch was in no position to refuse. In the clean-enough Rover, and following the uncomplex instructions the concierge gave, back they went over the Ohio River—it looked membranous in the dark—and into Kentucky. The big liquor store not only was still open but it turned out to be commendable, with an unusually wide wine selection. Brian ended up buying three full cases: a Pinn Creek Reserve as the big splurge, an Oreta-Kalfus zinfandel, and a second-label Coffard Chardonnay, a wine that was new to him but which the manager, a pleasant guy by the name of Craig, said was oriented to toasty oak. But when Brian asked for an empty box, to put a few bottles of each wine in for his companion, Baruch held up a declining hand.

"Of course, right. How's your selection of kosher wines?" Brian asked Craig.

Brian was surprised when they were led to the back wall of the store, where among the boxed wines and the Asti Spumante stood two measly shelves. "Really? Just in my neighborhood alone are two good new kosher wineries that aren't represented here."

A slightly paunchy full-bearded man, standing before the same woeful selection and loading his cart full of the bottles at hand, nodded his knitted skullcap at Brian in agreement. Craig said that he couldn't persuade his distributors to send him all that much. "With all my other volume, and they still won't. Isn't that right, Rabbi? I've been complaining about this for years to you."

"I'm Larry Gersh, Leib Gersh." The rabbi shook their hands. It turned out that the rabbi knew who Brian was. "I play ball with Nate Zwilling, he's one of my newish congregants. You've arrived, I guess, to make your movie."

"They're just scouting locations," Craig the manager put in, no less au courant. "I saw the thing in the *Enquirer*. Wow, that you came in here!"

"No locations," Brian said, "no scouting yet." Had the Tash been talking the movie up while here alone? She wasn't supposed to do that. She herself had told him so back in California: "Just a reconnoiter."

After plunking some more bottles into his cart and giving both Baruch and Brian his card, inviting them to Shabbos services the next Saturday or daily minyans whenever they had the time or inclination, the rabbi headed for the cash registers. Brian soon paid for his own cases, which the manager helped out to the Rover in the parking lot. The kosher bottles rested perilously on top of Brian's box, ringing and chiming with every step. The border-town lights burned with a slow gooey twinkle. The air was chopped into distinct odors: highway exhaust, fast food, diesel fuel from the railway spans, a happy dirty smell of briquettes and molasses from a drive-thru rib shack just across the street from the store.

When they were back in the hotel suite, Brian uncorked one of the bottles of Pinn Creek Reserve. Baruch sipped at a 7UP taken from the honor bar. "Which of your children is it that's . . . challenged?" Brian asked him.

"You mean the Downer?"

Brian winced, then sucked rapidly at his cabernet: God surely took angry note whenever you forced another soul into being needlessly clever.

"My fourth. Yitzy. The third boy. After him Myryam and I consciously stopped."

"And Myryam's wife number what?"

Exactly and amiably: "Two."

"Is birth control something you're allowed to practice, or is that why you married again, to have children with another wife? I'm so nosy, I'm sorry. Had it been her fault? Of course I don't mean fault, of course not. I mean, had it been her genes? Your wife's?"

Baruch said, "He's a great kid, Yitzy. Too bad you can't meet him. Definitely one of our most *menschedik.* Maybe *the* most. I don't do anything but fully count him in. We have a special love."

Brian immediately started to leak tears at this. "Me too with Tessa, Baruch. My daughter. Yes, yes, the same thing"—the Pinn Creek quite a wine, to have prompted a sudden relinquishment of feelings like this. "Yet I'll lose Tess and you'll lose Yitzy. Or in a big way already have. Does it seem even remotely fair?"

Baruch inspected a package of honey-roasted peanuts he'd taken from the honor bar. When he found the circled *U,* the kosher allowance, he started tearing at the little bag's crimp. "How do you know we'll lose them? And where exactly would it be that we'll be *doing* this losing?"

Brian had little taste or patience for this *faux-naïf* dreck. "In *life,* man. Where do *you* live, Godland? But say you're even right, that maybe you'll be lucky with Yitzy and I'll be lucky with Tessa and that only God truly knows what He has in store for them—still, Baruch, Barry, whichever you are, for them to be sent through life carrying the kind of weight He dumped on them in the first place—it's obscene!"

"You've got a pretty sentimental attitude toward your children."

"What a word to apply! You sure you want to stand by that one? Of course sentimental, Christ yes! Who in the world doesn't?"

"Kids are unlikely to sentimentalize you, their father. Over the long haul they won't. Maybe it's better to love them too without sentimentalizing them."

"And if there's not going to be a long haul? Listen, man, I am talking about *protection* here. No one else, including your God, seems to want to do it for these little folk. I do it for Tessa. No apologies for that. None."

"I guess it follows," Baruch said, "that you also never hit any of your children?"

"I certainly do not. Of course I don't hit them." This wasn't exactly the truth; on occasion the wild-boy twins had received a whack or potch from Brian. But he was being backed up into something here. "Never."

"Maybe you *should* hit them. Tessa in particular, when she's being bad."

"When does she have a moment *to* be bad? And look, I hit her plenty—it's what you do with CF kids to keep them opened up and coughing, you hit at their chests and backs, at the shit in their lungs. Believe me, that's more than enough hitting."

Baruch scrunched his nose. "There's not also shit in children's *lives?*"

"Yitzy too? No, not *him,* you don't. Wait, you don't *really* hit your children. I'm sorry, pal, I *know* that you don't hit your Down's child. He's already been hit. All of them have already been hit. A good person doesn't voluntarily add to pain. What a shuck and jive! Do you also beat your wife? Your *wives,* I mean."

Hip to the old line, Baruch brightened. "That wine smells pretty good even from over here."

"I'll send you a case of something almost as good but still kosher. A friend of mine is a partner in Chai-Vin Vineyards. They have a special reserve cabernet that's fantastic. Come back out to the valley with me sometime and pick it up yourself. While you're out there maybe you could, as a favor to me, beat *my* wife!"

Brian reached over for a few of Baruch's peanuts. "You see, I have three children. And what a hoarder they've turned me into! I save and store every doctor's frown, every scraped knee, every hint of criticism of them by a teacher or the nanny. All this stuff I've got dragging behind me like a crocodile's tail. Crocodile tears. But people who manage *not* to do this—despite what I rationally know—you see, I view those people as cold selfish worms who shouldn't have been able to have kids in the first place."

Baruch smiled crookedly. "Like me. You know, the problem may be that you're thinking of yourself as too crucial. After all, we're God's children. God's children simply have more of God's children."

"I'm not referring to ego here. You're wrong if you think that. I want to be important to my kids if I can *help them out.* If I can't, then fuck it. I want to be nothing. A speck."

Baruch played with his dried-foam *U* of a beard. "Well, you surely have got *that* ass-backwards."

Later, about two in the morning, Brian was roused inexplicably from a light, swashy sleep, a sleep that had felt more like a settling of all the wine in him than a rest for his body, brain, and soul. He woke from it feeling as though he was mounted at the end of a pike, made ludicrous by grievance. He'd come to nowheresville Cincinnati, and already had been here the better part of half a day . . . and had Selva yet acknowledged him? Tumbleweeds like the arts liaison lady and the nutty professor, they had, but not his own associate? At the number Selva had given him, the phone rang three times before she answered. Brian said, "It's your mentor."

"What time is it?"

Had she needed to reach over someone else's bare shoulder to pick up the phone? "Two-thirty or abouts."

"You forgot to set your watch ahead, I bet, didn't you?"

"I was saying to someone just tonight that it's actors who are relative, not time."

"Can't you sleep? Room service can send you up some hot milk."

"Grouchy."

"Brian, I was *asleep*."

"And me? I am *arrived*. I got off a plane and there was no one to meet me. Not a Zwilling great or small—no one!"

"The poet, whatzisname, weren't you supposed to meet each other? Your flights were going to get in at the same time."

"I met him, yes. By the way, have you been chatting us up? A lady with the cultural affairs department or something mugged me downstairs in the restaurant. And what, if anything, do you know about a drama teacher who also says he spoke to you? I heard there was something in the newspaper too. Incidentally, changing the subject, you think Tessie would still be awake? What time is it in California right now?"

"They're asleep, Brian. Don't call them. All I did was make one call to the drama department at the university. I thought I'd first look into some student volunteers before outright hiring anybody just yet."

"Why? We've hired the Zwillings and Baruch Steyne. Why not other people?"

"Try to sleep, Brian. It's very restful here in Cincinnati. Take advantage of it. We'll talk tomorrow."

"They haven't been hired or they have?"

Dear Dr. Guiamaraes, Brian began to write on hotel stationery, half an hour later, at one of the suite's two fancy desks, *You'll have to forgive me for my intemperate words a few weeks back. They were a result, I'm sure you'll understand, of an incomplete appreciation by yours truly of the ethics of human clinical trials—especially when it comes to blameless children being used as data that can't possibly allow smiles and hopes and precious futures into the equation but only scientific factors leading to a career-building outcome. Pardon me for not grasping this fully at that moment. Pardon me too—and I apologize for this—for instead grabbing your Daffy Duck tie . . .*

He threw it away in the trash. As he drank a little more wine, he realized that the only halfway decent greeting he had received was from that Gwen Filler, that big, disheveled piece of aging girl, her calves plocking out of the hotel restaurant on her high heels. She had told him to call her anytime. The only one, so far, who had greeted him with open-ended generosity.

Clearly Brian woke her up too, just as he had Selva. When she finally arrived at the hotel, she was wearing not her vaguely slutty party dress and heels anymore but powder-blue sweats and New Balance running shoes, things quickly thrown on. It was about four A.M. But she welcomed the Pinn Creek and drank it hard while they spoke. Actually, she did most of the talking. About Cincinnati's hosting of movies; how the city's antique look had been its original selling point; how she was a little worried that it would be the only one—they needed to broaden out.

Finally Brian bent a finger at her: "Come here."

Her giggle. Her breathing out of sync and through her nose as she prepared. Her saying, "Oh, how fun." A teddy under the sweats, and in her purse condoms not only still in their box but the box still in a Walgreen bag. Though summoned in the dead of night and roused from sleep, she at one point went so far as to get down on hands and knees on the carpet, presenting her considerable hams. Brian discovered with emotion that large women, when they take off all their clothes for you, are remarkably and movingly *vouchsafed* you: the generous flesh piles of butt, belly, and tits. From the rear vantage, the swell of her thighs was a sort of additional ass, a repeated cello shape from the waist down. It even occurred to him that Gwen might not be averse to a light slap, perhaps from the hardcover local city guide *Bravo! Cincinnati!* that had been prominently arranged on a coffee table in the room. She seemed happily adventurous.

Yet as soon as Brian merely touched her with a respectful finger (which would have to do until his dingus got into more robust trim, overcoming the hurdles of fatigue, wine, ambivalence, and the requirements of the Trojan), as soon as he touched her, Gwen was crying "Ow!" as if he'd cornholed her. She was too tight, too nervous, she said—a problem, a hang-up, given to mortifying reappearances. "Vaginismus," she wept, unable to forgive herself. Soon, in a viscous air of shame, she clothed herself again while Brian overheartily complimented her charms and frantically drank some more wine. Gwen said she felt she really ought to leave. Her parting words were: "You're very sweet, do you know that?"

Here in Cincinnati for the time being, Brian chose to believe this. It served him as a jerry-built equanimity. After she was gone, Brian fell asleep curled into Gwen's opinion of him as best as he could manage.

9

Barbara took an afternoon off to go shopping. Except for an occasional charity-board meeting, which were strictly things to suffer through, she almost never took time off during the week. The male partners routinely and loosely considered golf dates as rainmaking, but Barbara would leave the office only for illness, emergency, or something involving the house, letting a plumber in if Joel couldn't be around. Never pleasure, oh no. Ever so good, good a girl.

But Selva was drawing her away from such numb dutifulness.

At one point that afternoon the two women found themselves on the western end of Fourth Street, walking past the windows of an auction gallery.

Inside the gallery, Selva was halted by one particular display table. She held up a heavy, dull, flat-bottomed, pebble-finished cooking pot.

"I cannot tell you how long I have been searching for this stuff, and here's nearly an entire set. Incredible! Terrible looking, but they're truly the best pots. They were promotions—I think from the late fifties or sixties—and you mailed in a certain ridiculous number of coupons from a cake-mix box plus some additional money. Very little. I want to say . . . Duncan Hines?"

Barbara removed the pot from Selva's hands to inspect it. Selva was going on: "Armenians must have loved them. My aunt had a set. My father. *His* mother."

Duncan Hines was correct, that Barbara already knew. She still owned a few of these pots herself. All were stored away, permanently unused, for unlike Selva's, the memory Barbara attached to them wasn't a good one: high-school-aged Barbara needling her mother about falling for consumer gimmicks. For Barbara, Duncan Hines pots were less items of family nostalgia than tokens of pointless struggle.

Yet, because at the moment Barbara didn't want to date herself explicitly to the younger Selva, she kept quiet.

"How are they here?" Selva asked Barbara in just above a whisper. "What's their policy about whole lots?"

An excitable-looking man in shirtsleeves had worked his way to them: the auction gallery's owner, someone Barbara knew by sight. "A guess—but you're the movie people, aren't you? The producers? I'm Mike Yudell. Peggy Lomas is one of my wife's best friends. I understand she's hoping to put in a bid to do the catering for you."

Selva responded by turning half away from him. He offered his hand to Barbara instead, then reached for the pot Selva was holding: "Let me take this out of lot for you. Did you maybe want all of them? It's no problem to separate them from the rest. Anything else you see, just tell me—I'll pull it."

"But these *were* going to be auctioned, right? When's the auction going to be?"

"You're an hour early. It's at twelve." He appeared to be at a genuine loss. "But look . . . "

Selva turned away, setting the pot back on the display table, nearly rapping it down like a gavel. "I'm not interested in your putting them aside for me. I'll bid like everyone else. Maybe I'll come back."

Out on the street again, Selva said to Barbara, "He's probably wondering what he did to deserve *that*. You'll have to do business with him again sometime for all I know, won't you? Probably thinks he's just met up with the world's biggest bitch. Why do I *do* that kind of thing? I used to think it was gynecological. I'm sorry."

Barbara began to feather this away, but Selva held fast, contrite. "I overreacted. He wanted something very innocent. He wanted me to be special. Therefore *he'd* be a little special."

"Well, he did say his friend was going to bid on some work for you," Barbara reminded her, feeling very lawyerly.

"No, I don't think he was trying to buy influence. He just wanted into the loop a little. Nothing's wrong with that. You know, Nate was not all that wrong the other night. His aim just was sloppy. People don't always want to be special themselves. It's someone else they prefer to be different or unusual. They need the ideal of specialness more than they need to be it themselves. It lets them off a certain kind of private hook."

"Joel's still embarrassed about that night, you know."

"No, he shouldn't be. Tell him from me that it was fine. Even kind of fun. I'll tell him myself."

"I didn't know that your official title was Producer," Barbara said.

"You'd have to be one yourself to know how unofficial producers are. Whatever Brian tells people I am from day to day, hour to hour, that's what I am. Lately it's a little more fluid than usual, but not much."

"Why?" Barbara asked sincerely.

Selva looked surprised at the question—which immediately embarrassed Barbara. "Alter egos aren't really independent animals. What I am is basically whatever Brian *isn't* at any particular moment. I should go back there and buy all those pots, shouldn't I? Even though I won't."

In Saks they paged through piqué shirts. With a hanger in hand, Selva moved in closer to Barbara around the circular rack. "When Brian was my teacher in film school, he talked all the time about this idea, I think it was Keats. 'Half knowledge.' Half knowledge was knowing what you knew, realizing what you didn't, and also *allowing* yourself not to know what you don't know. You permitted yourself to stroll around inside your ignorance and observe its dimensions. Enjoy it. It used to be very impressive to me. It seemed so smart and wise and humane of Brian to care about this, to care enough to share it with us. It took me a long time to see it in another light."

Barbara did not miss a beat. "As privilege."

Selva didn't even nod, expecting Barbara to be right there with her on this with a faith in their likemindedness that gladdened Barbara no end. How very deeply Barbara understood what Selva was saying! Joel's trust in what he knew and how he knew it was what originally let Barbara fall in love with him. The faith he had in her too—that eventually she would reach an understanding of what she couldn't grasp yet—had flattered and bolstered Barbara's spirit as nothing before that ever had.

"*Of course* Brian is going to like the idea of half knowledge. He has women to help out with the other half. To know what he wants done and needs to do. Also to *forget* that we knew what he needed. He had me pretty well pegged for someone who forgets particularly well."

"You really don't, however."

"You know, I do and I don't. You're the same way. It's rarely in my interest to remember certain things too strictly."

"The lobby of my law school had a statue in it, the figure of Jurisprudence. The scales, the blindfold, the blind servant. It used to occur to me: Who else *but* a woman? She balances everything and makes as if she'd never even seen the mess." Barbara suddenly felt self-conscious. She pointed at the blouse Selva held: "That's an interesting color."

Selva gave the blouse a more than cursory repeat inspection before returning it to the rack. "The way I finally have seen it is a little cynical. It's that to half know means you're also provided with an excuse for screwing up fifty percent of the time."

Barbara found it a kind of miracle. Two childless, attuned women who did not depress each other. Barbara sometimes wasn't sure she didn't know more about love than she did about friendship. At times in her life, friendship had seemed like a boundless field seeded with landmines: comparison, competition, regret. She'd had a mother who used to refer to neighbors as "females." Yet being with Selva seemed like being alone in company, a basic exchange of underground currents running at the identical temperature.

Selva now held up a different blouse. "Like this at all?"

Barbara said, "Eh." The reason the auction gallery owner tagged Selva so readily was that she dressed like hardly anyone else did in Cincinnati. The night she first came to dinner in Fort Thomas, she had on a cream shawl-collared crepe jacket over a flared white linen tank top. With it she wore silky black pajamalike pants. Today she was wearing a long sleeveless white jacket, a big white shirt with the tails untucked, and white jeans. Her bag was a woven red sack grommeted in gold. Over the weekend, Barbara had bought herself what she had on today—a stealthy Calvin Klein suit, soft brown with a wrap top—which brought looks of appreciation and surprise at the office this morning. All thanks to the courage Barbara took from Selva's example.

Ultimately, Selva discovered something she liked enough to buy—a pair of blue tee-strap shoes, on sale, and the weighted shopping bag then seemed to act as the pendulum of a clock, because the notion of lunch seemed to occur to both women at the same time.

Joel would have wanted nothing to do with its posters under glass and its tall potted plants, but a new, would-be chic café up on Gilbert Avenue was snug and pleasantly melancholy, the lunch crowd all but gone. Shuffling sugar packets on the black tablecloth, Barbara was so swept away by a single glass of wine that she became forward:

"What you said before, about being what Brian Horkow isn't? Sometimes that carries along with it . . ." Barbara tried smiling. "Was there ever . . . ?"

Selva's look was indulgent. "At the start. Teacher and student. But I liked him more for what he was without any of my own influence. Brian builds up a lot of steam. I wanted to be sucked up into it without him losing much of it on *me*. Besides, I always liked his wife very much."

"I was going to ask."

"Shelley's been through a lot, which I know is neither here nor there, life's a vale of tears. But with her you can actually watch what gets her through. She's frank. She makes very specific demands on other people."

"You two are friends?"

"She wants either virtue or guarantee from people. Of course, she gets neither from Brian. From me she asks for and gets guarantee, I guess."

To Barbara, Horkow's wife sounded forbidding. The fact that Selva could so precisely analyze the woman made Barbara a little insecure as well. Would she one day be dissected this intelligently and dispassionately too? "Guarantee of what, do you think?"

"That I won't hurt her man. Nuts as he can be at times, I understand that he is still her man."

Selva at heart was a protector. Barbara hoped some protecting of Joel would be included, now that she was here. For instance, Horkow had brought into town, for no good reason that Joel ever knew, an old acquaintance of Joel's, a poet whom Joel was then forced to meet with. There'd also been some "idea" conferences from which he returned half dead. "A jitterbug," Joel would mutter to her about the director. "Flies at private altitudes." And Nate was in even more dreadful shape. He'd been polled for frivolous script ideas not even related to his father's book. He'd gotten a call late at night from Horkow asking him to act as a guide, taking the director down every single street in Cincinnati. Horkow then never brought up the ridiculous request again.

"You remember that scene in *Anna Karenina* where Kitty and Levin go to tend Levin's dying brother?" said Selva.

All that Barbara, suddenly miserable, could say was, "Joel loves that book."

"Levin's so wracked by pity and terror at the suffering and dying that he's good for nothing. But Kitty just immediately sees what needs to be done for the dying man and does it. That's Shelley. She knows it too. It's a problem for them both."

Barbara would go right out and buy her own copy of *Anna Karenina* this afternoon. It once was fine that she didn't share Joel's literary loves, but it didn't seem so fine to her anymore. "The two times we've invited Brian to dinner—well, you remember, he gave excuses. Just between us, Joel asked me not to try again."

Selva's candor was what Barbara envied above all. Secrecy was something she was growing to detest. Family secrets, client secrets, her own secrets—did she increasingly miss children because so little about them could be secretive? Other people's indiscretions, confidences, and problems all got locked with complete security into Barbara's icehouse. Where Selva was openness and moviemaking visibility, Barbara gauged herself as a study in tans and shadows. She looked out the restaurant's front window. "Is Brian that way with *you* too? Making it always uphill? My partners in the firm are that way."

"Brian's one of those men who, once you surround him with poised women, he'll pay them plenty of lip service, but in the end female competence isn't a fascinating enough trait for him. Doesn't speak enough to the unknown, the half known, whatever. It seems not to keep his attention very long. A lot of the men I tend to know are like that. I'm sure you know them too."

They continued the conversation on their way back downtown in a cab. (Barbara's feet, in heels, hurt; the kind of plain flats Selva wore made more sense.) Barbara admitted, "I'm never *not* confused by it, the protégée thing. I always expect some accommodation to arrive tomorrow: my being comfortable with them or them with me. But then it's tomorrow and the next day and the day after that, and still nothing has happened. It's a little like"—and the words unexpectedly climbed over Barbara's heart like a spider into whose web she'd walked unseeing—"pregnancy. I used to expect that to show up. And always . . . "

Selva took her elbow immediately. "No show?"

Barbara's eyes became moistly grateful. Selva looked out the taxi's window at the streets. "I have been. Twice. Once I miscarried and once I *had* myself miscarried." Barbara involuntarily drew in audible air, but Selva said evenly, "My guy at Alta Bates is very good. Painless. And now it's a moot point. I'm so messed up in there with endometriosis."

"I have that," Barbara said. "Some."

"Mine is more than some. But in a way it doesn't make a difference. I was alone and I still am alone. Any addition to my kind of life that was that enormous would have had a fight on his hands, on her hands—funny that I always assumed it would be a boy. And how could I possibly do that to my own dear babies, make them have to scratch around in my aloneness? For you it's different."

"Why is it different at *all?*" Barbara nearly was dizzy.

"You have a man who loves you."

"There isn't anyone . . . ?"

"And lets *you* love him. More important." Selva leaned over and for just a moment touched her forehead to Barbara's shoulder before taking it away.

10

"Well, that was unpleasant, so let's start again. I'm Horkow."

Horkow had rented a floor-through in a warehouse building on Scott Street in Covington, to which Zwilling never would have gone if Nate hadn't pressed him. ("You should come to supervise at least once." "Supervise what?" "I don't know. That's why I think you should be there.")

So Zwilling was here. The most consistent project of his life—truer than his quest to be a writer or a husband or even a man—had been to find an effective way to deny his half-orphaned son something, *anything*. Without success, he was questing still. Would he have been any better a father to his daughter if she'd lived?

The loft's windows were painted shut. So far, though, the large dark-ish space was staying morning-cool. Right behind Nate, in the back of the room, sat Selva, more vigilant-looking than comfortable. The summer-session drama students were in folding chairs arranged in choirs at three sides of the room.

Right now they were immobilized, stunned. Their professor, Dichteroff (who'd earlier introduced himself to Zwilling with a half-aggressive and grudgeful "Finally!"), had gotten up to introduce his class of interns to Horkow. Yet in the course of his rambling speech, during which the teacher made mention of Brecht and Grotowski and Artaud and John Berger and Peter Brook, he was approached by Horkow from behind and without a word or signal had his elbow taken by the director and was calmly led from the loft. Horkow then bolted the steel door.

A good-natured, I-can-take-a-joke knock came from the other side of the door. Then another. A fainter one again. After a minute, one more. Then silence.

"Over there, doing nothing much, are my associates. My producer, Mizz Selva, Selva Tashjian—the one with the clipboard, the vaguely jaded look—and my cinematurge, Mist Nate, Nate Zwilling, whom I hope will help us all write a script together someday. The man who looks like him but is older is his father. You see him back there, hiding all by himself in that corner way way in back? I bet not quite back far *enough*, though, eh, Joel?"

A check for sixty thousand dollars drawn on a Florida bank had arrived by mail at Zwilling's house the day before. Nate had received one too. Joel immediately had put his in a drawer, never intending to cash it, if it even were good: No contract with Horkow had yet been signed and he hoped none ever would be. Nate, on the other hand, certainly must have cashed his, though it seemed clearer day by day that he'd worked himself into a terrible jam, unable to deliver anything to the movie people for the money. Zwilling had been kept up the past few nights wondering whether or not this failure was going to lead Nate back to shooting crystal meth—and so in secret, the kind you want to keep even from yourself, he had two days ago begun to write a movie script based, repulsively, on his own old work. If Horkow ever suddenly pressed Nate for something he could claim as his own, there it would be, at least something.

"Also I'd like you to meet someone else, someone who's right here in this paper bag. This'll be our presiding pneuma, our fetish, our mascot—please great him warmly: Alf! My little girl must have ten of him and I filched one as a talisman before I left California. Makes me think of her."

Horkow peered back toward the left of the room. "It's funny, sir? You over there, yes you young sir, this is funny? I guess so. I'm no one to hold anything against someone who finds something funny that I don't find funny. Still, I think I better rest Alf right here on this windowsill where he can be undisturbed. And perhaps continue to amuse. 'Kay."

He picked up a clipboard. "Schedules. We're working only early mornings for a while, the time when your class over at the Conservatory normally would be, so I thought it wouldn't at all be a bad idea for us to make up a rough bathroom schedule. The clipboard's holding a piece of paper that'll be coming around to you in a minute. There is one small, primitive john in this place and that's why planning is necessary. I am myself already down for about twenty minutes after my second cup of coffee. I've figured that as about nine-thirty. I'll pass it around. Pass it among yourselves."

Rudderless with their teacher gone, the students were defenseless. Zwilling felt for them. Two of them—the sole males in the class, both of whom wore camouflaged hunting vests strewn with left-wing political buttons, anarcho-Brechtians like their departed prof—actually were bold enough to scribble something down on the clipboard. When one of them passed it on to a female student, though, she had the good sense to slip it disdainfully under her seat.

Half the girls had short perky haircuts: These probably were the musical-comedienne/ingenue types. The others wore their hair longer, the soulful tragedians, the Antigones-to-be. When Horkow later asked for opening questions or comments, the eager boys spoke right up, spouting trendy guerrilla-theater buzzwords. But though they were given an encouraging thumbs-up sign, Horkow refused to respond to them and seemed to be waiting instead for the girls. Finally, one of the serious Antigones obliged.

Horkow listened to her question and considered it a moment. "How do I treat motivation, the young lady wants to know. You all hear the question? Well, I see it's going to take some time to disabuse you of the notion that this is a master class, but meanwhile, so you'll never have to think about this again, at least with me, or with anyone else if I can help it, these, I guess, *are* my feelings about motivation."

He looked up at the pressed-tin ceiling of the loft. "There is none. In acting *or* in life. That's my answer about motivation. When I was home in California—this happened the very day I was leaving to come here to Cincinnati—one of my little boys . . . you see, I have twins. One of them was playing outside near the vines—we live next to vineyards—and he managed to step into dogshit, which inevitably he brought inside on his shoe later.

"So you all know how that goes, right? *What's that smell?*—and by then the kid's playing with his brother and the rug's starting to show these rusty spots everyplace he's been. My wife's not there at the moment, she's away somewhere else, for her sanity's sake—and where the nanny is right then I also have no idea.

"So I've first got to get the shoes off and stop the invasion. There are all these wads of fouled paper towels on the floor next to me in addition to the kid's shoes, plus I still have the rug itself to deal with. We like Lestoil in my house, incidentally, for this kind of job.

"But finally it gets done, cleaned up, of course just in time for the nanny to show her face. And I still have a plane to catch, I have to go to the airport. I kiss the kids good-bye. But on my way out with my bags, right by the front door, by the mat there, I see there's a *little* more shit, just a slight stain—which I take care of. And then, finally, definitely, I'm out of there once and for all.

"I go to the airport and get on the Cincinnati plane. I'm a good sleeper on airplanes, which is a blessing really, so I fall asleep and wake up just as we're beginning to drop altitude, making the first approach to land. I have two tips for you. Tip one: Drama workshops are bullshit, which is why you're going to have to fight to get one out of me. Tip two is that the best thing you can do to regulate the pressure in your inner ears when you're up high is a maneuver an ear-nose-throat doctor once taught me. You hold your nose and you make like Dizzy Gillespie. You puff out your cheeks.

"But you see I was groggy, just out of sleep, and I didn't remember to do it. Instead I just tried blowing my nose. I blew into what I *thought* was a tissue in my back pocket. What it was instead, though, was this particular piece of paper towel . . .

"*Capisce? Farshtayst?* Any other questions about motivation?"

Yet even the travesty of writing a secret script came as an improvement to the tenor of Zwilling's life ever since Horkow's invasion. Back when Barbara was made partner, Zwilling had given up his full-time faculty position; now he taught only one course every other semester, a single afternoon a week. But with summer come he didn't even have that. His days had turned into slimy snail tracks, non-days during which he'd snack desperately, without appetite, so much so that sometimes he'd throw up or have to run to the bathroom with cramps. He read inattentively. He did some reshelving of his overgrown collection of old records, LPs. Without seeing, he watched endless loops of cable news and the stock-market channel, which were good only for alarming him every half hour. Luckily, Barbara had been away a lot on business, so she was largely spared the pathetic sight of the mole he'd become, deeply impacted except when he pried himself out of the house in order to attend one of Horkow's "meetings."

The first had been a breakfast at the lavish restaurant of the Queen City Hotel two days after Horkow had come to town. Having planned it as a reunion between Zwilling and Barry Steyne, Horkow seemed disappointed by it from the very get-go. "Baruch here hasn't written another book since the one you wrote about so favorably, Joel. That's a shame. I haven't actually read his first book—I'm going to—but maybe your review of it made it sound so good that I didn't think I had to read it." Barry Steyne, meanwhile, had been smiling painfully (Zwilling hated to see children he once knew, grown into men), his fingers twitching and drumming nonstop. He sported a full but not quite sufficient beard and a pancake-sized crocheted yarmulke attached by a hairpin. There was a perplexed look in his eyes, as Horkow rattled on: "Sort of a tribute to you, maybe, Joel, don't you imagine? You stopped him dead. I wrote a book too, just one."

Horkow went on: "My wife writes books, you know. *Breathing Room: A Parent's Guide to Children with Cystic Fibrosis*—that's the big seller. But the one about international adoptions is starting to come on. Check these out sometime—not only her books, but books like hers. You discover what people want from writing. They don't want shrines, they want *guidance*. The whole thing's about usefulness. Us guys really don't get it. I'm learning, though. Even with this movie, I'm learning. It's been useful to *me* already. And, look, it got you two together again."

Years ago, a week after the accident—as if he had absorbed nothing from it—Zwilling automatically, unforgivably, disgustingly had tried to write a poem. Rhyming *cited* with *sighted* (when Rebecca and Liss were killed, the driver in the truck was held responsible only for reckless employment of a trailer, his sum admonishment a ticket; "I'm sorry," the town constable had told Zwilling, "but all I'm able to do is cite him."). Rhyming *Ditch Witch* (the machine that had destroyed his two girls) with *this which*. And committing such crimes as *Now that we're made no longer four- / but two-sided* . . . until he finally came to his senses and threw both the paper *and* the pen away in the trash can.

Yet a few years later, he'd received in the mail Barry Steyne's book of primitive poems. These were poems about the birth of a child with Down's syndrome, an unerasable screw-up; about the poet's inability to return merchandise to a store; about being too nice to a boor who criticized the fact that there was more than one Steyne wife. There were ones about talking to oneself, about having trouble changing a banjo string onstage, about snot-eating, about the quality of the telephone voice one of his wives used when she was talking to his mother. Moved by these poems that seemed to have awakened within art like a sleeper in a strange room, Zwilling experienced a moment of rededication. In one pass, he wrote an overly praising appreciation and sent it to an editor of a little magazine he knew. But at the last moment he lost heart and demanded it be published under a pseudonym. Barry Steyne, once it appeared, tried smoking him out by letter, but by then Zwilling had retreated back into his cave of secretive silence.

"You know," Horkow had said suddenly, "I think I'm going to leave you guys alone for a little," and he got to his feet and took the breakfast check with him.

"I met your son yesterday," Barry Steyne said. "Plays drums. I didn't know that. I even invited him to come tour with me sometime, but he said he had to stay here. You ever go back to Brooklyn?"

Zwilling shook his head. "Do you?"

"No."

Zwilling here felt he needed to explain something to this man, who was a genuine musician. "Nate, you should know, only really 'plays' drums in quotes."

Steyne fiddled with the rind of his honeydew half. "How much did I disappoint you, Joel? As a percentage, say, of your—or of 'Dan Fine's'—first interest in my poetry. Fifty percent? Sixty? More than that?"

Zwilling shriveled. "Well, to paraphrase the old crack, who are *you,* to disappoint *me?* Come on, Barry. You didn't disappoint me at all. There's no disappointment. I liked your book a lot. If anything, *I'm* the one—"

"The fact that you made the effort to write something about my poetry—and that then I didn't write any more of it . . . When someone expects good things from someone else, and that person then doesn't deliver . . . It's a breach of faith. *But . . . !*" he improvised—and produced a manila envelope from underneath his chair.

Horkow now was addressing the student externs. "Who's going to come up here first this morning?"

One of the musical-comedienne girls rose, a spunky one Zwilling had seen making whispered comments to her seatmate.

"Okay, petunia, bring your chair forward. Turn it around to face everyone else. Now sit back down and pay everyone else no mind, they're effluvia. Good. Now let's start this way. Say the word 'child' for me."

"Child."

"Can you try saying it not quite so much as though you're deciding between Sprite and Coke? The word *child* takes you somewhere, doesn't it? Do you *have* a child?"

With a risqué giggle, the girl said, "No, thank God *not*."

"You've been one, though."

"Well of *course* I have. Hasn't everyone? Of course I've been one."

"Or so you've heard tell. You know, I don't think we *really* remember being children. We let our parents remember all that time for us. That way we continue *being* children. Then, when our parents are dead and we want to remember, we can't; we get all fucked up and desperately fanciful. In any case, back to this: What about *knowing* one, knowing a child?"

"I know plenty of children."

"I see this isn't exactly working. So let's change—nonono, I don't mean you should go, you stay, leave your chair right where it is, don't go anywhere. Sit in front of us all. Let's start again. What's your name?"

"Deanna."

"'Kay, Deanna. Deanna, I'd like you to wave good-bye."

"Really?"

"Good-bye. That's all. Wave good-bye."

She waved.

"Fine. Now, allow me to tell you a little something. Try as hard as you can to believe me, too, since I am right about this. Deanna, you *really truly do know* who it was you were waving good-bye to just now. You know the one specific person. I'm not talking about some drama-class-bullshit personifying. A fact: *You know who it factually is.* And also *when* he or she was who he or she is. So tell all the rest of us, please."

"I was just waving. You told me to."

"But you don't ever wave good-bye to the air, do you? Or to the past? Or to the room you just left? Of course not. You wave good-bye to *someone*. So to whom?"

"I don't know."

"You *do* know. I want you to tell me."

"To muh-mom?"

"Great. To *maman*. Now we're cooking. You're French, I take it, Deanna?"

"Muh-*mom*. My mother."

"'Kay, got it, just heard wrong for a moment. So then where was *yuh-mom* going? Tell us where. To the hospital? Was she going to a funeral? Was she leaving you in the care of someone not as tender and gentle as she is in order to earn enough money to keep you in some degree of comfort, considering that your father ran off and left you two in a bad spot? *Where?*"

"I was going to school and I was saying good-bye to her. I had an eight o'clock class."

Horkow studied the rosettes in the pressed-tin ceiling of the loft.

"You asked me . . ." The girl searched her thumbs for some composure. "Even *I* can understand, you know, what you want. You don't have to be insulting. And I'm not the only one here who feels that you . . ."

"Stop right there, good. Good! Tell me what it is that I want."

"You want us to be expressive."

"Expressive? Maybe. Actually I don't—I don't want you *plural* to be anything! I want Deanna to wave in the now *as though it had something to do with the then!*"

"I could try again," whispered the girl.

"Mr. Horkow, I think I need to say something." Another of the female students, one of the pure-theater tragedians, had risen.

"Tell us. Tell us all what you need to say."

"You left Deanna with not much self-respect, I feel."

"Did I?"

"That's the worst thing you can do to a person."

"Worse than drowning her? Worse than clogging her lungs with crap?"

"You know I don't mean it like that."

"I do, but do *you* know? What about making a person aware of his speech affectations? A guy I know, you ask him a question, any kind of question, and he asks it right back to you. 'How was your vacation?' you say. He says, 'How was my vacation. It was good.' You ask him how he'll manage without the other car. 'How will I manage without the other car. Maybe I'll ask Meiko for hers that afternoon.' That kind of thing. It probably started out as an academic tic, repeating the question to the class at large, but then it became part of the way he naturally spoke.

"Still, it's enough to drive you up a wall, no? Enough to make you want to one day point out to such a person how incredibly annoying it is that you can't ever ask him a question without him echoing it right back. So then suddenly there are potholes for him whenever he opens his mouth, ones he never knew were there before. Without a comfortable way to say things anymore, he probably finds a lot less things worth saying. That might not be such a bad thing, but neverthesss, *that,* off the top of my head, might probably be something worse that you could do to a person."

The kids buzzed. "That's why you threw Dr. Dichteroff out?" one of the camouflage boys called out. And the serious girl, the original protester, who'd stayed on her feet throughout, said, "Well, isn't that what you sort of did do to Deanna too? About how she says her mom? A person isn't reliable for how she does or doesn't speak."

"Tell me, Deanna, did I? Did I stop you from thinking about your mom? *Reliably?*"

"No."

"Good, I'm glad. That was not my intention. And I applaud you all—a little insurrection is a good thing. What do you say we get back to the work at hand? I think what I'm going to do tomorrow—we're done, by the way, Deanna, go back to the others—is split you for the time being into acting groups, cadres. Try to picture yourselves in quilted uniforms with little red books. I think I'll make the division according to an unsurpassably useful scheme I stole years ago from Sam the Sham and the Pharaohs. The 'Woolly Bully' band? San Antonio Tex-Mex, drove around in a hearse and wore turbans? Nah, you're all too young. They had another song—it was lesser-known but it was a great Manichean song all the same: 'Oh That's Good, No That's Bad.' And that's how we'll do it. Some of you will *be* good, some bad. Some of you will *do* good, others bad."

The guy is plainly nuts, Zwilling thought, not for the first time. For minutes Zwilling had not dared to move his neck, for fear of catching Nate's eyes or Selva's from across the room. After Baruch had left town, maybe about a week later, there had been another "meeting," just Zwilling and Horkow, the two of them. It had been planned first as a lunch at one of the riverboat restaurants, yet once Horkow had parked near the boat, he'd made no move to open his door of the Range Rover. Zwilling, after a few seconds of hesitation, was compelled to let go of the handle of his own door as well. Perched together at a silly-feeling height, the two of them watched the river traffic from the parking lot, a concrete apron that sloped down to the water's edge. Forlorn ducks drifted around the riverboat's sternwheel. Men and women in leather-soled business shoes battled gravity on the waffled gangplank leading down to the restaurant. A coal boat pushing barges moved silently into sight west of the stadium, coming downriver.

Horkow reached around to the backseat, where his briefcase was. Zwilling remembered the same briefcase from California. When Horkow again pulled photocopies from it, Zwilling found himself holding his breath.

Yet in the end, the papers were ignored. Horkow maybe only shook them once or twice—and during one gesticulation Zwilling was able to rest fairly reassured that his old *Harper's* thing was not in Horkow's hand.

"Art-making sure is embarrassing, isn't it? Had you always figured you'd give it up? You hole up here in Cincinnati, you don't see people, you don't see me—why? All that happened to you was simple every-day failure.

"You know, I made three films, all three of which died in the am-bulette. So does that mean I should transform my life into a grand gesture of disposal? You wrote some novels that nobody read—what else is new? All that happened to both of us, Joel, are accidents. Accidents.

One thing standing in for another, that's all. Your kid and wife die instead of someone else's wife and kid. My kid gets sick instead of someone else's kid. Everything could as easily be anything else."

He began pointing toward the riverboat. "Did he just cut power?"

It looked like it to Zwilling too, who squinted at the boat's wash, the prow of the leader barge. Emaciated sounds of troubled engines were reaching the shore.

Horkow reached back and returned the papers into his briefcase. "Or is it just that you like to be *chased? That* why you play dead?" A fly had entered the car. "Am I talking to a dead man, a ghost?"

Out on the river, the tug then made a horrible grinding, its whistle blowing in alarm. "This guy," Horkow commented, "just pooped out in front of fifty thousand people watching from their office windows. How mortifying. Had to wait till he was going through a city."

Zwilling rolled up his window against the oily smoke coughed up by the disabled boat in the middle of the river. Then he thought better of it and rolled the window open so that at least the fly could find a way to leave.

Was or wasn't Horkow finally going to mention the Ramada story? Obviously he knew of it. Zwilling wished he'd just get it over with.

Instead, sounding heartfelt, Horkow said: "You know, I never counted on the fact that you wouldn't like me. That I really hadn't expected. Back in California, I'd hoped we'd be pals. I think maybe we still could be." He shrugged before turning the ignition key once again. "But you'll be the one who knows better about that than me."

Now being passed around the loft to the students as well as to Nate and Selva and Zwilling were copies of what Horkow called "a lyrical ballad" he'd been inspired to compose in Cincinnati. "*Nothing* on the radio here except country-and-western. Isn't that true, Joel?"

The students turned back to look.

"I don't think it is," said Zwilling. "No."

"Well, I've even started to like it, the country stuff. Emotion turned into kitsch, then back into emotion again. What I just gave you, cadres, is our last exercise for the morning. If, after a while, you could all sing along." And then, in a pleasant, high, utterly false twang, Horkow began to sing:

> Their problem was the chicken.
> Should not have bought it first.
> Once they hit the old motel
> They were about to burst.
>
> But the bucket on the dresser top
> Smelled of grease, smelled good.
> For chicken, though, they'd think to stop?
> And break the precious mood?

"Here it's still rough:"

> But stop in time of course they did
> One's always bound to be
> A little hungrier than the other . . .
> There's never—
> Uh-uh, never,
> Uh-uh never—
> Real parity

"Come on, everyone, sing. You've all got the words. Make up any old tune. Mumbling through a song you don't know is *good* for you. Sing!"

> So while she was his snack,
> And while he was her meal,
> One of 'em always was thinking:
> Soon we'll eat for real.
>
> The chicken sat there getting cold—
> Getting colder, colder, old.

People wait, bodies do—but the
   chicken it was cooling,
Shake it, bake it, fake it, take it—but
   chicken isn't fooling.

"Well, *God*," admired Horkow, "isn't that just piss-awful!"

"Certified pigshit!" one of the guerrilla boys called gleefully. He and his friend whooped it up with low fives like a couple of frat brothers. One of the girl students, though—in tears and muttering something that sounded to Zwilling like "An actress needs . . ."—started getting up to leave.

"And me?" Horkow trained his eyes glitteringly on her. "Do you have the slightest idea *I* need anything? It would help if, as my shock troops, you could figure it out on your own, though you won't, because we don't figure out other people's needs, it's not in the nature of the animal. So I'll just tell you. I need *pity*.

"You're laughing? Yes, you, the same redhead again—don't look at someone else—you. Yes, I do—that's what I need, to be pitied. *Everyone* needs to be, which is why pity is the holiest emotion of them all. You can provide it but never reap it. *It's the only thing you can take by giving it.* That ever occur to you? Now it has. 'Cherish pity, lest you drive an angel from your door.' Blake, 'Holy Thursday.' And so now all of you go home or back to school or whatever. Go, go."

Immediately the girl sat down.

"Everyone's staying? It must be a hell of a show. I mean it, I am dismissing you—without prejudice, as they say. Am I going to have to go in order to get you to go? Because I will, then. I mean it, we're done for the day. God bless you, God protect you one and all, and to all of you a good morning!"

11

Even though Joel Zwilling had chosen the place himself, the poor man was dressed up more than this casual restaurant required: He wore a tie and a sports jacket, possibly the exact same outfit he'd worn to California that time. So Selva felt she ought to make a little more of the place. "Giant windows. I really love airports." After beckoning for a taste of his iced tea, she then didn't return the glass to him. "Tell me the name again of the firm Barbara works for?"

"Steiff, Cloud, and Gaines."

"A big deal around here, I gather."

"Nearly two hundred lawyers."

"A lot of the partners women?"

Joel grinned at her as she took another sip of the now appropriated tea. "Maybe eight or nine. Something like that. I forget exactly how many."

"We've talked about it, Barb and I. I'd been under the impression, though, that there were more than those few women. Eight makes for a very fine line to walk."

"I guess she doesn't look down at her feet."

"Well, that's lonelier than you as a man could know, believe me."

"Barbara was an only child. So she's probably somewhat used to it."

"You expect people to be used to things, don't you? But sometimes it doesn't happen." Selva reached over and dragged away a few of his french fries. It actually was easier for them both for her to eat his food. Her salad had come piled so artlessly high that to eat it first meant dismantling it, logs of spice-charred chicken skittered off the greens, forcing her to spread the napkin wider on her lap. Joel had watched this fretfully, already concerned about his own order; his stomach had been giving him trouble lately, he told her, and so he'd ultimately settled on a simple hamburger.

Selva said, "It's a particular trait, expectation. I have it too. I don't know if it's a talent or not. You think it's realism but it may be the very opposite, I don't know. People usually *don't* get that comfortable with new situations easily. If you expect them to, you set yourself up for disappointment. You didn't have brothers or sisters either, did you?"

"Only my parents. As much of them as there was to have."

"They the kind of couple who lived only for each other?"

"Well, they were camp survivors. They had no good subsequent idea of what they lived for, exactly. Other than to keep living vengefully in order not to die. It was probably very exhausting, although I'm enough their son to find it perversely appealing, too. Any siblings for you?"

"My mother died when I was two. No, no one else. *My* parents—at least this is *my* myth, *my* family romance—would have been exactly that kind of totally in-synch, adoring couple. My father required it by temperament. No time for me especially."

"So did you then take over? A kind of wife-daughter?"

"I did indeed. I was happy to be that." Through the wall of windows Selva watched a small plane start to rise into the damp sunny August noon. "Those are our guys, I guess. The fishermen."

Because Joel once had made a paternal noise about the car she'd rented for her stay in town—a tiny Geo, something too unsafe to chance getting lost in, he'd said—Selva had taken it as a challenge to not only meet him on time here at the airport (a small general aviation field with a funny name, Lunken) but even to be early, to get here before he did. Standing alone at the hurricane fence in front of the terminal, she had watched the Cessnas and the occasional corporate jet arriving and going, disappearing down a long floodplain runway to pop back into view far away. The wings of the little airplanes seemed to give an extra tug at the restraints of the heated midday wind.

A pair of tanned, potbellied men in suits had come out of the terminal to take claim of one of two small aircraft parked on the tarmac right in front of Selva. As they stowed expensive soft-sided bags and long tubes of fishing equipment in the plane's belly, Selva chatted with them. She hadn't even heard Joel arrive, approaching her from behind, shyly tapping her on the shoulder. "Catch a lot!" she had wished the pair. One called back: "Sure you don't want to come? Ditch him and hop in?"

"They're going for steelheads in Montana when their meeting's over," she filled Joel in.

The fishermen's anticipation; her own consciousness of her rear in jeans, pitched out a flirty inch as she leaned on the fence; even the sight of Joel's unnecessarily nervous tie—all of it had pleased her deeply. Cincinnati seemed to have been poured around her like cake batter; she was baking and firming within it. Her very worst habit, overdetermination, was forfeiting itself to the damp, level unexcitement of the provincial city's summer days. Dr. Coffman had been right. So far, a slower pace had worked to her body's advantage; cramps came fewer and farther between now; sometimes there were a few consecutive days without any at all. She'd ceased to feel like a crowded arena of pain.

Now, through the restaurant's glass, she watched until the little plane slid into the air and left her sight. Joel, noticing that she was only picking at the mushrooms and dry sprouts, leaving the hard-burnt, uncuttable chicken, said, "I'm sorry."

Selva didn't especially care for this too-easy air of apology out of him. It seemed too matte a finish, too neutral an emotional coloring for him. She pushed the unmanageable salad away and filched another of his untouched french fries. "It's an odd position I'm in, here in Cincinnati with you," she said. "You make time for me, like now, which I appreciate. Which in fact I love. Spending time talking to you. Sometimes I'm afraid that you may be making the time because you think—considering the configuration here—that I have messages to bring. From Brian mostly."

Joel played with his silverware. "Ah, he makes pretty sure I get to know his thoughts and concerns directly." Then, mildly, a little sadly: "And even if he didn't—I don't think I've turned into that much of a Buckeye. I'm still able to see people as more than the sum of their errands."

Sometimes, like now, he didn't appear wholly healthy to her; there was a touch of pallor under the complexion dictated by his light eyes and reddish hair.

"Nor any messages from Barbara, either," Selva made a point to add. "She's so naturally discreet, anyway."

"What they say about good lawyers, isn't it?"

"Anyway, just tactically, how would I ever get to know you if you kept expecting information *out* of me? I know, for instance, that you once had some, but do you still have money of your own?"

At this, his head comically started to bobble back and forth.

"I'm not allowed to talk about this with you?" Selva asked.

"*Children,* Selva, with their big innocent eyes, ask such questions: '*Mister, are you rich?*' We're haute bourgeoisie of a bedroom community of Cincinnati. Barbara makes a very good salary, plus bonuses. Whatever I had at the time Nate and I first came out here I got good advice about, and I took it. I've had good luck putting it into decent places."

"Stocks? I'm only guessing stocks on the basis of that story you once wrote. The woman who didn't want to buy only mutual funds."

Selva had known from the time she first met him in California that this was someone you'd have to take a chance with. There was something doubled or mirroring about his intelligence. Like the two lobes of his brain. And he was someone who had learned a rare thing: to let a wound not heal completely, not a hundred percent. To let it act instead as a reference point, a backboard, a collator. Selva knew all this about him because she was much the same way. She had been told (mostly by men) that she was father-obsessed, father-obsessed or else cold. Cold had been ultimately easier to accept. Yet Joel Zwilling, she realized, quite out of left field, was melting an edge of that painful belief. She wasn't cold. Like him, she just was more prepared than some to cut her losses.

Now his hands were clasped upon the tablecloth in front of his plate, as if in prayer. "The suspense had been killing me," Joel said. "So you read my story. How did you first come to it? Nate give it to you?"

"I first found it on my own, months ago. I don't think Brian knows of it, nor would he be interested, anyway. Hey, finish your burger. Dr. Tashjian's approach to stomach ills is to eat *through* them. You know, you did once promise to give me a tour. You have any time to do that today, after we leave here? Take me someplace? I want to see more of the city."

"All that there is of it to see."

"There's enough, though, right? There's always enough."

Joel's car, largish, stodgy, American, was also not too new. When they were stopped at a red light not far from the airport, Selva said, "I've been around here before, I think." On one corner a knot of hillbillyish-looking mothers waited for afternoon dismissal outside a school building. "You know, I'll miss big bangs when I go home. And, look, there isn't one who looks like she isn't working on a major-league eating disorder. They're pencils or else bowling balls. Plus they all smoke, almost every one of them."

"Why were you around here before?"

"This isn't Northside?"

"The East End," Joel said. "The whole other side of town, right on the river. How do you know Northside?"

"Remember that drama professor Brian threw out, Dichteroff, the one whose students Brian's been entertaining? I went to his house to make nice."

"How did the nice-making go?"

"As you would expect it to, fine. People are craven for the tiniest personal attention. I wish hurt feelings could sometimes marinate more, at least until they turned into something useful. Besides which, he's a truly silly man."

"*Tenured,*" said Joel. "Worse than silly."

At the door of a fuchsia-colored brick townhouse, Selva had been met by Dichteroff's Japanese wife, who ushered her anxiously past the front rooms to the kitchen at the back of the house, where Selva found Dichteroff seated alone at a refectory table. A can of Sprite sat before him, as well as copies of *The Nation* and *Tikkun* and *In These Times* spread around the long table's surface like felled birds. He hadn't been expecting company; the look on his face was private and unformed.

At first Selva read it as guilt. In the gossip column of that morning's newspaper, brief mention had been made of "movie director Brian Horkow's unconventional rehearsals in a Covington loft—which, we hear, are yielding scratched heads from local talent and even some complaints from the Conservatory externs involved in the project." Selva had to be careful to make no direct accusation—yet as soon as the subject was gingerly advanced, Dichteroff vehemently denied ever talking to the newspaper. Selva believed him. "I never would even *read* that rag! Whoever did tell them, though, I want to congratulate him. Probably did everyone a favor."

Selva then had apologized for the even older business, the scene at the loft. She tried explaining Brian's "method," but Dichteroff surprisingly stomped onward, a cause mounted firmly on his shoulder: "No, this is *good*, yes! Let him treat me the way he wants to. Who am I to him? I don't matter. But shake 'em all up! This is *great!* Shake up this fucking dead place! Get their smug attention!"

When the light changed, Joel left the school behind and soon was making a series of turns and pointing the car up hilly streets. The sight of many old gingerbread Victorian houses prompted Selva to say, "It's like San Francisco, the Painted Ladies."

"You realize I've just provided you with a good definition of a provincial?" Joel said.

"I'll bite. How so?"

"Someone who shows someone else something in order to get the expected reaction—that's a provincial."

It was said with a touch of sorrow. Selva looked at him more intently. "But it *does* look a little like San Francisco. So what? Are you being contemptuous? You aren't really that, are you? I can see someone like our drama prof needing to feel that no place he lived was good enough for him—but not you."

Joel's response was to pull the car to the curb, leaving the motor on but yanking back the parking brake and staring straight ahead through the windshield for a moment.

"I upset you talking about your old story," Selva said seriously, hardly able to breathe. At that exact moment, her heart was surrendering to him.

He smiled queasily. "*The Thing That Came from the Deep*. It really wasn't Nate who showed it to you originally?"

He released the brake and started the car into the street again. Selva plucked a tissue from a box resting between them on the front seat, wrapping it tightly as support around the first two fingers of her right hand.

"I just had done some legwork. Your son adores you."

Nate Zwilling had been touchingly forthcoming about his father at first. The names of the three novels Joel had written. What life was like in New York when Nate was little. How Joel had worked part-time for the ILGWU writing public relations and teaching writing at Cooper Union. He spoke of his mother's and sister's accident, how the two of them were going out that day to buy sour cherries while Joel and the boy stayed home.

But then, as the girlfriend Polly sat watching like a duenna on a hard unforgiving chair brought in from the kitchen of their apartment, Selva had probed a little too wide afield. She asked about money. They had the insurance money from the accident, Nate answered, plus there'd been a grandfather, Nate's mother's father, who had died. Joel's survivor parents, in turn, died not long after—with all their savings from their hosiery store and from the reparations payments paid to them by the German government coming to the Zwilling men as well.

Then, suddenly angry, Nate had flared: *My father's not a bad guy, you ought to know. And he used to be a brilliant writer*—at which precise moment Selva knew she could have a film here in this for Peter Swainten of Channel Four if she ever chose to pursue it. A documentary about Nate Zwilling, done with slow intricacy and without pressure, a way for her to stay calmly centered in Cincinnati and perhaps save her womb. In that documentarian mode, she could easily have pressed on: If your father is in fact such a good guy, why do you suppose he's done everything humanly possible to make his son think otherwise? To lower himself in your and everybody else's eyes? To not be a writer anymore and give up his gift? How do you feel about being the son of a son of survivors? Your father experienced his own miniature Holocaust when your mother and sister were killed—do you think that a style of catastrophism had been passed down to you?

This last thing she regrettably *had* said to Nate that day. And into his eyes came a hatred for her that there was no mistaking.

"That sign I just saw," she asked Joel. "'River Downs.' What's that?"

"A track."

"Racetrack, you mean? Have you ever gone? Is there any racing there now?"

"I've gone, in certain seasons, more than occasionally."

"*We* could go, couldn't we? It's open now?"

"I think the question is would we want to. First of all, it's incredibly muggy, right on the river. Plus the fact that what they race can be appalling. Dogfood horses. Alpo candidates."

Selva laughed with shock. "Don't say that! That's horrible!" She flattened out the tissue in her hand in order to blow her nose. "My sinuses have gone loco since I'm here. Barbara's going to give me some of her prescription stuff." To their left, keeping roughly even with them on the two-lane street, was a car that had a passenger in back reading the *Racing Form*. "Look, would I even know the difference between a good horse and a bad? Come on, let's!"

"You'll remember that I warned you, though."

Outside the track, cars waiting to get in were lined up on the road. A single sheriff's deputy in a trooper's hat was directing them to different gates for parking. Once out of the car, Selva and Joel funneled through the turnstiles with the other horseplayers, and Selva could see that as soon as Joel was through the gate his face changed. He felt at home here. Oddly substantial.

Selva admired the sluggish Ohio River from their seats in the grandstand. The sun compressed the haze covering the track but never quite dispelled it, and the air smelled more of cigarettes than of horse. The bettors were picturesquely ragtag. Members of a ladies' club bussed in from Indiana were being officially welcomed on the public address system, and later Selva observed some of the club members flirting with male retirees near the pari-mutuel windows.

First Joel led Selva through a race on paper. He was endearingly serious about it all. He explained to her how to read the *Form* and what to ask for at the windows and how to watch the progress of the race itself. At this track, on days like today, he explained, when the surface was rated fast, he believed in trying to determine something called a *track bias.* It was harder to do without binoculars, but what you tried to do was take in as much of the whole field as possible. You wanted a sense of who was getting to where from what post position. To that end, did she mind too much if they watched just one race first on one of the TV monitors under the grandstand? More for the sake of the replay than for the actual running.

"Like looking at rushes?" she kidded. "You're turning Hollywood despite yourself, Joel."

But she enjoyed how unself-conscious he was about all this. There was a naturalness buried somewhere in him that stirred her.

Joel stood looking up at one of the ceiling-mounted monitors in the cementy cool of the promenade beneath the stands. He explained to her what he was seeing: the break from the gate, the run to the first turn, what the statistically best of the poor lot of jockeys were up to, where they were steering their horses to, and when. Selva could make nothing at all of it. All she really wanted was to be led just as soon as possible to a betting window, to be allowed to plunk down some blind cash.

The first race that Joel finally allowed them to bet on, they both lost. She'd chosen a horse solely because she liked its name, Poit; Joel had gone in with her for the sake of solidarity, and Selva liked that he'd done that. Afterward, though, as soon as the wire was crossed, he told her reproachfully: "Completely out of the money. Never came even close," and for about ten minutes after that he all but ignored her, concentrating harder on the *Racing Form* for the next race. Selva did not disturb him.

The next one they watched from their grandstand seats. Again it was an undifferentiated rumble to her. Exciting still, though. After the frontrunning horses crossed the wire in a clump, she looked over in ignorance at Joel.

He was grinning.

"What? What? You mean we won? Did we *win?* We *won!*"

Joel for some reason was studying her shirt. Having consciously dressed preppy today, in an invisible style she thought he might be more comfortable with than her usual clothes, she'd worn jeans and a man's pinpoint oxford shirt with two pockets. What was the matter? she asked him.

"Your favorite breast, which one is it? Which one's lucky?"

Selva managed an off-balance smile. This she hadn't seen coming at all. "Why do you want to know?"

He waved it away. "Just kidding."

"No, you have to tell me."

"I wondered where we should keep tickets from now on. For luck. Hey, I was just kidding."

"I can't believe that we won!" Selva said.

"Well, he was the favorite. So most people here did think he could do it."

"But you made hardly any noise! I might never have known we won. You're one quiet victor." Selva took the winning ticket out of his hand and inspected it. "Can I pass on the pocket?"

"The what?"

"The lucky breast?"

He frowned. "I was just *joking*."

"But can I tell you why, anyway? At heart I'm a primitive. Say I went ahead and picked this one here"—her right breast, the one farthest from Joel, which she now covered with her hand. "And we won. Two months from now, I wake up in the morning . . . I feel something there . . ." She removed her hand from herself. "I'm too superstitious to call any part of myself lucky."

Joel looked almost woozy with embarrassment. But Selva had to give herself a quick reminder: Chances, chances. When he began making some apologetic noises, she cut him right off, telling him she was still hungry, especially after that showpiece of a salad.

Touching shoulders, they considered the *Form* together over bratwursts and beers on the promenade near the betting windows. Selva's eyes kept drifting over to one particular longhaired man in a sleeveless bodyshirt who stood five yards away at an adjoining refreshment table. He too was studying his own copy of the racing paper. But whenever he closed his eyes in concentration, each of his eyelids exhibited a cross. Blue tattoos had been applied to his eyelids—in prison, was Selva's guess. It was thoroughly unimaginable.

Joel, in the meantime, had made a decision. He said he was going to "wheel" the three horse in the sixth race, a horse named Pulpo, a sprinter. "It's an extravagant, idiotic, sucker's bet that I usually stay away from like the plague. But I guess not today."

Selva, entranced, looked into his eyes. "I guess not."

"Ideally, you make thirty dollars for each dollar you've bet. What it does is guarantee the trifecta: You're winning no matter what horse comes in second or third. Of course we won't win. At a mile, plus this Pulpo creature hasn't even come close in over a year."

The intelligence in his face, coexisting with goofy pleasure.

"Then why are we betting on him?"

"Don't please ask me that. A hunch."

They found spots down by the rail to watch the race from, adjacent to the actual dirt of the track. Down here, the mood somehow was lewdly encouraging. Her butt pushing out like at the airport, Selva leaned her elbows against the rail and, almost floating with easeful-ness, had a revelation.

Having given up what surely meant more to him than anything else in life, his talent, Joel mysteriously seemed more of a writer to his wife and son, and now to Selva, than he would have if he'd still worked at it every day.

Before she lost her womb, Selva needed to start being more of a woman—in a somehow aggressive way—than she'd ever been till now. If she couldn't make new life herself, she'd sharpen her skill at draw-ing existing life *to* her, become a kind of great hostess with an ever-growing list of guests. They'd leave eventually, since everything leaves eventually, but they'd also leave valuables behind: love and warmth. Temporary things maybe, but still valuables.

She squinted up into the sunlight beyond Joel's head. "This is a part of you I never would have guessed at. How it squares with your pes-simistic, realistic, seen-it-all presentation, I don't know. It just doesn't, I guess. You don't come here to lose. You want to win."

"Yeah, I'm a winning kind of guy. We all of us are"—gesturing at the other railbirds. "Seers and visionaries."

The jangling buzzer of the gate sounded. The race was going off. In-toxicated by her great bolt of self-knowledge, Selva turned to watch. Joel gave her updates through the tumult: Pulpo, his choice, was sec-ond from the rail, keeping the inside. Then, at something called the quarter pole, he was out in front. Without any science whatsoever, Selva stared at the tote board's changing position numbers and screamed, "Come on, three!!"

Then Joel was telling her that Pulpo, incredibly, was not fading, that in fact he might come across easily. Which he did—by what Joel said was a good four lengths. The thousands of pounds of horseflesh thun-dering right in front of her thrilled Selva.

Calmly, Joel said, not to her but to another horseplayer, "Amazing. Wasn't even much challenged. Amazing."

Selva hugged him. "I am never again feeling sorry for you. Someone who knows how to win at the horse races!"

"You've been feeling sorry for me?"

"What else do you enjoy as much as this?"

"Look," he said, "maiden claimers are mostly what's left on the card. Those are races for horses that never won before. So they're less interesting and much much harder to dope. Had enough? We could leave now."

"Just a little longer, okay?"

Standing behind him in the cashing line, Selva wished she could just rest her cheek against Joel's spine. Instead she addressed the back of his neck, its not-so-youthful column. "Do you remember mentioning Turgenev that night on my boat?"

He turned to her a little. "Was this post-stinger or pre-?"

"I had said something about *Fathers and Sons*. Such a faker I am, since all I really knew about that book was the title. You said you liked his *Sportsman's Sketches* even better. Of course I haven't read that one yet either—but I *did* find a biography of Turgenev in a used bookstore downtown right here in Cincinnati. And he fascinates me. A little too suave for his own good, his own happiness, but he's very touching." She was speaking now fairly rapidly. "That business, for instance, with his mistress."

"Pauline Viardot."

"The opera singer, yes. How he once rented a house next to hers and her husband's in France. Then did the same thing another time too, going around Europe with both the wife and the husband. It's somehow very moving to me. Three people who asked so little yet also so much from one another at the same time."

Joel didn't immediately say anything, and then craned fully around. "Turgenev's critics had a great old time making fun of him, you know. They loved pointing out that he had the habit of describing sunsets in colors the sky couldn't possibly have."

Yet he'd heard. That she knew. She asked to see the winning ticket, to admire it once more.

"So tell me again how much they are going to pay us for this adorable little thing?"

12

"Go back to sleep."

"I need to say something first," Shelley said.

"Just tell me first: *Is* she all right?"

An exasperated silence. "What I was going to say was that, yes, you can come back to us here anytime you want to. Now's as good a time as any to talk about this. But I mean this seriously: If you *need* to stay there more, you should do that."

"I'm *working* here," Brian said. "Of course I need to stay."

"We both know, Brian, that you *don't* really have to stay. But I did want you to hear this, though: *You shouldn't come back too soon*. The children can't say this. I have to for them. And I mean just what I said: You can't come back if you're only going to have to clear out again quickly. Your longings take up a lot of room around here. There just isn't that much space in this whole house for so many longings. Stay where you are. Piece things out. Use them all up."

"Blake again! 'Sooner murder an infant in its cradle than nurse un-acted desires.'" This was a stupid attempt to charm. Longings? What was she talking about? He was here in Cincinnati on business. Making, God help him, a film.

"I just had to go on record about this with you."

"Well you're on it," he said. "You have. In like Flynn."

"I sent you some more of the Valporate. Did you receive it? If you've been taking them, your pills should have just about run out by now."

On record? Had to? Could a lawyer possibly have counseled her to say this to him?

"It's early," Brian said. "Look, I'm sorry to have called now. Go back to sleep. I wrote a letter, by the way, to Dr. Guiamaraes at UCSF"— careful not to say if he'd actually sent it. "Go back to sleep." And then, at wit's end, standing on the little spit of sense Shelley so often lately left him stranded upon, he hung up on his wife.

When the phone rang right back a short minute later, Brian's heart bounded at his second chance. Snatching it up, he started in right away: "What gets into me? I know what you said is completely right. And calling you so early your time, waking you, that of course was thoughtless. And I am taking the Valporate," he lied.

"Is this Brian Horkow's room? Brian? This Brian?"

"Who's this?"

"It's Jay Loftspring in Miami. You on another call, Brian?"

"Who?"

"Jay Loftspring, Miami, The Warshaw Foundation? Look, I'm in a *pay* phone, Brian, and I don't want to be in here too too long. It isn't quite light out yet here."

"Why a pay phone? What's going on, Jay?"

"Brian, is Selva Tashjian still there with you in Ohio? I have calls in to her at a number since yesterday at that same area code. But she hasn't gotten back to me."

"Back to you at the phone booth?"

"Please relay something to her, can you? Both of you should hold off writing any more checks right now—say as of this morning. Whatever's already been cut and working its way through, that's okay. That'll be fully covered: your own reasonable expenses. Anything new, though, you just better hold off on."

"Jay, calm yourself. Any day now I'm expecting something out of the Zwilling kid, a screenplay draft. I'm leaning on him daily. And did Selva ever tell you that we're using interns, students? You knew about that? We're being very frugal and working forward. *Why* are you in a pay phone, Jay?"

"I wish I could have been able to speak about this to Selva Tashjian first. What both of you probably should do is go home to California for the interim. You'll see it tomorrow or the next day maybe, if it makes the papers where you are—but it looks like Gates, Mr. Warshaw, is going to have to come back here to the States. The Israeli High Court ruled yesterday against his petition to stay."

"I'm not getting you, Jay. Not getting the quid pro quo here. You expressly told Selva and me that these were nonprofit foundation moneys. Seed moneys promised to support a project. What would have changed that at all?"

"All I'm suggesting is that you dry things up for the moment there. Not even nonprofit foundations are sacrosanct. So at least ditch your profile, none of this *Variety* stuff that I saw a few days ago. The clipping service sent me something from the local newspaper, too, that I didn't like to see. We all agreed from the beginning that you'd keep this as low-key as possible, didn't we?"

"*Variety?* What did it say in *Variety?*"

"I appreciate civic boostering and all that garbage. But you can't just feed them what they want to hear and then expect them to sit on it quietly. I don't remember—something about the movie, it had to do with the local arts agency."

Gwen Filler. Oh, Gwen! Those manila folders, the sheer black hose, the meaty calves, those slingbacks. All Brian had wanted to do was like everything about Cincinnati, his temporarily adopted home. To like the inappropriate as well as the forbidden. (In a place as sheltered as this, the inappropriate *was* the forbidden, he had estimated.) And though they'd proved themselves ludicrous figures in a sexual comedy of errors, there had been many subsequent calls from her, notes left at the hotel for him, small trinkets, her continuing audition to be reconsidered as his little local piece on the side.

"The new U.S. Attorney down here, Parich, is a piece of work," Loftspring explained. "Maybe once he bought a bad penny stock, but whenever he thinks he can use the SEC to help with a case, he drools. With Gates he may even get lucky. Assets could be frozen from all sorts of places—even philanthropic mechanisms. They could even, as harassment, try to call some back. Though as far as you two are concerned, you're probably fine."

"As *we're* concerned?"

"What's on the books for you is pretty congruent, I think, with the charter aims of the Foundation. You'll be okay, I think. Parich is a very devout Catholic, the kind who'd never forget that Jesus' parents were Jewish. And so though Holocaust might not be good enough to get him to back off completely from your project, just the fact that it's Jewish probably works in your favor."

"Now, Jay, I have to say you're scaring me. What have *I* done? Are you telling me I need to worry about this? I haven't done anything! Do I need a lawyer?" The only lawyer Brian was still on semi-speaking terms with was a guy in Sebastapol named Tim Poythress, whom he had used when he sued the town over an easement for the house remodeling. Poythress might still think he'd been stiffed out of a grand or two in fees—Brian had taken some exception to the bill—but he remained someone who at least still said hello to Brian on the street. "Shit!"

"Selva, though, must call me, as soon as she can, okay? Please please make your movie apart from us, Brian. Don't let this unfortunateness stop you. Aug says you're a genius. I'm sure you are. Someone else will come forward with the backing. And Brian, tell Selva to leave her number with my voice mail."

Immediately trying Selva, Brian as usual got only her pager.

For lack of any better idea, he then called Aug Jimmerson at home in Miami. "Shaneema, sweetheart, is your daddy there? Could you maybe wake him up, please? Tell him it's urgent, it's an emergency."

All the mean willfulness of his knockdown pitches during his glory days accompanied Aug to the phone. "Who *is* this? *How* is this an emergency?"

"Gussie, it's me, it's Brian."

"You okay, babe? So early, man. There an emergency? Your little girl okay?"

An athlete front man didn't stand to figure deeply in corporate consultations, so the story Brian then told Aug came to him as totally fresh news. "That's not good, Bri."

"I'm also wondering how entire *your* ass will be at the end of the day."

Aug chuckled. "Rest your mind about my black ass. I'm cool, always cool. You know me, always working on a few things of my own on the side." Aug couldn't hold back another small laugh. "Whoowhee! The Supreme Court over there in Israel not going to let him stay—now that *is* surprising. The way I was figuring it, it was a cinch. You a Jew, you go there, they hide you, they stash you—I had been led to understand that it worked out that way. *Hunh!* The *brothers* take better care of each other than that!"

"Let me know right away if you hear anything."

Aug yawned, unconcerned. "You take care, my man. I'll listen around. What have you got to do with any of it anyway? Nothing I can see."

"I'm in Cincinnati," Brian reminded him. "That's where you should try to call me."

"How come? *Cincinnati?*"

Brian could have cried. "That film we were there to talk about on Sea Island?"

"You actually *doing* that? How's that coming?"

As soon as Brian got off with Aug, the phone rang once more, though this time he was less than quick to pick it up. If it was Shelley, he was in no shape to do the delicate repair work required. If it was

Loftspring again, well, Brian was frightened enough for the moment. And if it was Aug, what else was there to say? Yet the little red bubo left to pulse on the phone once the ringing stopped finally sawed against Brian's nerves. He called down to the desk and was told that the rabbi was downstairs waiting—or would Brian like him sent up? Brian had forgotten completely about Gersh.

He had gone to a single one of Gersh's Torah-study sessions, partly out of heartland ennui, partly out of real curiosity—and maybe mostly to discomfort Nate Zwilling, who irritated him somehow. Why? Because he was shifty like his dad? A writer like his dad? *Anything* like his dad? (Tessie, after all, stood a less than great chance of growing up to be anything at all, whether it was like Brian or not.) Brian never missed an opportunity to needlingly ask the Zwilling kid, "How are the diaries coming? Anything good happen to you lately? Any good small incidents?"

But after the study session with Gersh had ended, with Brian admitting to the rabbi that he missed Sonoma, the conversation somehow got turned back to wineries, kosher wineries as per Brian's first meeting with the rabbi weeks back in that Kentucky liquor store. Not very seriously, Gersh and Brian agreed that someone should look into starting a kosher winery right in the area of Cincinnati. Plenty of wine used to be made by the Germans, after all. And so that night, at three A.M., unable to sleep, Brian casually read the real estate pages of the local newspaper. And there one was, in Indiana: a winery for sale.

Now, as Brian drove along with the rabbi, the Ohio River burped into view through low trees every few miles as they took the short ride in Brian's Rover. In his lap Gersh held a book on viticulture checked out of the public library. Of course it was a stage prop; the only reason the rabbi was actually along for the ride was to play the role of Nate Zwilling's defender. Brian didn't care. Keeping it Jewish had been Loftspring's admonition. On that score, things were in good shape, Brian felt. Zwilling. Nate. Baruch the Orthodox musician. Here now a rabbi.

Brian asked Gersh the question he seemed to ask everyone lately—in fact, the only thing he really seemed to care to know of anyone: How many kids did he and his wife have? The rabbi told him three.

"Me too. That Steyne guy you met, the one here with us for a while as a consultant, he has seven, if you can believe that. Could almost mount a scrimmage."

"That's, *baruch ha'shem,* quite a blessing."

"Yeah? One's got Down's syndrome. Where's the blessing there? I've been thinking a lot about how tired genes get. My own little girl has cystic fibrosis. Aren't genes supposed to *promote* the species? CF, cancer, Alzheimer's—who needs this second act, this encore?"

Not too immediately, the rabbi said, "I can understand you seeing it that way. But there are good human attributes too. Maybe we're individually put together the way we are in order to respond to what's required of us."

"*Very* metaphorical," Brian said to the rabbi.

Gersh raised a humorous brow. "Unless you're God, it's *all* pretty much metaphor, isn't it?"

"There really *isn't* any hope for us Jews, is there, Rabbi? Even poor little shreds of DNA extrude out as commandments. Choked by laws! Speaking as an illiterate kike myself"—Brian found himself speaking more hurriedly now; he did not know how much longer they'd be driving; if he floored it a little, increasing the pace and intensity of the talk, might they get down to even deeper matters?—"what is it with some of that stuff, anyway? Penance in the Bible seems to precede judgment. It sounds like my marriage! Yours probably too!"

Gersh smiled.

"And that's something else I've always been curious about. These laws of purity. Conjugal duties. What's with those? Doesn't that turn it into pure carnality? First not being able to do the deed for a certain time each month, then *having* to do it? How can anyone think laws drawn down from appetites *ever* work? Is it all right, for instance, for you to *fantasize?* To make believe once in a while that you're having *halacha*-fucky with someone *else's* woman of valor?"

The rabbi looked away for a moment out the window, then down at the book resting on his lap.

"I'm sorry," said Brian. "Forgive me. Overstimulated." But by then they were unfortunately just reaching the signs for Aurora, Indiana.

The realtor Brian had contacted, a fellow named Holthaus—who turned out to be a barrel-chested fiftyish, wearing a summer straw hat the color of stale chocolate—even was waiting for them in front of his office on the town's main drag.

More than once the realtor looked at the rabbi's skullcap. Brian declined when Holthaus offered to take them over to the property in his DeVille. When they were back alone in the Rover, Brian explained to Gersh: "I've been shown land aplenty. For a while in California, everybody and his brother had ranch fever. And when these rural guys haul you out into the middle of nowhere, the ride you're forced to endure going back to somewhere is all pitch."

Gersh said nothing. He hadn't said anything since the *halacha*-fucky remark.

They had followed for a mile or two when suddenly the realtor's Cadillac made an unsignaled turn that forced the boxy Rover to sway against itself like something from *Hatari!* The country road had gone completely to dirt. Holthaus finally stopped and got out of his DeVille at what looked like the target area for an ordnance range. A defined, cake-pan-shaped parcel of land was stitched through by maybe two dozen rows of sickly-looking vines. It was more like a diorama than a vineyard—there was no contour, no flow. A grimy and dishfaced boy in his twenties, the caretaker, came slowly over to greet them, since the owner hadn't arrived yet.

When Brian asked the kid if he knew what kind of grapes were grown, the kid smiled: "I sure don't"—classic *muh-mom,* satisfied with any fact, even the fact of ignorance. "Something with a B," Holthaus tried pitching in. "Or maybe a V? I've heard Sandy say something along that line." The rabbi, finally coming back to life a little, said, *"Vinifera?"*

"In their dreams," said Brian. "Maybe a weird *vinifera hybrid* in this part of the country, but probably not even that."

The sound of a car had reached them. "Here's Sandy," said Holthaus. "He sees us."

Jogging toward them was a white-haired man who'd unfolded himself out of an old Volvo station wagon. It seemed to pain him to run, and Brian held out a dissuading palm, but the man kept slogging ahead anyway.

"Really sorry," he wheezed as he came abreast. The white guayabera shirt he wore bespoke interesting vacations, but his immune system couldn't have been much to boast about: Brian saw chalk-pink points of psoriasis on the man's elbows. The hand he extended was clear-skinned enough, though: "Sanford Rowen."

Rowen showed them around. In a consciously equalized manner, he asked the rabbi and Brian what kind of yield they were looking for and did they plan to do their own casking and aging? They toured the modest free-juice tank, the cellars, the newish bottling equipment.

Little by little, Rowan's story emerged. It was the sad one Brian guessed it would be. A chemical engineer, thirty-five years with Procter & Gamble in Cincinnati, Rowan with his wife had built up the vineyard as their retirement dream. But now the wife was in a home with dementia—lost to her husband, to life itself, and certainly to amateur winemaking.

"This could be a very nice commercial boutique operation for someone," Rowen said. "The wine world's no different from anything else, you know. What goes around comes around. There's always a need for novelty. Australia, Chile, Argentina—I mean, my God, I understand they're even producing good cabernet on *Long Island* now! We'll never have the climate, of course, but I'm positive this valley springs right back up *on its own terms* if given the right push, the right people making the appropriate wines sophisticatedly."

"*Sophisticatedly*," Holthaus chimed in.

The rabbi wandered off by himself to look around as soon as Holthaus tried to take them aside for a few private words after Rowen left them alone. Holthaus and Brian leaned like bored summertime pals against the vermilion thigh of the DeVille. Its paint gave off both heat and a submerged cool at the same time. The broker wiped his face against the rubbery humidity, the lack of breeze. "You should see it here in fall and spring."

"What's the gent angling for again?" Brian asked.

"Vineyards, house, winery, outbuildings—two ninety-five."

Brian gave it back calmly: "Two ninety-five."

Had he somehow missed this in the paper? There must not have been a quoted price, for certainly it would have made an impression. Brian's chest began to collapse slightly, air seeming to leak upward into his throat, his shoes turning so leaden it was lucky he was leaning on the car. Good fortune always tended to do this little bodily number on him: puffing him up like a duck while at the same time nailing him to the earth like a mailbox post. Scale didn't matter. Undercharge him a dollar a pound for veal, and he likewise got lighter on top and heavier below.

Holthaus was staring straight ahead, not at Brian at all. "My gal in the office told me you're in the movie business. She read about you in the Cincinnati paper. You thinking of retiring here eventually, or moving your operations here now?"

"Retiring?" Brian swiveled around, bending down to look at himself in the Caddie's side mirror. "I look that bad?"

Holthaus laughed—but not too freely, for now the formalities were being untied and together they were stepping down the first few yards of the real deal, its hallway runner. The business about what purpose Brian wanted the property for was Holthaus's way of letting Brian know that he, Holthaus, knew that Brian had money—and that Brian was experienced enough with money to know also that he was, at this stage, being overquoted.

"He put a lot into this place, Sandy did, with the wife. It was their baby, their dream."

As efficiently as anything else, that word *dream* told Brian the property could be his for a hundred fifty. If even that much. "Mr. Holthaus . . ." Brian began slowly, deliberately.

"Norb."

"It is a honey, Norb. Definitely a honey. Of course I'm going to have to think about it and talk it over with my associate," gesturing over to the rabbi who, standing on the rise near the vines and seeing them talking, slowly was starting to head back their way. "But you mention dreams. In so many things, a dream *itself* is where the real value is. You've seen this a lot, I know. We overvalue our dreams. It can even be a kind of disappointment to find that someone else *can* care as much about your dream as you do."

Hardly a virgin when it came to a haggle, Holthaus locked right on it. "There is a time factor," he said dispassionately. "It's been listed a while. *Someone's* going to walk away with a sweet deal for themselves, I'll tell you that."

At some point in his progress, the rabbi decided not to join them after all and went to sit alone in the Rover. Holthaus handed Brian yet another of his business cards. "Look here. Down on this you've got the office number, the home number, the fax, and my car numbers—I couldn't hide from you even if I wanted to. So you give me a call anytime, night or day."

"I will do that, Norb."

To Gersh, when they were in the Rover, heading back to Ohio, Brian said, "What does another undrinkable wine get you? Especially if in the beginning you had to use the trashy rootstock he's got in the ground now. Sure, you could bottle *something*, but who'd ever buy it? Anyway, a kosher winery—would you even have enough observant Jews around here to do the winery's work? Dermatologists aplenty, but winery workers?"

While all the time Brian was busily thinking to himself: *Where could I call up the cash?*

"Although it is lovely land, granted," he continued to Gersh. "What about a kosher B&B, bed-and-breakfast? The observant could use a nice weekend getaway sometime too. Your marriages are so perfect with all those kids? We could market Sunday-Monday packages."

Gersh picked at the edge of the plastic library covering of his wine book until finally he could hold back no longer. Twisting almost violently in his seat, he was looking directly at Brian's ear.

"You know, I wear Nikes too," pointing down to one sneakered foot, making sure Brian glanced down to see as well. "I live in the same world you do. I'm aware of your condescension. The way you see it is that either I'm fooling myself with foolish contracts with God— or else I'm fooling *you*."

Brian heartfeltly said, "No, not at all. I believe in your belief. There are things I just don't get, though. Don't you make yourself unnecessarily childish? You all need a Daddy so much? Nagging at Him with endless prayers. Or else sinning, acting out, so that you manage to get His attention through punishment at least. You need the attention so much, Larry?"

"And you don't? You make movies. You don't hope people will see them?"

"What about the *quality* of the attention, though? God's goods are not exactly good. Ask my daughter. Ask Baruch's Downer boy. His attention isn't always so fucking sterling in those cases. In us His little lapses translate big."

Gersh took some time before speaking again. "There isn't a single person alive who doesn't have sufficient reason to be seriously angry at God. But that's anyone's individual business. Please leave me and my wife out of your argument."

"I apologize," Brian said sincerely. "I said so before."

Now Brian had to pee. The rural road had urbanized and turned itself into a midden of strip malls. Brian steered the Rover into the parking lot of a Starvin' Marvin convenience store, and once he'd used the facilities he called Selva from a pay phone. He got no answer, only her voice pager.

Neither of them restarted the religion conversation after Brian returned to the Rover, which was just as well since there wouldn't have been much time anyway: In a matter of minutes they were back into the Cincinnati limits proper, the rabbi giving Brian directions back to the lot downtown where he'd parked his car.

Home at the hotel, the Queen City, the concierge handed Brian a sealed hotel-stationery envelope.

Got your message. Came by, thinking you'd be here by now. Couldn't wait very long: a jogging date with Mrs. Zwilling. Call me, though. I need to speak to you also. Somewhat urgent. S

Upstairs, in Brian's suite, all the morning's developments—Shelley, then Loftspring, then Aug—seemed to stale the air. He was just at the point of turning around and leaving for God knows where when the room phone rang.

"Mr. Horkow? Norb Holthaus. Glad I reached you."

"Yes, Norb."

"Mr. Horkow, I hope you don't take this as if I'm pressuring you. Because I am not, I am sure not. But I did neglect to mention something to you this morning that I think you at least might like to know about. Something you might want to at least throw into the hopper when you and your people get to the point of making your decision on the Rowen parcel."

"Information's never not welcome, Norb. Shoot."

"Riverboat gambling, sir, is on the horizon for the Ohio River. It's only a matter of which state lets the deals go through first. That state, I happen to know this for a fact, will be right here in Indiana. Ohio politics are bound to foul it up over there, so at least for a while it's a pretty clear shot for us here as the only gambling in the area.

"Now, I know you saw the stretch of river the property overlooks. My bet—and it's also the bet of a number of people in the know—is that the first casino goes into Lawrenceburg. That's just a few miles east of Mr. Rowan's land. If there's one boat, the feeling is, there'll be at least one other as well, so what you might find is yourself owning property that would be considered central to any kind of development."

"I see. Hmnnn. I'm glad you called, Norb. That *is* good for me to know. And yet the property's been on the market a while, right? You did tell me that, didn't you?"

"Not all *that* long, but—"

"So the promise of eventual gambling notwithstanding, it sounds to me like it's been an opportunity other people figured they could pass up. Even you yourself, Norb—a guy like you could have swept together investors and snatched it right up. That you didn't gives me a little pause."

"Well sir, *if* that's true, Mr. Horkow, which I'm not saying it is or isn't, it just may go to show that folks around here—even me!—are not sufficiently *sophisticated*. Maybe too conservative by nature. Don't pick up on the future implications quickly. I'm telling *you*, though—"

"Because I *am* a sufficiently sophisticated person?"

"I think so, yes. I'd consider you that, sir, that's right."

"Well, as I said before, Norb, you'll definitely be hearing from me about this."

Brian felt an even more urgent need now to move, to be in motion, to distribute some of the ether that at this very moment was enlarging the packet of his destiny. Sweet God! You start off planning to make what you discover is a false-bottomed movie in nowheresville—you end up a millionaire from selling land to Las Vegas sharpies!

In the cocktail lounge area fitted out of a corner of the lobby of Selva's apartment hotel, where three skinny off-shift nurses wearing green scrub suits were throwing down wine coolers and giggling a good deal, Brian sat at a café table. He worked indifferently at some crappy claret, the only half bottle the bar carried, and kept a watchful eye on the lobby door. After half an hour, Selva sashayed in. She was wearing satin shorts and a none-too-dry running bra.

"Why are you here?"

"*La vida es sueno*, Sel. Have a seat—though even in celebration I won't offer you a glass of this Château Pishachs. But life really is fantastic. I couldn't wait. I had to come over. I think I'm going to buy a vineyard."

She sat. "Where? In Sonoma? When you go home?"

"No, here!"

"Here meaning *here*? In Cincinnati?" That slightly terrier expression of hers came to her face. "Why? With what?"

"You heard from Loftspring too, huh?"

"Yes, and he told me he'd spoken to you first. Can you see why I'm more than a little confused right here, Brian?"

"Look, Loftspring has nothing to do with this, he's not germane. In fact, that's the beauty. I have had a morning out of the fucking *Faerie Queene!* I met Opportunity on the road!"

"I would have thought that limited partnership you were in—what was it called, Château Kore?—it would have cured you once and for all on wineries. Your word for it at the time was *fiasco.*"

"You're not hearing me. This is around *here*—in Indiana, not California."

"Brian—"

"The Germans, they settled here originally with winemaking partly in mind. The hills, the river. It reminded them of the Rhine. They planted vines."

"Brian—"

"Not only is it criminally cheap, but it could also be multifunctional. Do you remember that Baruch character who was here the first week? Think about him. Wouldn't his be a much better story than Zwilling's beat survivor-family book? It would still be *extremely* Jewish, right? We're still keeping a prayer shawl over our heads. We completely dump these Zwilling duds. You and me do a script together: Baruch, Brooklyn bluegrass musician, poet, Orthodox bigamist, running, say, a kosher B&B and winery on the banks of the River Ohio! Not wonderful? Not hilarious? When you go back over to England, you right away try to sweet-talk a money actor, someone like Ben Kingsley or that Branagh guy. Those guys like stretch roles. We slap a beard on Branagh, we teach him basic banjo licks . . . "

"Brian, what did Loftspring tell you? Their tap's been turned off. It's what he told *me*."

"Selly! Selly! Fuck Warshaw and Loftspring! I *myself* would buy this place! Third-mortgage the house if I have to. Borrow . . . "

"Slow, slow, go slower for me. Why would *you* buy the land if all you wanted to use it for was a location?"

"*If* it's only going to be a location! Follow me. No one in the business is going to plow money into a picture about Baruch, either. I know that. Yet we try to get something rolling, just a little, and when it doesn't fly, a no-go, then at least at that point we'd also have improved land!"

"Cimino, Brian? Isn't that exactly what he did? You know better than I do the kind of trouble it got him into. It finished him. He bought his locations for *Heaven's Gate*, then once it was shot he had a package of real estate. It's called *fraud*."

"Not at least worth sailing past your London sugar daddies? Tell them *you* want to make the stupid thing."

"Brian, look, no, no, enough. Have you—"

"'Kay. Forget it. Fuck me, then, I guess. Forget it. Terrible idea. Forget it. I'll manage it somehow myself maybe."

Almost as though she planned to grab him before he ran, Selva leaned closer. "I know from Shelley that she sent some medicine on from California for you. Did you ever get it? Have you taken any of it at all? Is it still up in your room at the hotel?"

Brian stood up. "Goodbye, I'm leaving."

Selva, sighing, stood as well. "Wherever it is you're going now, I'm going there with you."

13

Barbara did errands or went to the Y or jogged with Selva at lunchtime; it wasn't a time she usually took for eating. Thus she was just heading out of the office for a window-shopping walk around downtown when a call came in at her desk.

Polly was calling from a video store in St. Bernard. Other than to report trouble, she'd have never phoned Barbara at work. And trouble it was now exactly, "some shit" that was happening and that she needed help with. The shit was left unspecified, but from the sound of her voice Polly was clearly not in good shape.

Barbara took a cab to the St. Bernard address Polly gave her. It was one of a small local chain of video stores. Inside, at each corner of the ceiling, video monitors played mutely, on one of them a cartoon, on three others the identical unheeded movie.

Polly had on what Barbara took as her work attire at the group home: a green cook's apron over a red tee shirt and cutoffs. She was standing frozenly about a yard away from a life-sized cardboard publicity cutout of an eyes-wide, similarly dressed Goldie Hawn. Meanwhile, a policewoman was taking down information provided by a bony-faced young woman wearing a store badge at the front counter to Barbara's right.

In back of the store, police officers and a pale man in a windbreaker stood around a stocky, plum-colored boy who was weeping. He wore a molded black-and-orange bicycle helmet, and certain defenselessness to his mouth led Barbara to assume that the boy was one of Polly's group-home residents.

A gray-haired, scholarly-looking sergeant was walking toward her. "It might be better, ma'am, if you could come back a little later. We have a small situation here. Give us maybe a half hour tops."

Barbara introduced herself as an attorney. It elicited a double take from the sergeant: "For *who*?"

"I'm a relative of Miss Doecklein's," pointing at Polly, who still had not moved toward them at all.

"What's *she* need . . . ?" The sergeant shrugged. He motioned for Barbara to follow him outside to the street.

The story was this: The retarded man was being accused of stealing bowdlerized adult tapes. According to the manager, he'd first rent these, then substitute blank tapes for them in the boxes he brought back. "It's all bogus, naturally," the sergeant told Barbara. "He doesn't have a driver's license or a credit card—how was he going to rent the tapes? This kid Wheels—this *man*, really—we all know him around here. His nickname's Wheels. You always see him around on his mountain bike. The kid's a citizen. I only wish there were more like him in the neighborhood. He helps the store owners on upper Vine sweep up."

Barbara asked the sergeant—Simmons, from the nameplate—what this then was all about.

"Well, see, the salesguy who usually opens here knows that Wheels loves movies. Sometimes he lets him in a half hour early to watch anything he wants. Well, to me at least . . . a guy like this, lives in a retard home, you know, he might want to get a look at *certain stuff* sometimes?"

The sergeant pointed through the glary window back into the store. "The one monitor way back there was accidentally left on. One of those sexy movies was playing with the sound off. But the salesguy must have forgotten about Wheels back there, and he unlocks the doors at ten and, lousy luck, his first customer was a mom with little kids. The movie got turned off, but not fast enough. The mom wants to speak to the manager, who had just walked in herself. The manager is brand-new, was brought in from another store. Some bad blood apparently among the staff that she got the job someone else was expecting—I'm picking that up. The manager absolutely loses it. She's maybe having her . . . she's maybe having a bad day already. She fires the guy who let Wheels in, then she calls us! Wheels, in the meantime, is so confused and scared that I figure he accidentally knocked down the cabinet of posters over there. But now this manager girl's claiming he got violent too."

He shook his head. "I have to tell you, though, that your relative, she isn't making things any easier. With my fellas back there is Mr. Heigle, the retard home's director, and anytime he ever says anything, tries to wrap it up, your person flies off the handle. If you could maybe just get her out of here. She's making things worse."

"What *are* her objections?" Barbara asked.

"You really want to get into this?"

"I'd like to know."

The sergeant frowned. "Mr. Heigle made a promise to the manager that he'd look in Wheels's room at the home for any of those tapes. He knows he isn't going to find any, but it's to make the manager feel better. He's being diplomatic. That seems to tick off your relative there *way* out of proportion. Foul mouth on her too. She's just scaring Wheels worse."

As Barbara and the sergeant reentered the store, they found that Polly had moved, gone over to the group in back. Her raised voice carried: "Take Jacob out of here right now! Walk him out! Do your job— *protect him!* They're not letting *me* do it! This is so obviously *bullshit!*" She addressed the patrolmen: "You don't have better things to do than persecute someone who isn't even able to know the *time?*"

The younger-looking of the two cops had been keeping an arm around Jacob. He therefore seemed to take special offense at this persecution charge, and in a stage whisper to his partner—but meant to rankle Polly—he smirked that *everyone* knew when it was time to be horny.

Polly turned and fled the store.

"I'd keep an eye on her for a little while," Simmons said. Polly could be seen through the window, recovering against a parking meter out on the street, and Barbara was surprised she hadn't already vanished altogether.

The group home was a large old house sided in a brown vinyl, with added-on wings lurching off in a few different directions. It was set down in a neighborhood zoned for mixed use, and therefore stood shoulder to shoulder with a warehouse on one side and a fenced-in auto body shop on the other. Inside, though, it was clean and cheery and domestic enough. Polly did some perfunctory grumbling to Barbara about the low-quality ingredients she was forced to use, yet the kitchen was far from primitive or cramped . . . and chopping and stirring and setting endless strips of cooked lasagna noodles into pans, spending more time alone with her quasi-stepdaughter-in-law than she ever had in all these years, made Barbara at some point realize that she was in the middle of a fairly pleasant afternoon, hookey-playing once more. At one point, Polly suddenly dropped what she was doing and ran to one of the kitchen windows—it was Heigle arriving back at the home with Jacob, which caused Polly to swear aloud: "Over my dead body is he going to search"—but other than that, keeping Polly relatively calm and at bay was a real satisfaction for Barbara.

Some years ago, Joel had taken Barbara to an art exhibition of Polly's. It had been one of their earliest dates, and Joel probably had meant for it to be an introduction to his world, one that largely revolved around a late-teenage son who'd forsworn college. Nate's girlfriend even at nineteen, Polly was semi-estranged from her parents, and she had landed a job at the county courthouse, filing property-tax records. It was there that one of her immediate superiors had put moves on her. But rather than complain to a higher-up or confront the man directly, Polly responded by creating an artwork, *Stations of the Crass,* which she then arranged to have exhibited at Ravage, the clubhouse-like gallery space where on weekends she and Nate took part in Cincinnati's small alternative-arts scene.

Foamcore placards had been carefully but crudely crayoned, as though to highlight the fact that Polly was nearly underage: "GOOD GOING, POL. NICE JOB." LITTLE KNEAD OF MY SHOULDER. Next: "PLANS FOR THE WEEKEND?" Next: "LUNCH? BUSY AFTER WORK? HONESTLY—REALLY NOW—HOW YOU DOIN' WITH THIS JOB? DO YOU LIKE IT? THERE ANYTHING I COULD DO TO MAKE THINGS BETTER FOR YOU?" Next: "READ THAT ARTICLE IN THE ENQUIRER THIS MORNING ABOUT 'SEXUAL LITERACY?' AMAZING, HUH?" Next: "I HAVE KIND OF AN ODD FAVOR TO ASK. BE HONEST. HAVE I BEEN SEEMING A LITTLE DOWN TO YOU LATELY? YOU NOTICE THAT? LINDA AND I . . . WHAT DO I WANT TO SAY HERE? WE'RE REALLY NOT IN SYNC LATELY, DON'T SHARE INTERESTS. THAT'S THE MAIN THING, I THINK, THAT WE DON'T TALK—NOT LIKE YOU AND I HAVE BEEN DOING." Next: "EVEN IN THIS CRAPPY OFFICE LIGHTING, WITH THE FLUORESCENTS, YOUR HAIR'S ALWAYS SO NICE." And finally, lettered first in pale pink, then in brutal black: "AT THE OFFICE PICNIC, WIFE AND KIDS 50 YARDS AWAY AT MOST, PRESSES YOU AGAINST A TREE ON THE FRISBEE GOLF COURSE: "OH COME ON, OH NO, COME ON, DON'T BE THIS WAY . . . "

Barbara recalled the exhibit not just for the consuming fire of its indiscretion but also because she and Joel went back to her apartment afterward and to bed for the first time. She'd had an almost uncontrollably exciting, propulsive time with him there—and, looking back, she always knew that Polly's exhibition had had a hand in that. A secret flavoring: Joel, her teacher, an older man taking advantage of her.

Polly got in trouble as a related consequence of the art show, however. One of the older Ravage kids, who worked part-time for the IRS across the river in Covington, mentioned to her how easy it would be to file a phony 1099 income statement to Internal Revenue against her harasser. Polly less than brightly had gone ahead and used Ravage's tax

ID number on the filing. And though her lecherous ex-boss wanted no further publicity, his loyal middle-aged civil-service secretary turned relentless and soon Polly was easily caught. She received a fine. A few months later, she and Nate left Cincinnati altogether for New York.

The two years the kids were gone turned out to be Barbara and Joel's extended honeymoon. Newly wed to her brilliant, injured man, going off every morning to her new job at Steiff, Cloud, Barbara had been happy. She was never much concerned whether or not Joel, left alone in the house, would be writing that day; either way, she'd restored a nest for him. It gave her deep pleasure, the providing of stability and time for something to gestate in him. When he was her teacher at the university, he hardly ever stood up during class, sitting instead in front of the room behind a long table, his shirtsleeves folded up twice, arms and legs pushed out straight. He didn't urge, he never quite dazzled; but to every inch of him there was a languor of confidence that she'd later discovered in his lovemaking as well. Joel's unfixedness seemed expansive and profoundly free.

Yet, once the kids did return to Cincinnati, it never was that good again. With his son in range, Joel became a slightly different person. Nor was there anything about Polly that could give Barbara peace: Polly made it seem as though, by living with the son, she also had married Joel first; that the two men came as a package; that Barbara must therefore always remain Polly's student, never to know quite enough on her own about the fragile, batted-around Zwilling men.

The one Barbara truly enjoyed being with back then was Nate. Newly off drugs, wobbly, depending on the Midwest to reform and rehabilitate him, Nate often was in need of a sympathetic ear. Barbara became it. The secret crush she began developing on the boy was one she allowed herself; she trusted herself to keep it breezy and humorous. Sweet poor Nate, who talked and wrote his journals into cassette recorders, in cheap school notebooks, on the backs of automatic teller machine slips, even on his wrists. The motherless boy-man, eternally shifting for himself. Barbara was sometimes sorry she couldn't do something particular for her stepson, something involving her mouth.

According to their horribly indiscreet published diaries, Nate relished oral sex, though Polly had grown weary of the effort required. Barbara herself loved to suck Joel, liked it even more than he did being sucked, she suspected . . . and if only, under some spell of forgetfulness, she could draw Nate out this way too, relieve him, enthrall him as peasant mothers occasionally did to calm a colicky baby son. She'd feel as though she'd accomplished something good. Something *fun*. For if she didn't have some fun in her life soon—fun or else an obligation more sacred than this endless *straightening out* she did for everyone—Barbara surely was going to shrivel up and die.

Done for the day at the sheltered workshops of Goodwill where they made labels, or at McDonald's, the home's residents came off their schoolbus at four o'clock. Their heavy, unrhythmic footfalls could be felt as well as heard mounting the porch steps. Polly wiped her hands on a dishcloth; greetings by the staff were part of the daily routine.

Yet, quite unfortunately, Barbara's bladder got the best of her just at that moment. She'd been putting off going earlier, leery of whom she might run into in the house.

She hoped it didn't look as though she was *creeping* past the five retarded men who'd gone to sit together on a sofa that could comfortably hold only three. The spartan bathroom and its hospital-cleanser smell held no surprises. After washing her hands extra well, Barbara was just stepping out when she found one of the female residents blocking her path in the narrow hallway.

Right behind the woman was Heigle, the home's director. "Marie would like to invite you to see her room."

The woman was obese and ageless looking, with hair sheared down almost to a crewcut, and dressed in baggy-seated jeans and a Bengals sweatshirt. A rictus simulated a sweet chaotic cheer in her expression. Marie reached out to take Barbara's hand: "Check my ancestors."

When Barbara just stood there, a frozen and self-loathing stone, Heigle's brooming fingers urged her forward. "We don't have visitors very often."

In Marie's room were two single beds and a pair of individual metal lockers. Heigle took a post at the doorway while with her foot the woman fished a shoebox from under one of the beds. Then Barbara was shown a collection of postcards from *The Stephen Foster Story*, the outdoor drama pageant of Bardstown, Kentucky.

"We're big Bardstown boosters here," Heigle commented. "Marie's hometown."

"These are very nice," Barbara told the woman. (And to herself: *Try harder.*) "I was once in Bardstown."

"You liked it?"

"I did like it, yes. I did."

"You *loved* it?"

Heigle started to gesture Barbara out of the room. "Everyone loves Bardstown, Marie. You know that."

As they made their way back to the living room, Marie insisted on holding Barbara's hand. Polly was nowhere in sight, and as Marie's trophy Barbara was introduced by Heigle to some of the others in the room. A frail man named Arthur sat on the sofa talking down into his clavicle. "What the dog went for, so he couldn't put it in, the carton, and my hands were slippery. Couldn't." He stopped talking for a moment to gauge Barbara, then declared to Heigle: "Green!"

"Major compliment!" Heigle told Barbara. "Everything Artie likes most is 'green.'"

Beside Arthur sat a man named Jess, pewter-haired and wearing a windbreaker-and-tie ensemble identical to Heigle's. Jess was involved in carefully picking at the nubbins of fabric on the couch's arm. A much younger man was next to him. "Gilly, meet Barbara."

Heigle pointed to a small electronic typing device hooked to a lanyard hanging from the young man's neck: "Gilly's got atrophied vocal cords. That's his communicator." Gilly raised his device and punched at it surehandedly for some seconds. Then he pulled himself forward by the neck in order that Heigle and Barbara could read the digitized letters: MARIE IS CAROL BURNET JESS IS HARVEY KORMAN

"Gilly's our other television and movie fanatic," said Heigle. "Gilly and Jacob."

Arthur at that moment turned to Jess and ululated, "Let me alone!"—although to untrained eyes Jess seemed to have been doing nothing at all.

"I used to love the Carol Burnett Show," Barbara said weakly.

Once she was back in the kitchen, Barbara's hands trembled a little as she watched Polly portion out lasagna onto plates. How did the girl manage to work here even a single day? In her there had to be some core of harder stuff than there was in Barbara, whom pity swamped. Pity or worse, like out in the living room: disgust. No, it was a *good* thing that Barbara had no children. Shouldn't you always be less fastidiously upset than your child? Not suffering parallel to, at the same pitch with, him or her?

The lasagna was nearly ready to be served when Heigle ducked in to the kitchen to report that Jacob was refusing to come out of his room for dinner. He appealed to Polly. "I don't think there should be a gap in the group dynamic."

"Maybe he knows *why* you want him out of his room, *Kenneth*."

Heigle left the kitchen without another word.

Barbara helped Polly load and bring in trays. Friendship was something that Barbara again wasn't confident about lately, yet Polly at that moment seemed almost like a friend. (After a propitious beginning, it sadly seemed that Selva Tashjian was about to fail as friend material. Maybe the harmony that Barbara had wanted to believe was there actually wasn't. Selva's endometriosis turned out to be a horrific case, and because of it she'd long past accepted that her body was a useless receptacle. Then, too, Selva every so often lately made a cutting remark about Cincinnati that Barbara couldn't help but take as coming from someone who was growing tired of the place, of the people, of *her*. Selva once or twice even expressed something like surprise that Joel could live here. This was the kind of thing a wife takes one way only. Especially a wife who knew hardly any of the film or literary or art figures Selva and Joel both knew. Selva even *jogged* differently than Barbara did—with a purpose that seemed less than casual.)

The group home's dining room looked pretty; its sheer white curtains, the two brightly colored and vinyl-covered long tables; and the physical work of serving felt good to Barbara. Overcarefully, she set the full plates down, only hoping that the residents didn't advance on the tables too quickly, too oddly. On her third trip back to the kitchen, she found that Heigle had returned there as well. He was saying to Polly: "Where in *hell* do you come off saying a thing like that!"

Polly calmly filled a pitcher with milk. "Just what I said. I wouldn't be surprised at all if it was *you*."

Noticing Barbara, Heigle turned to her. "Thanks so very much for your help. We really appreciate it, but—"

Polly continued tonelessly to the man: "You only care about your own ass."

She went over to a drawer and serenely removed a large kitchen knife. At first she held it in an ambiguous position, near her forehead, as if shielding her eyes with it.

It was only theater. For years Barbara had tried getting a handle on the girl, and finally knew this much at least: Polly was never as lost as she liked to seem. She was always well-positioned near a door, something to disappear through, an exit. Did it partly have to do with Nate? Women drawn to artistic, literary men learned some lessons quickly enough. These men were not ones to leap or exult; the combined mass of fine antennae they came equipped with weighed them down, and their freedom was slow, syrupy. A woman who sought change or a new idea of herself had better take the lead. Polly's leads were operatic.

Heigle froze, but Barbara moved swiftly and intently. She made a circle around the kitchen, sweeping up her own and Polly's handbags.

"Big deal, he'll fire me. He's also going to drag Wheels out and do his precious search."

"He's *not*," Barbara was resolute. "You're not going to do that, are you, sir?"

"Oh, of course he is. He is because he's such a coward."

Polly returned the knife to the open drawer and she slipped off her apron.

"No, he won't. Mr. Heigle knows that these people have civil rights too."

Heigle seemed to be softened by Barbara's trust. "Look, Polly, I know Jacob's no thief—"

"I hope you do, asshole!" Polly pointed a finger. "And I'll tell you this too. I'm coming back here, to visit everyone, whenever I want to. You tell Wheels. Actually *I'll* tell him . . ."

But Barbara caught hold of her by the arm. "Not now. Come on, let's leave."

Polly refused a cab ride home. Barbara wasn't willing to leave her while the girl was this worked up, though, and they walked away from the home together. Past the body shop and around the corner, they came to a nondescript neighborhood tavern.

Inside the bar, Barbara turned hostess, her usual role with Polly, but the girl declined to order anything. Slumping in the booth, she scratched at the Bakelite of the table.

Barbara brought back two glasses of white wine from the bar anyway. "That Marie is very sweet. All the stuff about her hometown."

The brassy air-conditioning was making Barbara aware of how clammy her blouse had become, of how much she must have perspired during these last few hours. Polly was leaving her wine untouched, instead ripping her napkin in a circle around the glass's damp base.

"Wheels waves at children in cars when he's waiting next to them, you know, on his bike, at a light? When the light changes, though, he's all business. His head may look loose and swivelly, but he's checking out the traffic, paying attention to how to get where he's going in the safest way. He's the only person I know who *does* drive that way. Wonderful *Nathan* doesn't, who can't talk and drive at the same time. Who gets insulted if I mention he missed a stop sign. He wants the rules of the road to be suspended while he makes his precious point."

Barbara leaned back in the booth. She felt a little revived when the backrest's cold tufted vinyl met her damp shirt. "Well, it must be genetic. His father's the same way."

"Nathan's the kind of precious genius who can't be *bothered* to really be driving."

They were plainly splitting up; the relationship was past rescue. Barbara thought back to her last lunch with Nate. He had looked terrible.

Not everything he said made sense or was to the point, any point. He'd told her about an experience he'd had in a Hardee's. "Maybe there were three customers, plus me. One of them was this light-skinned black guy—Latin-looking, Caribbean-looking—wearing a Forty-niners stocking cap. He was sitting alone at one of the longer tables and spread out in front of him were like these sheets and sheets of paper with writing on them. Really dense penciled writing. He'd study one, smile, and jot something else down on it. Then he'd hide the papers with his arm like in school during a test, when you suddenly think of the right answer.

"He saw me looking at him. He goes to me: *'All my friends are here in these notes. All my friends in forty-one years. I'm forty-one years old.'* And, you see, it hit me later, after I left the Hardee's. All *my* friends are in my notes too. Pops the same thing. The notes *are* our only friends. What's the difference then between the madman and myself, or between the madman and Pops? Nothing. We're each monsters.

"Well, fuck that, I'm thinking. Why should I even write *anything* anymore? Your husband, you know, isn't the only one who's able to throw it over completely.

"And so I'll tell you what I'm seriously considering doing. Want to hear? I've even priced the ticket. I'm thinking of going to live in Jerusalem and study at a yeshiva there. That guy that Horkow brought in: Steyne? Baruch Steyne, from Pops's old neighborhood? He'd done that. Gone to Jerusalem to learn. I know myself a little better now. I'm like a Holocaust survivor-kid too, in my own way. Pops and I had a Holocaust of our own. I haven't been able to do the damn script because it's like straining to learn something I already know!"

Remembering Nate's bleakness, and staring now at Polly, Barbara wondered whether she and Joel shouldn't maybe divorce also. She was worn down flat by these grotesque past few months. How Joel for instance wouldn't cash Horkow's check, stuffing it instead inside his desk as though it were a shrunken head brought back for him from someone else's gruesome vacation.

Did it all have to be so painful for him? Did *everything* have to be? How draining it was to be loyal in your heart to someone else's scouring disaffection! Which by now probably included Barbara herself.

Polly was digging into her bag. Then, with a mean smile, she hauled out two individually wrapped bags of microwave popcorn. She slapped them onto the table next to Barbara's glass of wine:

"The lady policeman even *saw* me take these!"

"Oh Polly, for God's sakes!" Barbara's fingers covered the flat packets of popcorn. She had to restrain herself from crushing them in frustration. "You have got to cool down. You have to."

Polly gave a suggestive snicker. "What, you're worried that I broke a law? Well, the holy law *saw* me break it and didn't give a shit. Jacob does nothing and they're all over him as if he robbed the place!" She retrieved the packets and tossed them back in her bag, saying, "But you're right, I do have to cool down. I shouldn't be this excited, this stressed."

"It'll blow over back there. You'll be able to go back tomorrow. Just not today." Barbara pushed Polly's untouched glass closer to the girl: "At least a little of this, a sip."

"No. I'm not drinking alcohol anymore." Polly then looked directly up into Barbara's eyes. "Do you want to know *why* I shouldn't be this stressed out?"

"Because no one should be, that's why."

"No, but me in particular—do you want to know? Ask me if I'm pregnant."

"*What?* You are? You're *pregnant?*"

Polly's tight grin cranked open. Barbara swirled down hopelessly within it.

Part Three

14

Brian had spent a large part of each day alone in bed since returning. His excuse first was a zonking jet lag, then loginess from too much sleep, and finally the mood regulator he now had to take faithfully. All put together, they allowed him to lie there undisturbed. He had tried to rejoin family life, really he had. But on the first day home, anything he did—whether meals or a walk around outside or even watching television with the boys—these things all felt to him as if he were walking on the bottom of a swimming pool. Everything was that slowed and strange, that hazy, that unlicensed . . . and finally he just went to bed.

Today, however, he was going to get up for good. He'd be able to start out slowly. Shelley's widowed friend Karalyn had undergone arthroscopic surgery on her knee the day Brian had reappeared unannounced. Today, two days belated, Shelley had taken herself and the two boys down to the city to Karalyn's house, perhaps to stay overnight.

Brian reached under the bed and found the Monopoly set. It was dug in deep, forgotten, long unused. (He and Shelley occasionally played the game at night, stashing the box under the bed because the game sometimes ended up as a horny-landlord-and-strapped-female-tenant scenario.) But at least it was still there, unremoved. On his first day back, he'd discovered Shelley's night table to be completely barren, not even a single magazine on it. His own night table was swept even cleaner, as immaculate as old dried death. Brian pulled the Monopoly box out from under the bed and dusted it off with the sleeve of his pajama top. Then, in the master bath, he showered, shaved, and put on fresh clothing.

Tessa's door was closed. It never took Brian too long to picture his daughter gasping for air or unconscious on the other side of a closed door, but the reason he'd been exiled in the first place was for being overly rash, so he had to govern himself here and first simply knock.

"It's Daddy. I have a need to play a game. Have any such need yourself this morning?"

Tess called back that Brian should instead play with Marta. But then: "What kind of game?"

"Monopoly. Holding it in my hand. But we have plenty of others too. I felt like playing *something* with you."

"Oh, Monopoly's *fine.*" Moralists and punishers, she and her mother both. But at least Tessie had come out of the house three days ago at the sound of his rental car's horn. "Selva called Mom," Tess had told him as she gave him his hug. "We just didn't know exactly when you'd arrive." Yet Shelley and the twins had stayed inside.

He'd found them at the kitchen table (which was set formally, Brian noticed, for lunch: a water carafe, flowers, not one but two little amber bears of honey—Shelley making a theatrical point here: DOMESTICITY IN PROGRESS. DO NOT DISTURB). Of course, once presents were produced—earrings for Shelley, a bracelet for Tess, two inflatable German bounce-on-'em balls for the boys—the twins came out of their chairs as though launched (making it doubly clear that they'd been restrained until then). Nor could they sit still for the rest of the meal: Bim getting up from his chair, coming around the table, and in his grave little voice ("For you") offering Brian a carrot stick, after which he ran right away as though his father might conceivably refuse it. Bom, not to be outdone, came over next and punched Brian twice, one time in the belly, one time lower, screeching, "Your wiener!" with delight. "Ow," Brian had said joyously, "don't do that." Bommie naturally did it again. "Someone help me, please!" Brian said, almost dizzied by hope.

Yet Shelley he'd been able to look at only in pared glimpses, as if she were God or the Wizard of Oz. It wasn't possible in only three or four weeks' time, but her braid looked as though it had grown a good half foot longer. Her skin was so tanned, beautifully/frightfully tanned, a kind of leather that kept her face immobile against whatever joking remarks Brian tried to make at the table. (Pointing a thumb at her mother, he cracked once to Tessie: "Fyodor Dostoevsky's *The Unimpressed*.") But Brian still hoped to get through to his wife yet. When the kids all were asleep and he and Shelley were in bed, he planned to go down on her, to eat her out regally, not just for a minute or two but lavishly, an elaborately overdone payment of respect, with tongue as well as nose, chin, and eyelids, inside and outside, where she wasn't yet wet and where she already was soaked, teeth teasing first around her bud, then lapping with ever more steady accuracy until she'd eventually relax enough to let herself direct him in gasps.

Yet when they actually reached their bed that night, Shelley firmly removed his hand from her nipple. "There's a lot of business we have to get done first. It's good you're home, it's good for everyone, but there's work for you to do, Brian. Things to straighten out first." She'd drawn the cover around her and turned away. "I'm pleased you took the medicine finally. Selva told me you finally did."

Meaning she also knew from Selva that he *hadn't* been taking the Valporate for almost the entire time he'd been in Cincinnati. Harvesting his lies to the contrary whenever they spoke on the phone.

"Are you still gonna use the top hat as your marker, Daddy?" Tessa asked as she opened the door. She was dressed in short shorts and a skimpy blue tee shirt that read MODE across the front. Together they began setting up the board. "What does *mode* mean?"

"The company's name. I don't know. Nothing special."

"Mode's a store?"

"Mommy bought it. Why does it *matter* so much?"

He and Tess distributed hundreds, fifties, twenties, tens, fives, and ones. But then Marta the housekeeper appeared at the open doorway. A coffee mug in one hand, she was dressed today in an outfit of sweats, both shirt and pants, with the word HUSKIES written down the outside of each thigh. As usual, her hair was not quite dry. "I figured to find you in bed," she told Brian. "I went looking for you there."

"We're *playing*, Marta," Tessa said snottily.

Marta waved Brian up from his sprawl on the floor. "You have a visitor."

Tessa snatched up her little lead Scottie from Go. "You can leave. I don't really care about playing." She slipped her fingers underneath the board, to tip it shut over all the cards already stacked there.

But Brian held her skinny wrist. "Wait, wait a sec. Marta, we've just started here. Can't they come back later, whoever it is? They asked for me? Probably they want Shelley. Tell them I can't come down now."

"*I don't think so, Brian,*" Marta singsonged. "You ought to come down."

Following Marta down the overly bright hall, Brian asked who it was that could be so urgently important.

"Don't blame me, Brian—he didn't call or anything first. Believe me, if he'd called I'd have told you in a second. But he just was suddenly at the door."

A sickening thought pushed down at Brian's guts. "Securities and Exchange?"

"Securities and what?"

"Is it a *fed*, Marta?"

Brian hadn't yet officially submitted expenses to Loftspring after the shutdown. Back in Cincinnati, he had begun keeping late-night calculations in a spiral-bound steno book, numbers that might be found reasonable and credible, but they were hardly in showable form yet.

Nor had absolutely everything been switched off. Getting out of the leased office space down in San Francisco was something Brian was planning to do in person this week, taking the landlord to lunch. And he had expressly asked Selva to burn any iffy receipts. She thought that would be unnecessary at the time—so who knows if she even did it? Was he going to be busted on top of all this? marched out of the house in handcuffs in front of his daughter? How cheesy of the SEC dicks to ambush him at home!

"Look, all I can say is that I think you'll be happy," Marta said, leading the way. "I'm *sure* you will be. *I'm* happy." And then, at long last, Marta was able to relax the smirk she'd bottled up until they came downstairs completely.

Standing in the living room for all creation to see was Phil Dreyer.

He wore a large-brimmed straw *latafundista* hat, he had on hexagonal wire-rimmed glasses, a version of the old hippie Ben Franklin frames of decades past, and all that Brian could think to say to him was "Hey."

"Me barging in on you like this. I know it's absolutely no good, man." This somehow agreeable neurotic dissatisfaction that was one of the actor's most attractive trademarks on screen. "Such a long time."

Phil took off his hat and put it down on a sofa before offering his hand. "But sometimes you just respect the patterns, the circumstances. But I always did know that when we *did* get to really talk to each other again, it would be while looking into each other's eyes."

"Marta, this is Phil Dreyer. Phil, Marta Spora—our helper."

(*The patterns, the circumstances* had cold narrow shoulders when my ass was seriously and profoundly on the floor, Brian thought.)

Marta was hardly pleased. "Like I really wouldn't *know*, Brian, right?"

"Marta and I are new old pals already," said Dreyer. "Just now, Bri, upstairs, were you very busy?"

In Phil's universe, *busy* ended up with the *done,* but not in Brian's. "My kid and I were playing Monopoly in her room."

"Would it be all right if I joined you? Can I . . . ? Well, great! On then, Macduff," taking Brian's elbow.

On their way up the stairs, Phil mentioned to Brian's back that he liked the house and found it handsome. Brian discovered that Tess had left her door open, a good sign. She was even still sitting on the floor before the Monopoly board, which remained open and stocked.

"Honey, you were just a really little baby, so you don't remember him, but this is—"

"Well, who *wouldn't?*" she said to her father. *"God."* Phil made straight for the Monopoly board, sitting down on the floor before it Indian-style. In shock, Tessa stared at the star a little in the way that Brian had looked at Shelley his first day home: as though half prevented, as though measuring the direct bitterness of the sun. All her life, she had heard how Dad knew this solar entity, and now she was compelled to completely believe it.

Without looking at her, Dreyer snaked out his hand flat to Tess, for five. Tess smilingly slapped the charmer right back.

"You guys must have just begun here. Can I join in, you think? People my age and your dad's age, some of them used to not approve of this game. Can you believe that?"

Brian sat too. "That's true." His eyes dusted at the wall shelf near Tessie's dresser, where sat her mist machine, her stack of teal kidney-shaped emesis pans used for the postural drainages. In the nimbus of Phil's stardom, all things familiar to Brian had turned strange and it was a little shocking to see the mechanisms of his daughter's disadvantage.

"Capitalist sublimation, was the line, if I remember," said Phil. "Of course, this was at the same time we all were also hysterically buying up bulk acreage somewhere wild and cheap so we'd be out of range when the 'repression came down.' You any good at this game, Tess?"

"Yes, I'm good. I'm *very* good, in fact." Tessa's right knee metronomed with ecstasy at being spoken to so adultly by Phil Dreyer.

"I think she's purely lucky," Brian said.

"Skillful!"

Dreyer reached over to grasp Tessa's hand in solidarity. "According to my old *roshi*, it's what skill is best for: games. Luck is better reserved for *life*."

Well, you should know, Brian thought. Phil seemed to live a longer day, a bigger week, a fatter year than other people did. All his myths relaxed into facts. He really had been in the service of a Kyoto *zendo*. He really had beachcombed in Sri Lanka. He really had studied sand play with flippy Jungians in Zurich. The eccentric private interests he pursued—trout farms, Himalayan trekking tours, meditation compounds in Big Sur—turned without sweat into gold-standard business ventures, hatched out of virtues that transcended themselves.

As did the fucker himself.

Phil was asking Tessa if she intended to buy railroads or shoot for it all and build hotels.

"Hotels."

He turned to Brian. "Speaking of which. We've been staying the last two nights at the Fisher Inn, you know, down the road here? They've been peachy over there, too, letting us alone. On the phone one day, Minna and I were talking, and we realized we hadn't done the wine country in such a long time. And so, since there now was a chance of me catching you here . . . She flew up with me. But I do have a funny story for you. Cracked me up. Maybe it's even funnier later, since I couldn't laugh at the time.

"It was just last night. We're eating a nice quiet dinner, when someone I do actually know a bit, an agent, is there too, I find, also eating there. Used to be with United Talent, now she's somewhere else. Linda walks over to us, and with her is a guy, and she asks me if I know H. Bruce Johannigson. Makes no gesture whatsoever toward this guy she's with. Plus she does have that bored, flattish, agent voice. So you never know for a moment whether you're being asked something specific or general, whether it's the guy who's with her or someone totally else."

"I know someone just like that!" Tess broke in. "In my school. Caitlin Mabbs."

Phil chivalrously nodded at her. "But I shake the guy's hand at least anyway and I ask them to sit. They do. But I'm still holding off consciously calling the guy by name. That 'H. Bruce' threw me. Maybe it was some writer whose book she was trying to get a deal for, someone who wasn't even present. But the guy sits and soon enough asks me to

call him Bruce. So that part's solved. Except that this Linda immediately butts in: 'No, Phil,' she tells me, 'call him *H. Bruce.*' Then she
says to him: 'I'm sorry, sweetie, but you can't have it both ways.'"

Tess picked up the dice and started jiggling them.

"Let's play, yes!" Dreyer said.

Playing around Phil's presence, which tucked in the edges of the
very air, caused the game to quickly fizzle and sink, however. Tessa in
time excused herself and went not to her own adjoining bathroom but
over to Shelley and Brian's down the hall.

"Great kid," Dreyer told Brian. "A whip."

"She has cystic fibrosis, you know."

Phil pointed in confirmation over at the mist machine, which he
had noticed after all. "Your others don't, do they?"

"They're adopted."

"That's right, I knew that. So of course not." Phil himself had children in an astonishing range of ages born of a half dozen women, only
a few of them wives.

When Tessa didn't soon return, Brian suggested they go back downstairs to talk.

Phil moved like butter within his clothes. Neither shirt nor slacks
argued with his will to sit when he reached the leather sofa where his
hat was. Fine reddish shoes were on his feet: London shoes, maybe
from Lobb's and handcrafted off a personal last with Phil's name
burned into its wood. They were held on by thin clear laces that
looked like cellophane noodles.

He patted at the side pocket of his soft green jacket—"Anyone
smoke?"—at which point his face went down in a heap: "I'm sorry. Of
course not. She looks great, your girl, though."

"She *is* great, always. She's in remission, or so they're telling us."

"A pretty abstract proposition, though, remission, isn't it?"

Gratefully, Brian said, "The *most* abstract." Marta was in the room
with them now, bringing in a tray with coffee, the good china, and
petit beurres. She was clipping Brian with a look, for Tessa, he'd learned
since returning, hadn't had a single congestive episode in all the weeks
he'd been away. The female-led household had even weaned the girl

from her twice-daily postural drainages. No bad news had ever been withheld from Brian when he was in Cincinnati because there simply hadn't been any.

"How big is this porch?" Dreyer asked, getting up to look out one of the windows when Marta finally left.

"Eighteen hundred feet worth or abouts."

"It wraps all the way around?"

"Our only big selling point."

"You selling?"

"Oh, perpetually. You buying?"

"How come up here in Sonoma in the first place?"

"A need to be around my betters. Making believe I was Coppola or Lucas. Actually, Tessie's doctor moved from Harbor Medical to UCSF up here, and we followed."

"Good. Good. Location's basically an illusion; no place is ever different enough to really matter, excepting maybe holy ground. To follow a healer is maybe the *only* good reason to ever move." Phil returned to the sofa. "You had something in preproduction out in the Midwest, I understand. I called your office up here and they gave me a phone number out there in Ohio. But the woman I spoke to out there said you already had come back here."

Selva never told Brian she'd heard from Phil Dreyer.

Pouring coffee into two cups, Phil went on: "They have a lottery in Ohio, don't they? Most every state now does. Maybe not Utah." He got up to serve Brian his cup of coffee and then took his own to the window that faced down the hill, the house's best view.

"A lightbulb went on for me after I read that you were working in the Midwest. It's stayed on, too."

"*Variety*?" Brian said morosely. "Where you saw it?"

And what else had he heard about, read, garnered from the buzz? Did he also know about Warshaw? The student interns? The bombs? It was the ludicrous bombs that ultimately had finished it all off for him in Cincinnati. The two pain-in-the-ass male acting students from the Conservatory, the ones forever trying to get Brian to talk about Artaud and cruelty and Peter Brook and to stop paying attention to the girls—they had tried to snag him exclusively for themselves by making a tongue-in-cheek attempt to bomb the rehearsal loft. Two comically fake bombs, amusing plastic spheres painted black with the word BOMB stenciled on them in white letters, had been set down right outside the front door of the rehearsal building. What the boys must not have realized was that the loft building stood only a block or two away from the county courthouse. Cops were nearby at any hour. The two morons had been caught in the very act.

"I need you to tell me first off what your time is like," Phil went on. "Tell me honestly, since there's no particular rush on this idea. I've sat on it for so long it probably smells of my anus by now. Twenty years, I figure. See, I don't want to intrude on any other of your projects."

Could the bastard be cruelly mocking him? "There are no other projects at the moment, Phil."

"Well, then reassure me as well, please, that doing only the script wouldn't bother you unduly. I don't want you put in a position where you'd be doing less than you want just as a favor to me. I think you're a great director, but this one I have to do myself, a promise I made to myself a long time ago. But if your work is done out there in Ohio, maybe we could start talking about blocking out a script together? You think?"

Police, Brian had found, had very little sense of humor about anything involving explosives. Detectives paid him a visit at the Queen City. Not wanting to say directly that maybe he'd had a part in staging the incident himself as publicity, they somehow said it anyway. And of course by then the local newspapers were all over it, stoked by the two young guerrillas and that professor of theirs, Dichteroff, a guy who adroitly knew just where to take it: Performance art! Artistic freedom! Apparently it flattered rube cities to be even adjacent to such cutting-edge matters.

Nor had Brian been above milking it for his own purposes, either. He'd gone on to a reporter about Cincinnati's tight-assedness and (with a nod to the shadow of Loftspring) dropped a gratuitous suggestion of anti-Semitic frame-up. At the time it had seemed as good an exit line as any.

Phil now paced beside the windows. "Here's the kernel. A guy, a kitchen remodeling salesman, works on commission. He was a pretty bad suburban druggie at one time but he went through rehab and was able to get his wife and kids back. Inside, though, he's still dying. Respectability isn't enough for him; he can feel the tide going out and not coming back in."

(At this last part, Brian prayed that he hadn't winced involuntarily.)

"One of the secretaries at the kitchen gallery persuades the guy to go in with them on a lottery pool, the Powerball. And they win! Four people, twenty million each. Once the guy's family is squared away, and after taxes, what's he then going to do with the smack? He decides to buy and reopen a factory in his town, which was crippled by plant shutdowns a few years earlier. What kind of factory I don't know yet— maybe a small steel operation or a foundry. Whatever it is, though, the guy knows jack about manufacturing. But precisely *because* he's at that spiritually cleaned-out point—died down to the root like Henry Thoreau says—he sees the lottery money as something to *lose*, not necessarily to make more money with. In the meantime, let him at least create a few dozen new jobs. Do something for other lives than his own. So he buys the factory—"

"And the company," Brian anticipated, "really takes off."

Phil came back to the sofa. "Like huge. It's still small enough to grow, but it does great also because it operates off love and faith, not just money. Is this too disgustingly feelgood for you? Capra crap?"

"It makes *me* feel good," Brian said sincerely—though probably not in Phil's context. Did Phil have *any* inkling of what kind of burnt offering he was talking to?

"Now here is where I think there really may be something to it. In my idea of it, there's an actual, *embodied* Spirit of Luck abroad during all this with the guy—a Spirit that's setting things up, arranging the pieces, doing the directing. We actually *see* the Spirit on screen, like in that Wim Wenders angel thing. This salesman is a throwback enough to still read the *Ching*, one of his cultural hangovers from college days. It was by throwing the *Ching* in the first place that he came up with the idea for the reopened factory."

Tessa had entered the room as Dreyer spoke, wordlessly taking a place by her father's side on the sofa. "Now I go back and forth about whether I'd rather play the hero or the embodied Spirit. Both would please me equally."

Tessa's presence untracked Phil, though. "What *was* Cleveland like?" he asked Brian.

"Daddy was in Cincinnati, not Cleveland," Tessa corrected.

"Do they make any steel there?"

Tess did the answering again: "*Soap* is what they make there."

Phil wants to make this lottery film in Cincinnati? I'll have to go back there? Gwen Filler had begged him for a last private meeting. "I was too uncomfortable with you, Brian. I'm sorry about that. You deserved someone more experienced—professionally *and* . . . " In the very public lobby of the Queen City, where every late afternoon a mock-English tea was staged, Brian had taken her hand tenderly. *He* should be the one giving apologies, he told her—by which time Gwen was reaching across the low table for Brian's *other* hand. "But I will always be touched by your vulnerability, Brian. Your openness." Her dropping voice began to shred. "Not everybody likes a big girl. You were not so high and mighty that you couldn't see the *me* that's under the weight . . . *and* despite my little, you know, problem. You considered *me.*"

"It's more a business town than an industrial one," Brian explained to Phil. "Sort of the upper South with a cork up its ass."

"I was in Cincinnati for about a week maybe, back in the sixties." Dreyer scratched at his perfect stubble. "My memory of it isn't sharp."

"Cincinnati or the sixties?"—and Tessa, who'd never heard the hoary line, was tickled.

"Both," said Phil, deadpan.

But Tessie's laugh unfortunately also tripped her up. To the laugh had hitched a cough, not excessively phlegmy but still and all a cough. And in front of the great star, not about to risk something worse, like a paroxysm, Tess panicked. She shot herself from her place on the sofa next to Brian and ran from the room, pounding up the stairs, faster than she probably should have been going.

"She'll be okay." Brian capably urged Phil—who looked wobbly (which was more than all right with Brian)—to go on.

"You need to go up to her?"

"We can let her be a bit."

Phil shifted around uncomfortably. It was delicious. "Well, so where was I? I also used to think about maybe one day doing something parallel, maybe about Andrew Carnegie. It could be the same film, for all I know, a double-tracked kind of deal." He paused, seeming to listen for any Tess sounds from upstairs. "All those local libraries he started. I've come to think that what you *do* with your money is a big big cosmic test. It has dramatic potential because basically it's moral."

"Not always." This just escaped from Brian, tickled out by subconscious considerations of Gates Warsaw, of Aug, of himself.

"You're right about that: Sometimes gray areas only get grayer. I don't always spot that. You, though, always had a terrific nose for the double bind. I think this is going to *work*, Brian."

"What is, Phil? Talk to me specifically."

"Do you need to go up to Tessa?"

"Is this project a ball that's actually begun rolling? You have—?"

"Look, you know what? Go up and be with Tess now. I'm going to stay at the Fisher another night. You come to dinner there tonight with Shelley if she's back. Bring Tess too." The actor rose. "One other thing just for now, though. This came to me in that same original dream. *The recycled improbable.* That's the key. Reopened factories. Local libraries. Gene therapy."

Brian for a moment thought he was talking about a person. Maybe the name of a character in one of his films that Brian had missed. When he realized what Phil actually had said, tears began to crowd Brian's throat and he got up blindly and bounded across the rug to embrace Phil. Phil, surprised, hugged him back.

They walked out to his car together, a rented black Cherokee. Phil gestured down at the beginning of the valley, the southern perimeter: "Your vines?"

"Yeah, I wish."

Marta was in the kitchen defrosting ground beef in the microwave when Brian reentered the house. "Tess is okay," she told him. "Embarrassed. Leave her be for a little."

Brian sat down on one of the stools at the prep island and watched as every few minutes, between microwave cycles, the young woman clawed off softened chunks of the dull red-brown meat onto a plate. "This is the deal—as I'm sure you overheard. A guy comes into massive money and so can do good deeds. What's good about these deeds specifically is that they restore something in the past that was valuable. The doofus wants to term it 'the recycled improbable.'"

"Brian, you're calling *Phil Dreyer* a doofus? Don't!"

"The past, the good old past. He wants back into the fucking womb like everyone else does. He still *smokes!*"

"You sometimes smoke too, Brian."

"Cigars. Out of the house. And with me it's *strictly* an affectation. It isn't an act of prior allegiance."

"Cigarettes are an *addiction.*"

"And, pray tell, what's an addiction? A last-ditch *choice.*"

The final chunks of the defrosted meat were in the bowl; Marta now was breaking eggs. "Well, I thought he seemed great. *Very* nice. Why not just be happy that you're going to work together again? And I will tell you something else, *señor,* which is that you better get hold of Shelley right now. She has to get back in time to get *ready.*"

The mysterious Minna turned out to be one of Dreyer's daughters, a junior at Penn. Brian could tell that this disappointed Shelley—that it wasn't a spouse or lover—but on the other hand Tessa, though she'd said very little for fear of being too obviously and nakedly her age, shone in the company of another daughter, no matter how much older. Happily drinking a bottle of Rutherford Reserve with Brian (despite Shelley's whisper in her husband's ear when Phil was asking to see the wine list: "*Should* you, with your medication?"), Dreyer laid out his idea once again for Shelley's benefit. She, in turn, took her best opening shot:

"Since it *is* so inherently classic a story, Phil, maybe you could even try first to shoot some of it here in California. For instance, Richmond has *plenty* of factories. And that way, if you needed Brian for rewrites at all during shooting, he would be able to stay close to home."

Brian didn't care. Let her say what she wanted. He didn't care about much. The only reason Phil was coming to him with this now was because he knew Brian would come cheap, desperate cheap. But even a cheap Phil Dreyer film still would yield more than was necessary to pay off any Warshaw funny bucks. As he was shaving before leaving for the hotel and dinner, Brian even began to see some charm and justice in the phrase "the recycled improbable."

The Fisher Inn's slightly fussy food was served and eaten appreciatively. The two men tried hard but patchily to reminisce. Minna and Tess went to the bathroom together (but vigilant Shelley not even once), and the wine, the blessed blotting juice, kept pouring forth.

It was like falling in love again with a huge handful of the world. That had been what Brian tried and failed to do in Cincinnati. There, the handful of world had been either too small to squeeze without dropping or else his hand had been too big and clumsy.

But not now, not here. Comfortably, he groped the recycled improbable. A man who's just been so baselessly saved, he could get with such an idea, couldn't he?

15

Although at the last minute he'd seen a parking spot on the street, Zwilling still went ahead and paid the few dollars for an indoor lot. Unable to know just how long he'd be, he didn't want to leave the car baking in the downtown's late afternoon sun.

Polly's choice of a place to meet, Lytle Park, was a surprise. It offered no illusions of escape, of oasis. More like a planted square than a real park, its sheets of dull grass were bordered by humdrum floral plantings. The square itself was too close to a precinct house to be a daylight haven for the homeless, and too severely open, lacking nooks, for lunchtime office-worker flirtation. Across the street on one side, the white-framed Taft Mansion dozed. To the west were the bland window walls of the appliancelike financial towers of Fourth Street. In the center of the park stood a statue of Lincoln, so ineptly huge-handed that Zwilling had once meant to show it to Selva.

Polly was nowhere to be seen. Zwilling sat down on a bench. Despite the problems with her boss, Polly had gone back to work at the group home, yet refused to take calls there and never seemed to be at home. Home now was Polly all alone. Pregnant *and* abandoned.

Would he and Barbara be asked to keep the baby themselves? Did they maybe even want to? Zwilling had to leash his penchant for adding a burden as soon as another was lifted. After a disgraceful last little bit of publicity, Horkow mercifully had left town for California. Last week Selva had flown off too—to London, on unnamed business, telling Barbara that she'd return to Cincinnati again only to clean her stuff out of the apartment hotel. Then she'd be headed back for good to California.

Selva had called him at home before leaving town. "It's important to me that you know that Brian wanted there to be a film until the very day he went home. It was me who thought there might never be one. I may have told myself that I was dropping hints like crazy to you, to Barbara, and especially to Nate when he started being so upset about not getting a screenplay in. But hints aren't ever enough, are they?"

After what she'd had a part in doing to him (and, worse, to Nate), all to no real final purpose, Selva was someone Zwilling ought to have written off, as Barbara already seemed to be trying to do. Despised. Yet Zwilling's emotions weren't as simple as he wanted them to be. The fact that she'd wronged him, *especially by withholding something from him,* this mysteriously seemed part of the essential dialogue between them. And so, somehow, he was now feeling more complexly abandoned by Selva than he ever had been by Nate's various departures.

One of Sir Walter Scott's Waverley novels rested in Zwilling's hand as he sat in the park. He had checked out the book as the most harmless thing he could find to read the last time he'd gone to the Fort Thomas library, and today had brought it with as something to hold, to keep his hands busy with while Polly cried, since Polly wasn't someone who'd allow herself to be held for long. Yet he actually had been reading the Scott too. Years of writing had effectively ruined the pleasures of reading for him. Eventually, he only read the long and safely dead, who made him feel less like an antagonist, even if one retired from the ring.

A female voice sent a male-ish "Yo!" from benches hidden by the statue of Lincoln across the park.

"Kemosabe," Zwilling said when he reached Polly, bending down and kissing her cheek. "I got here about five minutes ago."

"I know you did," she smiled.

"You were watching me?"

"I was buying something at the newsstand over in that building. I saw you through the window. You fidget very little. You're more peaceful than you think you are."

Zwilling checked his watch. "Was I late?"

The sun's slant forced Zwilling to look at her under a visor of fingers. Despite the season, Polly was dressed in black. The only color on her was a pair of orange high-tops on her feet and her persimmony hair, which didn't look very clean. Areas of her cheeks and forehead were broken out. "What'd your guy say about your Subaru?" Zwilling asked.

"Maybe water in the gas tank, I don't know."

"He sure? Water? That's a fairly left-field diagnosis." Zwilling knew her car being in the shop was merely her excuse to get him down here with her, but he still didn't want her being ripped off.

"They'll probably tune it up too."

"Can I see?" Zwilling asked—for a black shininess was peeking out from under the knuckles of Polly's right hand: a string of beads. "Greek? Tibetan? You've got the worries, I guess—why not the beads?"

Polly stashed the chain into a pocket of her black pants. "They aren't that. What's it that I have to worry about? You think I'm a wreck but I'm not."

"I think you're far from a wreck." Nate, in his disastrous bug-out mode once more, was on the lam from life. Leaving pregnant Polly, he had had flown to New York, eventually en route (or so he had threatened to his shamed father on the phone, once he was safely gone) to Jerusalem. But what if Polly did not see the loss of Nate and the prospect of single motherhood as crosses of cement? As a parent naturally drawn to the protective status quo, Zwilling had thought Polly and his son would always be together. But then how little he personally knew about the behaviors of unmating. In his limited experience, that fissure was something death took care of, neatly, neatly.

A pair of sparrows neared and moved closer to the bench. They then were joined by a single delicate goldfinch. Polly planted her feet subtly, adjusting her carriage in order not to make any quick, frightening motions.

"I'm going to be twenty-five years old," she began saying quietly. "Lately I've realized that in all those years I've never stood *for* anything. *Against* a lot—just not *for* much. And most of the things I was against I was against not because I had any better idea about them. Just to be against something."

"You and the great majority of young human animals," said Zwilling. "Don't beat yourself up."

"I've never made anything like a positive statement that could have come only from *me*. Personal in *that* way," she said passionately. She stood up abruptly, almost kicking one of the sparrows; the birds moved away in a coordinated hop. "In case there's traffic we'd better go."

"Now can I know where?" The least Zwilling could do in payment for his boorish son was let her have a chunk of his afternoon. The fact that she'd even asked him cheered him. On the phone she'd said only that she had an appointment and needed a ride because her car was in the shop. When he'd asked specifically where to, she'd changed the subject.

Now she partially confessed: "Mt. Auburn, Corryville-ish. Around there."

This in part was a medical neighborhood. "Obstetrician?"

"So where are you parked?" She gave nothing away in the car on their way uptown along Vine Street, either; and when they reached Mt. Auburn, she said simply, "This next corner and then a left. One last right, then into the parking lot of the Catholic church. You'll see it. It's obvious."

Now Zwilling was unmoored. Polly opened her door of the car. "They let us park here. Aren't you going to get out?"

It disturbed Zwilling. Nate going synagogish, now Polly churching it. People accepted protection wherever they found it, but Zwilling honestly wished these kids would stay out of dens of prayer. God to Zwilling had proven Himself a fine executioner, first and foremost. To go into a synagogue or church, therefore, was like asking the guillotine master for a calming smoke. It was when you gave Him something other than death to deal with, *then* was when the serious fumbles and diminishments and compromises clattered forth. Zwilling asked Polly if she needed him to wait.

Her face registered alarm. "You have to be somewhere else now?"

"I'm not terribly good in churches, Pol. I'll just wait here in the car, if that's okay."

"I'm not going inside, silly. We just park here, I told you that. It's only a few blocks from here. Please please please walk with me."

Zwilling got out of the car, locking it. His tolerance was starting to kink. "What's the intrigue?"

"If I had told you before now, I figured you'd spend the time between then and now worrying about it too much. You'll see, though, that it's fine. You know, Joel, life is good. It really is."

"I'm glad to hear you say that."

"Your son's the one who thinks life's not good enough. Maybe in New York that's a useful attitude."

They walked two, then three hilly blocks in saturated air. The streets searched for a tone, a way to be a neighborhood: crummy student housing, medical offices, a grim laundromat with bars on the windows, a grocery advertising clean chitterlings, on one unusually leafy block a drab rooming house that styled itself a bed-and-breakfast. Zwilling sweated heavily.

As they crossed the street, the letters of the sign on the corner building they were approaching—THE WOMEN'S HEALTH CENTER—seemed to rush up at Zwilling almost three-dimensionally. He lost all momentum rapidly. Joel had seen the abortion ads from this place in the back of the newspaper. Polly had reached the curb first, her eyes suddenly growing big. A turning car was headed for Zwilling on his left, forcing him to scurry to safety beside Polly on the sidewalk.

How could she be doing this?

His heart cawed harshly. "Talk to me," he pleaded to the girl. He couldn't take another step. "Nate's aware you're doing this?"

"Just a little further, Joel. Come on, they're the nicest people."

This is my grandchild you mean to destroy!

Two middle-aged women, neat as pins, one of them wearing a light-weight cardigan despite the heat, walked toward them on the sidewalk outside the abortion center. As they paced, their heads were slightly bowed. It took Zwilling a few moments to focus on their hands, to see that they were reciting the rosary.

Polly mined her own pants pocket to lift out the full strand of beads, complete with crucifix, that Zwilling had misidentified in the park. "See? They're the *opposite* of what you thought, Joel. They're hope beads!"

In four more strides, the two walking women reached them. "Eva, Mary-Louise—this is my father-in-law, Joel Zwilling."

"We've heard a lot about you," the one named Eva said, while Mary-Louise told Zwilling he was more than welcome to walk alongside them. The more the merrier. Then they swung away, too polite to put him on that much of a spot. They walked back in the direction they'd come, along the sidewalk fronting the clinic.

"So now you know," Polly sighed. "*This* is why Nate went ballistic. I've been coming here for a couple of weeks already. We had the worst screaming fight over it. Maybe we should sit. What about over there?"

Zwilling let himself be led across the street, to the stoop of a brown-stone that housed an insurance agency. Before sitting down on one of the steps and drawing Zwilling down next to her, Polly seemed to scan the street for something particular, even consulting a watch on her wrist. Zwilling had never seen her wear a watch before.

"I'm sorry I had to fool you, Joel, but I needed you to see me here with your own eyes. The one who got me here originally was you, after all— but I know that if I told you about it beforehand you wouldn't come."

"How do you mean I got you here originally?" A fatigue—one that almost had a rank, decomposed smell to it—had overtaken him. "Be clearer, Polly."

"Nate wants me to get rid of the baby. I'm sure you guessed that, at least."

"We never discussed it," Zwilling said—an unforgivably damning admission right there.

"He's saying he doesn't know if the baby is even his."

Out of Zwilling's mouth popped, unforgivably, "*Is it?*"

Polly didn't seem offended. "Of course it is. He knows it too."

"Then Nate will do what he has to do," Zwilling said, although in less than total faith that he was correct. Screwing up and bad conscience were his own provinces—his masterpieces, in fact. And it suddenly dawned on him that Nate, with his delinquencies, his Bohemia, his drugs, and now his domestic irresponsibility, was perhaps always trying to obtain a piece of the disaster pie for himself.

"Don't assume I *want* to be his have-to-do thing," Polly protested. "I never have before. Why should I start now? My attention's totally on my baby. You, I know, can appreciate that."

"Yes."

"Like I said, no one more than you *got* me here, Joel. You're already more of a grandpa than you know. That asshole film guy was toying with Nate so badly. Giving him no direction. It was driving Nate crazy, not knowing what the guy wanted, and so he went back through all your stuff and dug out that story you published when he was little, the one about the dead wife and the motel. I think he gave it to that awful woman, the producer. Maybe they'd want to do *that*, he thought."

Polly tugged at her rosary and again looked at the watch on her wrist. "I love your son, you know. Still. There was always more between us than you could ever know. I was wild with him, then I helped pull him out when the wildness got *too* wild. But I'm not sure I can save him twice. Having a kid changes things. It changes *me*."

With a mouth gone dusty, Zwilling asked if Nate was back on speed.

"No, I meant it generally. Saving him from himself. He's clean, as far as I know." Polly stood up. "Nope. Thought it was their car," and sat again.

"Whose car are you looking for?"

"Anyway. *I* at least got to read that story you wrote—which I've now read four times already. I have some things to say about it to you too. It changed my life, Joel, but it also makes me so very angry!" She pointed at Eva and Mary-Louise as they trod the abortion center's sidewalk. "I could never show it to those two over there, for instance, could I? They would be appalled."

"Yes, they would be," Zwilling agreed pridelessly. "*I* was."

"So I guess it's some kind of pattern with you. You do things and then withdraw them. You write something true and useful but surround it with *such sick shit*: a fake wife, fake dying, fake women, fake terrible guy, fake sex. You light a candle, then sit on it and snuff it out with your asshole. Nate and I, in our own different ways, have *never* understood any of that."

She put an arm around Zwilling. "But the reason I wanted you here with me today was so that you could see that something you wrote also had a *good* effect for someone. What you wrote was true, for me at least it was. You don't have much use for a truth once you've finished writing it down, do you? But somebody may."

Again Polly checked her watch. "When I was here yesterday, a lady from the *Post* happened to walk by, and we got talking. People aren't used to seeing someone on vigil who dresses the way I do. She said maybe she'd come back today with a photographer. But I guess not."

"A reporter, you mean?" Zwilling automatically got to his feet.

"You could talk to her too. Your name has been in the local papers a lot lately about the film. You *should*."

"It's a false position you put me in, Polly." For what she'd said was scouringly true: he *didn't* have much use for a truth once he'd used it.

"*A false position*—I don't think so. Really? I think a *really* false position is when you hide a strong truth inside a cheapo lie. It's like before, when I was watching you in the park. A person has no control over being watched or being thought of a particular way. You can't control what I think of you. And what I think is that there's a difference between being brave and just being bold."

She scanned the street. "Don't stay if you really can't, Joel. Eva's been giving me rides home."

"Where now *is* 'home,' Pol? You're always out." And, flailing desperately, Zwilling added: "Walking back and forth in this hot weather—is that even healthy for the baby?"

"Eva makes sure we all have plenty of water. Look, Joel, go. I just thought maybe you'd tell me how proud you are of me for doing this. Did you *ever* believe what you wrote?" Polly suddenly skipped down the steps. "Is that? . . . It is! I see them!"—and she began waving at a man and a woman a block away.

She came up the steps again to hug Zwilling. "Go. It's okay. I never mentioned your name to them. They won't know you were here. But *I'll* know."

16

Barbara had grown to hate the way Joel was watching her right now from across the kitchen, that monitoring, pessimistic way. Hoping to shake off his scummy stare, she blew extra long at her too-hot reconstituted soup in its cardboard cup.

"So late a flight," said Joel—who disliked nighttime travel, an inheritance from his mother, the storied mother-in-law Barbara had never met. (". . . *Scowling in the front seat beside my father; the fact that we had to still be schlepping along in an overheated Pontiac, passing houses where people were already settled in, in their pajamas. The worst part for her had been the transports. My father's boxcar apparently hadn't been as bad. Hers, though, was—very.*") Getting herself a glass, opening the refrigerator, filling the glass from an already opened bottle of sauvignon blanc ("To help me sleep later, what the hell. It's the last flight in, and they have me scheduled for a breakfast meeting at seven-thirty"), Barbara approached the table. She had noticed two Lean

Cuisines sitting on one of the refrigerator's wire shelves, food moved unnecessarily from the freezer to the fridge, tokens of Joel's good intentions but also of his failure, for Joel would eat neither of them if he continued going at the bourbon the way he was doing.

She sat down at the table opposite him. "Tell me one more time," Joel said to her, tight-shouldered and intent, "exactly what John Cloud said to you."

He just would not let it be. Barbara wished she'd been able to go straight from the office to the airport, and then, fait accompli, have called him from Pittsburgh. It would have made things so much easier. John Cloud's little debriefing talk with her had come early in the afternoon. Then, an hour later, Barbara learned she was being dispatched to Pittsburgh, an urgent matter for a client there who was not even one of her own but who had requested an intellectual-property consult. She'd be gone a few days at most.

She had been sent off by the firm with equally little notice in the past, though Joel was not in a mood to remember this. His mind, instead, was made up upon a quid pro quo. She gave it one more try now. "He was extremely nice. It was not a *summons*."

"Although of course it *was*," said her husband.

Joel essentially was still a child, which in most ways she found dear. But as a child, annoyingly, he saw all things as meaningful. "You know the way John is. He both likes and dislikes having the firm get into brokering situations like this. He feels it's easy to get squeezed if you don't watch it. And he's right about that. But if he had any hesitancy at all, that was it. He asked me how the meeting went, about what finally had been the disposition of the movie project—was it old news? history?—and what I'd been hearing about it from you. I said what's true: that you didn't know much because you never had been really involved to begin with. John said you were a lucky man, since his feeling was that they hadn't packed up and gone a day too soon. He'd been sensing and hearing an exasperation, a losing of patience."

"Hearing this from whom?"

"It would have shut him right down if I'd asked that—John hates being called powerful. But you can just guess. Business muck-a-mucks."

Joel rubbed his eyes under thumb and forefinger. "Happy to be a powermonger, just doesn't like being called one. A man of delicate sensibility."

"That really fair, Jo-jo? I don't think of John that way." If anyone had played the role of mentor at the firm for Barbara it was John Cloud. It wasn't surprising, then, that Joel would show some amount of jealousy. Not precisely sexual jealousy, but more wisdom jealousy, influence jealousy, an-older-man's-regard-and-protection jealousy. Up till this very minute, Barbara used to find this pleasing. "He went out of his way to let me know that no one was connecting any of this to me or you. He knew it was all Horkow, who was stirring up people better left unstirred. Meaning, as I took it, the arty crowd and the punks and the kid actors."

Looking up from his drink, Joel gazed at her as though she were extremely backward. "He meant *me*."

"Of course he didn't, not at all. That's what I was just telling you. That was my *point*."

"He did, though."

"You think you're on people's minds that much? You aren't. You may *wish* you were . . ." Immediately sorry for this, her face burned; she drew at some wine. "But say he even *did* mean you—do you care? Do you really care? It's what writers do, what they're *supposed* to do: make people uncomfortable. Though in this case you're wrong. He even said directly to me that he wanted us not to be hurt by this. That Horkow had come and gone, the whole thing in a month would be a memory, but you and I will be here permanently."

Joel reserved a long moment to inspect the tabletop. "Ah, well, there now we have it. 'Permanently.'"

Barbara had to act as though she didn't understand. What a weakling he could be, a blackmailer to boot! Last night, worried about today's meeting at the firm and unable to sleep because of Joel's snoring, she'd gone through the house depressed and irritated, carrying along a hollowness that seemed to fluoresce inside her bones. One thing she knew for sure: She had to bulk up somehow. She needed *more*—which was why, tucked safely deep in her bag to read later on the plane, were booklets about the fertility injections Dr. Mahr said he'd probably start her out with. She'd gone to him a few days back for an initial consultation. Mahr had seemed only mildly surprised that no husband accompanied her.

As he tended to do, Joel was now taking advantage of the silence. "He means, of course, that if you were conveniently *not* at Steiff, Cloud, and Gaines, if you were to go somewhere else, then *I* would be gone too, no longer drawing flies like this crazy movie director. That's what he was telling you. A scenario—and a threat."

"Don't drink any more, Joel. I mean it. Stop now. The way you're unfolding this is totally wrong, a totally wrong way. That's not what John was implying at all. He *likes* you."

"Sometimes I've wondered," he said very quietly, "if I'd ever recognize the more or less precise moment I finally ruined your life with mine."

The showy and more than slightly vain way he said this sent Barbara jumping to her feet. *"Oh fuck all of it!"* she shrieked.

But, bowed over the table like some goddamned old rabbi, he kept on: "Not necessarily me. My life. It once looked appetizing to you, but it was always poisonous—and I should have insisted you face that right from the start."

"Shit! Christ almighty! The self-*pity!*" Anything less dangerous than a glass in her hand would have been thrown directly into his face. The best she could do with her fury was to whirl around and chuck the wine glass toward the sink, where it shattered just at the countertop's edge. "That's *all* you have. Self-pity! It's all you ever *let* yourself have! Then you complain you don't have *enough!* I give up. I'm done. I'm tired of figuring it out!"

She ran upstairs sobbing, thinking *Let him clean up the fucking mess.* And also, more sickeningly: *I just said what he probably hoped I would.*

Though it wouldn't be fully dry before she had to leave for the airport, Barbara washed her hair in the shower anyway. Her head smelled of smoke from this morning's meeting and she couldn't abide it any longer. Malinckrodt, the Covington police commander, had chain-smoked Marlboros throughout the whole thing, and no one else had been in a position to object.

The meeting had started with chairs moved chorally closer to the table. The genius of law firm conference rooms: the table inevitably so large that no one could be too close to his neighbor, each just far enough away from the other to discourage too-easy alliances. Malinckrodt, Steve Lannigan—Steiff, Cloud's other janissary—and Ben Barone—the kids' lawyer—had come alert. But the longer-haired of the two acting students simply doodled on his thigh with a fingernail, a display of dull apathy that especially irked Malinckrodt. When simple glares had no effect, the police commander finally had to say to Ben Barone: "Have your clients *seen* the estimate of expenses incurred by the division on account of their little game? Maybe it would be profitable for *everyone* around this table to study the numbers one more time."

It was then that the *other* kid, bizarrely—as if making up for a missed cue onstage—suddenly began to bellow at Barone:

"And what *else* should everyone know, huh, Mr. Ben? Huh? HUH?"

Secretaries who were moving down the corridor outside the glass-walled conference room froze in their tracks at the ranting. Wearing painter's pants and ratty sandals over callused feet, a black tee shirt with John Lee Hooker's name and face on it, the boy did not seem benign; Barbara wasn't sure he wouldn't turn violent.

"How about how rotten the apples are? How corrupt this fucking cozy anti-art city is?"

"Be quiet, Kevin," said Barone. Ben, one of the few civil-lib specialists in town and thus hired, unusually, by the parents of both students, fancied himself the owner of a mean professional streak; but he basically remained a nice boy from Chicago who, in this case, was too good an attorney not to know what he was getting away with here. He'd sat barely animate throughout the meeting, his fingers interlaced only to the first knuckles, his thumbs waggling and occasionally going left or right to make a point, to direct a fragile emphasis.

Excepting maybe Malinckrodt, they *all* had a sweetheart deal here, in fact. As soon as the kids' professor, Dichteroff, had started to make noises in the media that the bombs had been performance art, the bigshot legislator Fred Shafer in Columbus had stepped in. Since his baby was the Ohio arts, which he never failed to refer to as "world-class," the last thing he wanted was another art scandal in Cincinnati, echoing the Mapplethorpe mess. Shafer had put in a well-placed call to Jack Walthaller, the Kenton County judge-executive across the river, and that, essentially, was that.

But now, to justify *his* billable hours, Steve Lannigan dropped in two cents as well: "Mr. Barone, you've *talked* to your clients, right? Explained the situation? Do they have a problem with it?"

The kid Kevin yelled, "*I've* got a problem with it, yeah. *Shit*, do I have a problem with it!"

"We don't, no," Barone said quietly to Lannigan, who then asked the group around the table if there were any last questions. A last percolation from Kevin— "Yeah, I've got a question! Aren't you all *ashamed?* Just plain fucking *ashamed* of yourselves?"—prompted Bob Barone to warn, "Kevin . . . ," but people were already putting papers back into briefcases even before Lannigan concluded with the fine print: Charges of inducing panic wiped off the record after a suitable time of no repeated behavior, and so forth.

Kevin let out one more bleat—"Someone's got to *know* about this!"—and then they were pretty much done.

In only her underpants, her hair wet, Barbara was in the middle of packing for her business trip when Joel came into the bedroom. His showing up only now wasn't nearly soon enough; he should have been waiting for her in the room when she got out of the shower. And so she gave him no chance at all to say anything first:

"I can't defend you. *You* have to defend *yourself.*"

To speak to him again cooled her anger somewhat, but also hardened it, casting it into an ingot.

"Defend yourself against *yourself,* I mean," she went on. "You're always giving up exactly the thing you need to protect the most—your concentration. You let Horkow play with it, take it away, dump it somewhere. And you suffered horribly for that. Now you're letting this screwed-up, pathetically *afraid* city take it away. Do you ever try and get it back? *Do you ever try to do anything but feel so goddamned sorry for yourself?"*

Barbara came within a hairbreadth of crying at him: *What kind of father are you going to make?*

But this was hardly the time or the way to tell him about Dr. Mahr. Besides, he already *was* a father—and the kind he'd made before he'd probably make again. This she did not want to think closely about just yet.

"You have to rub their faces in the truth. You're an artist—you *know* what's true. Be like that poet you used to tell me about, the one you admire so much, who recited his poem about Stalin's mustache. And, yes, I do know what happened to him. You don't have to remind me. He was eliminated. But you *still* have to!"

Barbara was crying again, which intensely disappointed her. Turning her back on him to remove a bra from her dresser, she could feel that Joel was coming forward silently. If all he wanted was to turn her and have her look at him, she was prepared to shoot him an elbow if that's what it took to get him to back off. But when he did reach her, his flattened hand set itself first on her behind, then traveled to the small of her back, and finally softly upward.

She didn't want this (although the fertility doctor had told her that intercourse would have to be fairly constant once treatment commenced: "Almost like putting a crop into the ground"). Exasperated that she'd have to assent now, of all times, Barbara leaned back hard into Joel's hand, hoping to hurt him a little, bend the hand back at the wrist if she could.

Angrily, she slipped her panties down and backed him up toward the bed, down onto his back. Unexpectedly excited, extremely slick, she knelt to peel off his pants and shorts. He was already responsively thick, aroused by her nakedness and initiative, but Barbara's zealous mouth enlarged him more—to a point where she hoped there'd even be discomfort. She tried getting at some of the thin skin of his shaft, get it under her teeth—to nip him, to bite him, to cause him to protest.

But all that resulted was that her aggression jumped to him like flame. Joel maneuvered her to the edge of the bed, where he engaged in some biting of his own, high up at the insides of her thighs, next at her outer lips if she'd have let him. She pushed his head away. Half kneeling, half standing, with Barbara's feet still on the floor, Joel went into her as an intruder, and seemed to be searching for an unprotected plane of bone that he could batter with his own pelvis. Anything but a softness.

Barbara began to climax. She came in an accumulated but blaring way, like the all-sounds scalded chord at the end of "Sergeant Pepper's Lonely Hearts Club Band"—but her first rough cries were taken by Joel for pain, and he quickly stopped assaulting her. They settled into supportive lovemaking, a binding married wrestle that was exactly what she *didn't* want.

Barbara thrust her legs into the air afterward, urging the sperm to make the journey upstream (though conception was a tiny possibility before she'd be adequately prepared by the Lupron or whatever she and Mahr finally settled on). She put her legs back down when her thighs began to ache. Joel never asked what she'd been doing. Barbara turned her face away on the pillow.

What had made her go to Dr. Mahr in the first place was Selva's departure. Selva, if she'd built up the nerve, must have already had her hysterectomy in London. Barbara never wanted to end up as lonely as Selva was.

Getting onto her back again, she lifted her legs straight upward for a few more seconds. Lowering them, she turned to stroke Joel's shoulder tenderly. "It was Mandelstam, right? The Stalin's mustache poem? You didn't think I'd remember." She kissed his shoulder. "Tell the truth—you didn't. Are you going to be okay?"

It was a dangerous question to pose to a man who had a narrower definition of *okay* than anyone she'd ever known—and he too knew better than to answer it with anything more than a nod.

She'd never had any real business marrying this complicated a man, who himself could not stand his hundred facets. How perfectly Barbara had failed to uncomplicate him!

Joel later drove her to the airport, where in the terminal, on the automated walkway, someone going in the opposite direction accidentally brushed Barbara's elbow. She didn't even turn around until she noticed Joel looking backward. He was grinning and pointing. A receding Selva, pulling a bag on wheels, was getting off the other walkway at her end and U-turning to ride the one Barbara and Joel were just stepping off of at theirs.

"Small world, guys!" She had just now passed through customs. Her flight had been late—a long delay at the other end at Heathrow. "Where are you two off to?"

Quickly, Barbara said to Joel: "Girl talk for a second—excuse us."

She pulled Selva aside a number of yards until they were standing before a croissant kiosk. "You look great." In fact, Selva looked tired, beaten up. "Did you . . . ?"

Selva shook her head no. "Chickened out at the very last minute. But I made a firm promise to myself and to the doctor there that I'd do it in California. You two headed someplace romantic?"

"Pittsburgh. Just me. Business."

With a slight British accent, Selva said, "Ah, just my luck. I have my last packing up to do before I go. I could have used some company."

"I'm gone for three days max, that's all."

"My ticket to San Francisco is day after tomorrow."

"You could change it. Change your ticket. I have things to tell you." The hug Barbara gave Selva then was one compounded of forgiveness and fear. "Look, get Joel to help you pack—he could use the distraction."

"What time is your flight?"

Barbara looked down at her watch. "Oh my God."

17

Selva let them in and, once her bags were down, directed, "Sit there."
She looked around her in distress. She truly was a wanderer, she realized. "Did you ever see such an amazing mess? Take those off the seat.
I wasn't expecting anyone to come back with me."

Joel, fingering them, said, "These the notorious drapes?"

"In the end, I decided yes, I would take them back to the boat with
me. When I get more shipping boxes, they're going to go into one.
Something to remember Cincinnati by. The first of many nice things."
She looked around. "Somewhere, though exactly where? I have a bottle of the bourbon you like. Dickel, is it? It's unopened. I was going to
give you the bottle before I left. I was going to put it on your
doorstep."

Joel set himself down into the severe bentwood rocker. It cradled him inadequately. "No whiskey for me. I've already had. More will erase me."

"Celebrating, were you? Unfolding like a flower as soon as we all left you alone. Are you sure?"

"Well, only maybe if you're having one. Very small, though, very light. Lots of water."

Selva made two drinks and brought her own glass to the sofa opposite him.

"Nate's in New York," Joel told her. "You maybe knew that. He says he's fine. I'm not sure why, but this time I tend to believe him. Polly's finally there with him too. They dealt with it, worked it out. You knew she's pregnant?"

"He just needed to sort things out," said Selva.

Zwilling sighed, "A long process."

"My father used to say that when we don't know what's ailing us— he meant spiritually—it usually means we're unsure at the moment of who is loving us. The ones *we* love, of course, they're covered, we know them. He meant where love is coming *in.* I feel for Nate. Being a broken twin can't be a trivial thing. He tried having Polly be his sister, but Polly isn't someone who can be Alissa for him."

Seeing Joel's mouth twitch prompted an unconscionable thrill in Selva. "Should I not use her name?" To be this desperate and windblown was a hateful state. The problem would soon be moot—she'd be cut open, sewn back together, and thereafter be a hag. Yet, exactly *because* she was going to be that, her recklessness seemed to increase now day by day.

"I like to think I can talk about anything," Joel said slowly.

Selva put up a hand. "You know, I want nothing better than to talk—but I also have been sitting in these clothes for a whole day. I can't do it anymore, not for even another minute. Do not go anywhere. And don't look around too hard—remember, I'm packing and I didn't expect to be quite so acquisitive in Cincinnati. I'm not usually so much of a slob—though it's true I never did let Barbara come up here."

Selva scrubbed at herself intently in the shower, in order not to think. Then she faced another difficulty while drying herself. To get fresh clothes out of a carton would have been complicatedly public. So she came back to Joel wearing merely the kimono from the hook on the bathroom door. He had remained in the rocker, still grasping his no-less-full drink.

"Now I'm not so disgusting."

Selva took a place on the sofa facing him. "I thought of you, you know, while I was in London. I passed a record store. I went inside and it had thousands of records, of LPs. I was going to buy you a present but there was too much. It wasn't too well organized and I didn't really know what you'd like. Or—the biggest thing—what you already didn't have. But I did think: Joel would love this place. The last man in America who listens to records."

"Oh, not at all, no. There are thousands of other dinosaurs left, but we're generally up in the hills, keeping out of the way, out of sight— getting ready to evolve into birds."

Selva curled her feet up under her, making sure the kimono was tight around her knees. "Have you usually controlled yourself and consciously tried *not* to be funny with me? There something about me that you thought wouldn't like it?" She couldn't help herself. "Something, by the way, I've been meaning to ask you for some time. Who is Dan Ingram?"

"Dan *who*?"

"Nate once mentioned him to me. He said he was sort of a hero for you. I *think* the name was Ingram. Was he a writer? A comedian?"

"Nate remembers me talking about Dan *Ingram*? Jesus. No, he was on the radio, an AM station in New York, a deejay. A wonderful old pro."

"A *deejay* was one of your heroes? This was when? Was I born yet?"

"Oh, thank you so very much. He was the afternoon man in the late fifties and into the mid-sixties, I guess. This was back when AM radio still was subconscious and not self-conscious."

Selva wanted this to go on and on, to never stop. "Do you have a tape of him or anything I could listen to? What did he do that was so wonderful?"

Joel, while he sipped at his drink, laughed strongly into his glass; this then required him to take out a handkerchief from the back pocket of his rumpled chinos and blow his nose.

"When he wanted to, Ingram could have the single dirtiest-sounding voice ever heard in the history of man. Lesley Gore, for instance, would finish up and Ingram would say: 'Don't Make Me Over.' Then he'd mumble, really *evilly*: 'Once, thank you, was fine.'"

Selva squealed.

Joel, himself cracking up, went on, "He'd cue up a Clearasil commercial—the dramatized ones that radio never could pull off but always was trying to. You know the kind. *'Oh, Mary, I'm so unhappy.' 'What is it, Sue?' 'It's these darn pimples! How will I ever go to the big dance?'* Ingram would break in, this dark *commendatore* voice climbing up into falsetto: *'Don't worry, Sue—it's a masquerade dance. You can go as a cherry pie!'*"

Selva wept with laughter . . . and after that simply wept. It seemed to take Joel, who'd been laughing hard too, a long moment to notice.

Still crying, but trying to brake herself with hard simple facts, Selva said to him whisperingly: "I'm all alone. Worse, I know what I want. It isn't fun to be alone *and* to know *and* not to have. Can you bear to hear something that I like to think about?"

"I can"—and his nicest smile came along with it, his fatalism exhibiting all sides of his heart.

"On my boat? While you were helping me get the salmon served in one whole piece? I was holding the platter and you were sliding the fish onto it from the poaching basket. Well, you made a little joke. Do you recall? You spoke to the fish. *'Upstream now,'* you said, *'don't forget.'* You could tell it was important to me that it look pretty when it was served. You made fun, but your eyes also told me how used to paying attention to people you were. It finally dawned on me after I got here to Cincinnati that *Dummy, one of the people he pays attention to is you!*"

Joel wanted to look away for a second, she could tell—and yet by force of character he didn't, he held on to her eyes. Selva wished she was able to cut herself off right now. "Once I realized that, I became extremely hungry for even a little bit of that attention. To hang on to you was something I couldn't have done and didn't, but it was very difficult not to. You're going to be someone whose high-grade attention I always will need to have at some dose or other. Maybe I stayed here—which was so wrong to do in so many ways—in order to have a little more."

"Selva—"

"You're married. And you're still married to your work, I think, at whatever level, past or present. You don't live anywhere near me. You don't care at all about films. And a lot of the time you make me feel idiotic. But I need to tell you this. When I *am* being stupid I'm usually being it about *you.* Confused. The constant underselling you do of your life. Whether or not you're maybe the world's biggest coward. I don't even necessarily *want* you to want me—since I'm not positive you *could.*"

When she stopped, Joel's lips flattened involuntarily, an unconscious face of loss. After that, there was no way she couldn't continue: "It would get in the way of my wanting you."

He looked down gravely at his ankle in its sock. "*Don't* want me."

"You telling me what I should want?" Turning the smallest bit hysterical felt very good, like a partial rescue. She sat forward, setting her drink on the floor, the glass's base leaning partly on the edge of the fake Oriental rug. "You may have a say in whether I get it or not, but as to *what* I want, that's really my show completely."

She noticed that Joel was trying not to look at the still-good gloss of her red-painted toenails, the nails she'd painted for Peter Swainten in London, who'd come to her hotel for drinks and, in due time, had sucked the toes. The fact that nothing could have prevented that sex didn't make it any less disheartening to her. And the next day, when she'd called him on the phone to cancel the surgery, Dr. Coffman's gentle paternalism had grown a little scratchy: *Good luck to you, by all means and truly. But if you were my daughter I still would beg you to re-*

consider. How much pain is it that you judge you deserve? Find a good surgeon in California.

"That's going to tip," Joel pointed out. Still crying, Selva moved the glass. Now he was getting up and coming to her—but so apprehensively that it offended her. Selva stood to take an evading step away and turned her back to him. She didn't want to be a figure of pity.

Then, defiantly, she turned back to him. The wrap of her kimono winged up, exposing a great deal of her before she pulled the robe back around. "I'd like to be one of your successes, that's all. One of your winners, like at River Downs. It would be good for me. God forbid, maybe it would be good for you too."

Joel delicately sat on the sofa next to the spot she had left. His eyes alone asked what she wanted by way of a possible response.

Selva softened. "You're thinking of Barbara, which you *should* be—but I am no threat to Barbara." She sat again. "I don't look to break up your marriage, Joel. If you fell in love with me at some point, if some mutual level of . . . oh, I don't know. For now it would be enough for me only to love you."

Taking his hands, she sat back more fully and tried to relax. "I *need* to love you. You maybe also need me to, or maybe not. Remember, I am disgustingly capable. The barest minimums leave me content. Men don't know how little women will settle for. It would be impossible for us if they did."

Selva's own heart tore a little then at the small fading laugh she gave out, a kind of swallowed burp. "I'm just a woman, Joel. We're supposed to be the more complex animals compared to males, right? But in the scheme of life we're still simple creatures. If you let me love you, and occasionally *showed* me that you're letting me love you, I'd be happy. Maybe you'd be happier too." When he sighed and drank from his glass she said, "Not *too* much. Don't get worried. But just a little."

Selva took Joel's right arm and wordlessly moved it across her shoulders; a moment later, she led his stunned hand into the front of her kimono to hold her right breast.

"*This* now is the lucky one," she whispered to his shoulder.

The smell of the whiskey, of her own dried-on bath oil, of the slight must of her wrapper—she was being led strictly by the senses now. "Do you remember asking me?" She adjusted his hand so that his fingers chopsticked her pebbly nipple more securely. "When I'm gone from here I won't almost ever see you. It'll be maybe only once a year, like in that play."

Then, though she guided his hand away from her breast, Selva retained one of his fingers and used it to trace one of his own eyebrows. "Dear heart."

Just as suddenly, she found herself missing his touch terribly. She had had too little of it, and she wanted Joel to at least once know her belly, her hair. She brushed the kimono back even more, directing his hand down along herself. She parted her legs.

It took next to no time, she came right away, silently—a slight sideward twitching of his situated fingers, a clutching, a squeezing with her thighs, her other hand sensing that the muscles in his back were singing a shivery song.

Once recovered, Selva asked him: "Let's kiss a little now?" Finally, for the first time in her life, she had willed a dream fragment completely into being. "Can we do that?"

Joel's mouth approached hers. It was almost at her lips when the phone's obscene clamor stopped him, causing them to share a look so undone it was comical. Under sparkling pain, Selva smiled bravely and pulled the kimono around her. The ringing stopped before she got to the phone.

Joel said, "Selva, I—"

It was almost to laugh. She'd be reading Montaigne again tonight. No vain hopes. No illusions.

"Reality can be gruesomely real, can't it? It was Brian or Barbara, don't you figure? And since Brian wouldn't know I'm back, it had to be Barbara. Go home. She'll worry. You never had to be here, Joel. If she calls here, I'll say you weren't here at all, that you never came back with me. Go. Go. And by the way, when you're home, do me one favor—hide a few of Barbara's *Vogues* and *Elle*s. She told me she's planning to throw them all out, all her fashion magazines."

There was a certain kind of tardiness in Joel's eyes, the look of someone who'd begun to pull himself together too late. She'd seen that look in his son as well. "That didn't *have* to be Barbara on the phone," Joel said.

She returned to kneel by his knees, once more taking his own limp hand, this time to caress his own cheek with it. "Maybe I'm *your* sister," kissing the back of his hand. She stood up and recrossed the room to sit in the rocker he had vacated, a final journey. But when the phone rang again, and as Joel groaned at the abomination, it made Selva almost lose control and go back to him.

After a while, tonelessly and sadly, he asked, "What does throwing out the *Vogue*s mean?"

"You see, we find ways to see off our illusions ceremonially. Barbara is preparing to be old. I don't think you have been persuading her much to the contrary, either. You should be younger for your wife."

"And . . . for you?"—looking astounded that he'd said it.

"Oh, I told you already, I'm a cheap date. I'll take care of what I need you to be for me." She stood up and walked to him. The embrace she gave him was already crapey, like an old newspaper. "No salesman will call."

18

As he sat down on one of the chairs on his porch, Zwilling noticed the moon still struggling in the morning's waxed sky. It looked vaguely the way he himself felt: historical, older than its energy allowed for. Although he had showered, he still could catch from his lap the faintest whiff of the morning's sex: Barbara's odor.

An architect was coming to see him about drawing up plans for an addition to the house. Zwilling had been unfairly imprecise to the man on the phone—"More options spacewise." Yet imprecisely was how Zwilling and Barbara still approached the idea themselves. A new office or studio for him. A separate apartment for Nate and Polly and the child if and when they came back from New York. They didn't yet admit to themselves what the final idea might be.

Nor would they dare utter the words *baby's room*—far too superstitious for that.

On the dot of ten, a late-model Acura, ink blue, began its way down the cul-de-sac toward the Zwilling house. Standing up to wait on the porch steps, Zwilling watched the architect emerge from the car. Enrique Chodorov seemed a little old to still be doing home renovations. His hair, a tinct of gray and black, was carried long in back. But in front it was holding on for dear life. The stylish gray suit he wore nicely favored his potbelly, a true embonpoint. Previously, on the phone, he had mentioned to Zwilling that he, a Chilean Jew, was also a Survivors' kid—Buchenwald to Santiago.

Chodorov paid specific compliments to Barbara's decorating while Zwilling showed him through the house. But he had something more on his mind. "I know your book about the camp family," he said while jotting down approximate dimensions in the kitchen. "Accidentally I saw it in the library years ago, after I'm here long enough for my English to be okay enough to read novels. The subject interested me, naturally."

Zwilling deflected him as they went back outside through the kitchen door: "What brought you to Cincinnati?"

"Airplane."

Zwilling grinned. "I myself drove."

Chodorov was putting his yellow legal pad up over his eyes. "For a house on a ridge, this to me is a surprising amount of room you have back here."

"We thought so too."

"Enough maybe for another small structure, if that's how you wanted to go." He sketched a few joined lines. "You don't know it, of course, but I meant to look you up always. We all get so busy, so lousy busy, and people drift out of mind."

"And aren't you thankful they *do*," Zwilling said.

"But then I'm seeing your name in connection with this movie. And a little bit after that, you're calling me about your house. Coincidence. You maybe sensed from speaking to me on the phone that first time how pleased I was that you called me. I hope so."

"We heard plenty of good things about you." But suddenly Zwilling was without patience for his *own* small talk. "Both parents were in Buchenwald?"

"The *tateh*. *Mameh* was in Theresienstadt. Afterwards, in the DP camp, they got together. It was common, you know? Who else was there to marry? One had to know what the other knew."

"Which," Zwilling agreed, "was everything." The phone was ringing inside the house. No friend of ringing phones, Zwilling chose to ignore it, letting the answering machine take it.

The morning air was fragile and delicious, though bound to degrade soon as the humid afternoon neared. Chodorov tossed his legal pad onto the grass and, with some difficulty, lowered himself onto it like a Parisian park-goer, swiveling back toward the house every so often to once more ponder its lines.

"I always hoped maybe we could get together like this and talk about your book, about our parent's lives. Maybe not now, but sometime."

"You should have called me up."

"Well, yah, I should have. The fear I have, though, you see, is that I am not good at it anymore. I hardly remember my childhood and my early life now. Like I was *made* to forget. Forced to, somehow."

"You think that's a wholly bad thing?" said Zwilling. "I'm not sure it is. Even better would be if we could figure out a way to forget *their* lives too."

"I know." A soft shadow in the architect's eyes signaled that he was unembarrassed at having been recognized and flushed out. "Not them as people, you're saying, but their terrible lives. I completely agree. But it's hard to do, isn't it?"

Chodorov got himself up from the ground and dusted himself off. "Arrange please, won't you, with your wife, when you will have me and Juanita to dinner. Call and tell me."

To Zwilling's intrigued expression he explained: "I don't start a design until I've seen how the people who are living in the house actually live in it. My little *mishegoss*. About two times, maybe three, you have my wife and me to dinner or lunch or brunch or something, even just drinks, and by then I have a good sense of in what direction we could go. If you then don't like what I suggest, *nisht iz nisht*—you're out a couple of dinners. My wife tells me that I sound with this like a prima donna, but what can I do: it's how I go about it."

"Sounds like a reasonable approach to me."

"One life, one way—what can you do? We're stuck."

Joel, Barbara, the message on the machine announced when Zwilling hit the button after Chodorov had gone, *this is Selva Tashjian. Something bad has happened back here and I'm sorry I'm not able to speak to you guys directly and tell you, but for now I'm just going to leave this message . . . I'm not really sure I'm even* up *to talking to you directly right now. But if you could please call me eventually. One of Brian's children has died, one of the twins—I'm going to get cut off by your machine soon, I'm sure—but it was an accident, Brian was playing with them in their room, and he hit his head, Bommy did, Jeremy, his son, one of the twins, against part of the metal bedstead. They were having fun, they were flinging themselves around, they were having such . . . I'm sorry . . .*

In the airport men's room, as Zwilling washed his hands after urinating, he took a hard look at himself in the mirror. Despite the dark suit, the light blue shirt, the ever careworn face, what possible kind of ambassador did he really make? What was he bringing to whom? Whom was he kidding?

As soon as they were up in the air, with the plane leveling from its great first climb, Zwilling experienced a great desire to eat. To be hungry right away, considering his mission, felt inappropriate, but lately he was always hungry. Some quality of fermentation to his days that turned him into one large open mouth. Even when he went with Barbara for her appointments with Dr. Mahr, the potted plants and fish in tanks in the waiting room, the framed posters of Cincinnati scenes decorating the walls of the examining rooms (to remind patients of what they'd be reentering when they left such solicitude?)—all seemed restaurantlike to Zwilling. Even Mahr himself, the young fertility specialist trained by the in-vitro whizzes in Norfolk, seemed as though he was reciting to them the daily specials. He spoke respectfully of Barbara's wrinkling drying inner eggs, and cautioned against hopes too great, yet at the same time the doctor betrayed an excitement about microscopic, improbable life that was infectious. It left Zwilling, as he and Barbara exited Mahr's office, in a mood of increase, his mouth awash in dreams of strip sirloin or large Italian sandwiches.

Was food even promised on this flight? Nor was Zwilling able to read now, either. He'd tried, but his eyes couldn't bite into a page. To avoid the prospect of sitting here and just *thinking* for four and a half hours, something that would wreck him, sleep seemed the only hope. Yet this was an especially long shot. Worried about airsickness, about his ears clogging, about jet lag, he had dosed himself in the airport with enough Dramamine and Afrin to hike up a horse.

Still, one particular reverie sometimes worked as a sleep inducer. To map in his memory the block of stores on Brooklyn's Avenue J on which his parent's own store stood sometimes got Zwilling to nod off. He closed his eyes.

The corner drugstore (name forgotten). To its right the two half stores, a shoemaker and a plumber, their doorways angled off a pentagonal white-and-red-tiled entrance. The overly large barbershop to the right of that: yellowed *Police Gazette*s on the deep windowsill; at Christmastime a plastic Santa face in the window whose eyes followed you. Next Simon's: Simon Antelek's fruit-and-vegetable business; Simon a Galitzianer without a family, with a numbered arm like Joel's parents but, unlike them, someone who was happy in his cells, who had been liberated from his psychic *Lager* by his body and muscles. A sort of Jewish Jack LaLanne able to carry two cases of apples on a shoulder or rip free the wooden slats of a lettuce box with his bare hands. Simon, his demons pinned and flattened, was *healthy*.

And then, finally, next door, the Fairview, the Zwilling family store: hosiery, foundations, and in the waning days, very briefly, some men's clothing too, as many sample sizes as his father could pick up in the menswear showrooms in Manhattan and haul back on the Brighton line in their thick canvas rack bags. The Fairview's light was yellowish, made that way by a glare shield affixed at the corners to the inside of the front window. Nothing in Zwilling's young first novel had more hurtfully confused his skinny nervous parents than the way he used the glare shield's jaundice to tint the whole book: sallow pessimism, anxiety, depression. To his mother and father, the glare shield had represented genuine action, something positive, a modernizing, a moving ahead. They'd debated buying and installing it for nearly a year, the Master Issue. His mother didn't see why they needed it at all. Zwilling's father would respond, Oh come on, Pesha, look how badly the hose boxes fade. Her reply: We sell *undergarments*—what's to see? Then his father would counter: Why not then board up the window altogether and *shoin!* What can be shown *ought* to be shown.

Sitting up in the air over Nebraska, perversely more distant from sleep than ever, Zwilling had to acknowledge that he was his father's son, after all. Artist, perfectionist, illustrator, fatalist. The glare shield had ended up making the ivory-colored hosiery boxes look even sicklier. It was succeeded by an expensive awning, also worth nearly a decade of contention—up, down, ripped, fixed, a nuisance, a godsend.

Unlike his last time in California, the arrival on the ground was strictly do-it-yourself. In a rented blue Toyota, Zwilling manfully figured his way out of the airport exit roads and proceeded to drive northward in light that was like a polymer, coating hummocky San Francisco, the Golden Gate, the mountains of Marin County, the green of the valley country as the highway led him up into where the Napa and Sonoma vineyards began. All the aggressive visibility made Zwilling feel exposed as well, a surface awaiting painting. His will, in an already loose socket, slipped back and forth. More than once he thought about just turning around and going home.

Other than Barbara, no one knew he was here in California. Selva, after Zwilling finally reached her on the phone, never once suggested he come out. All she did was tell him about the accident:

"He'd been trying to make it up to the boys, giving them more attention. Tess usually gets most of his focus. So he and the boys were roughhousing. The twins were mobbing him. First one and then the other, and Brian was flinging them away. Bommy—Jeremy—got flung too wide and he hit the metal bedstead with his head."

Edward Lear's two lines landed in Zwilling's head as he had listened to this: *"Long ago he was one of the singers, / But now he is one of the dumbs."* Horkow must avoid this somehow! As an ex-singer turned

dummy himself, whom had Zwilling ever helped, least of all himself?
When he called Barbara at the office a half hour later to tell her the
terrible news, along with his unlikely thought, she was not surprised
at all, for some reason:

"Sure, I can see you going. Do."

In Sebastapol's town center, Zwilling stopped at a drugstore for more
specific directions. The palsied middle-aged woman behind the store's
front counter, when she heard that it was Brian Horkow's house he
was looking for, gave him another once-over, an adjusting look. This
so unnerved Zwilling that he ended up buying something from her—
a pack of filtered Camels for lack of any better idea.

He knew he had finally reached the correct house when he saw cars
parked on the grass. The house was attractively white, with a porch
belting all the way around and tracts of widely spaced grapevines
barely an acre away. People were standing around on various sections
of the wraparound porch, and in the foyer women sipped from bright
red coffee mugs.

Zwilling stepped forward like a diver going over the side.

He had not expected to see the mirrors of the main room covered
by tacked-on sheets. They were actually sitting a traditional shiva.
Horkow was seated upon a mourner's bench in the immediate company of a man and woman in their fit seventies, likewise seated on the
low stark shiva benches. He wore slippers as well as a gray cardigan, a
torn black ribbon pinned to it.

At the sight of Zwilling, Horkow rose in shock and bounded to
him, his loud "Oh my God!" snipping every other noise in the room
short. "*You came?*"

He kissed Zwilling full on the lips, then held on to his cheeks for an
additional look at his face, searching for what must have been re-
arranged beneath it. "You came to me," he whispered brokenly, greatly
moved. A grime of emotion lay over the normal impishness of
Horkow's face, plus a few day's growth of beard. Zwilling took the director's hands down into his own and squeezed them. "I'm so very
sorry, Brian."

Horkow then pulled Zwilling in the direction of the elderly people on the benches. "Thelma and Maury Horkow, this is my friend. This is Joel Zwilling. Dad, this is the Joel I worked with. The writer."

The parents barely looked up. Horkow's father, tanned and very bald, was wearing the jacket of a black worsted suit over a solid pink golf shirt. The mother, equally tanned, was more conventionally dressed in subdued dark blue. A knowing face, a wiry alert body: She was a dynamo disabled. "He lost a child, too," Horkow seemed to demand of his mother and father.

"Recently?" the father asked. But he couldn't look at Zwilling, only at his son. Horkow's mother quickly stared off over his shoulder when Zwilling bent to one knee.

"A number of years ago," he said to the father. "It's a devastation."

"He *knows*!" Horkow spat furiously at his unresponsive mother. "*He knows*!"

Horkow's mother wasn't happy to be pestered. "I'm sorry he knows. I'm sorry for him." Adding: "Though what's to know."

Zwilling nodded. "There's nothing to know."

"Go change," Horkow's mother instructed her husband.

Horkow dogged her, "Also a twin!"—though all it achieved was a brimming-up in the father's eyes.

Again Horkow's mother told the old man: "Go up and change."

Zwilling rose from his knees and at that moment he first spotted Selva. Horkow's mother had been blocking her out, even though Selva was sitting merely about six feet away, alone, on the floor, her back resting against an inactive ceramic hearth. When Zwilling saluted her with his fingers, she immediately looked down at the floor.

To even only see her was like climbing a gate for Zwilling. He had come for this. It was time to confess that to himself. By merely seeing her, he might find out how he felt. Almost daily now he made love to Barbara in attempts to start a baby, and yet there remained over his life a hanging question.

Closely watched by Horkow too, Selva finally did raise her eyes, holding her gaze on Zwilling for a moment before waving back. But she never got up or motioned him forward.

"There's coffee or tea," Horkow said to Zwilling. "Wine too."

"Brian, your wife—could you take me over to her for just a minute?"

"God! That's true, isn't it? you don't even know her, you know only me. Come on. This way."

Shelley Horkow was small and sun-whipped, with a tight foxy face. She looked younger than Horkow by a few years, perhaps because of the extremely long single braid hanging down her back. She sat not on a mourner's bench but in an upholstered chair pulled arm-to-arm with one of a number of long leather sofas in the room. Seeing her husband and Zwilling approach, she rose with a springy, get-it-over-with dispatch—like someone just called at the dentist's waiting room. Two red-eyed women leaned protectively toward her.

"Shelley," Horkow said, "Joel's here! Joel Zwilling from Cincinnati!"

Shelley Horkow extended her hand, crowding her fingers inside Zwilling's grip as if more than ready to slip them out. "You shouldn't have come."

"I just wanted to tell you how terribly sorry I am."

"Oh, sure he should have," Horkow parried. "I wanted him here, I *needed* him here. Now that he's come I realize it!" Hugging Zwilling's shoulders: "Somehow he knew that!"

Shelley Horkow asked what Cincinnati's weather was like now.

"Indian summer. But the heat's supposed to break."

"The muggiest place on the face of the earth," Horkow declared proudly.

"Well, not here," said Shelley Horkow. "Here it's always nice. Here we're always great."

She sat down again hard on the chair. The chat was over. And as she did so, there was a commotion at a corner of the room: a little boy, tearing across the floor, heading straight for her. From a woman in the room came a soft cry of unreconstructed immigrant pity—"Ayayay!"—as the child jumped into his mother's lap with a laugh.

Horkow's wife cradled her remaining son. "Did you get a rice cake? I'm glad! And is this peanut butter I see on this mouth?"—and she leaned down to lick the child's lip.

Zwilling withdrew, tacking his way toward a wall, any wall. He then had the luck to catch and follow a scent of coffee to the kitchen, where a young Hispanic woman approached to ask him if he'd like anything to eat or drink.

With his own red mug of coffee, Zwilling hung around in the oversized kitchen. He assumed he was waiting for Selva, wanting her to float up out of this nightmare like a buoy, someone he'd be able to hold on to, but when she continued not to arrive, Zwilling after a while stepped out the kitchen door and onto the wraparound porch.

Stiff gusts of wind piped through concentrations of afternoon shadow. Zwilling momentarily saw Selva through a window to his left. She had moved. Now she appeared to be sitting with her cheek resting against Horkow's mother's back. As Zwilling turned away self-consciously, his jacket touched the white wooden porch railing. The pack of Camels in his pocket pressed into him.

A cigarette hadn't been in Zwilling's mouth ever since his wife's and daughter's deaths. He'd held fast, never wanting to turn Nate into a total orphan before his time. Now he opened the pack and smelled the tobacco. Then he took one of the Camels out.

Unpracticed, Zwilling couldn't get a match started in the strong breeze; he'd need to go back inside to the kitchen to light the thing. And there he happened to walk in on Horkow, who was in the middle of speaking heatedly to a stooped, kind-faced older man: "Because that's the way it *is*, Carl! That's the fucking way it *is*! Tell her—don't tell me." Horkow only then noticed Zwilling. "Hey, here's someone!" He took the writer's elbow—"Let's walk"—and led him back outside.

"And I thought my verandah was long," Zwilling commented as they traversed the porch. He was careful never to let up his stride; he could sense how much Horkow wanted to stop and look at him full-face.

"I never knew you smoked, Joel."

Zwilling dropped the unlit cigarette into his jacket pocket. "I bought these just now in town, don't ask me why. No, I don't smoke."

"You staying with Sel?"

It almost caused Zwilling to jump. "I flew in and my ticket back is for tonight. I'm not staying anywhere."

"Well, you got to meet my folks. Got to meet Maury. He was a furrier, my dad, before he retired. To this day, you can watch him fold down the *Times* with his elbow as he reads it along with his oatmeal in the morning. You realize that someone who works with fur all his life stays hungry for a decent crease."

A knot of people drinking wine from plastic cups lay just ahead. At the sight of the bereaved father and his companion, they naturally slipped to the sides of the porch. Horkow marched right through them without a look or word.

"A decent man, that dad of mine. Pussy-whipped, but what else is new. And as far as I know, he had just one vice in his life. Pistachio nuts. Twice a week he'd hike from Twenty-eighth Street up to Macy's and bring home a bag of the big red ones. Not the showoffy biggest ones, but big enough."

Horkow stopped walking. "When he'd get home he'd put the bag in a kitchen closet that was once the apartment's dumbwaiter. Remember that kind of bag they used to sell bulk nuts in? Crinkly paper, like an English newspaper?"

Zwilling smiled. "I do."

"We'd all take from the bag. My brothers and myself and Maury. Not my mother, nuts didn't agree with her. They never were poured out into a bowl or anything. You opened the door of the dumbwaiter closet; you undid the folds of the bag; you reached in. But because the apartment was so small, everyone meanwhile was *hearing* how many nuts you took."

Horkow began to shake his head. It kept shaking. "You don't choose what you hear. You can't edit. My sweet poor little boy! I saw him later. He looked so serious lying there! He can't hear anymore how much I loved him."

Zwilling put an arm around Horkow. "You know he *had* heard. He already had heard plenty."

Horkow started to sag, giving way under Zwilling's arm. "You know that I killed him, don't you? They jumped me, so I threw them; he

jumped me again and again and I threw him back. They were screaming with laughter. Intelligent monsters throw things." Breaking away
from Zwilling to lean at arm's length against the porch railing,
Horkow came apart.

Then, a minute later, once he'd caught his breath and wiped his
face, he said to Zwilling: "How did *you* do this?"

"Badly. I did it badly. You will also. But just get it done, Brian. It's
the only thing you're really asked to do."

"The stupid things I used to say to you, Joel. Now I understand why
you stopped writing. Really understand."

"All you want to do is get through today and tomorrow."

Horkow reached for Zwilling's hand. "Let's find my darling—you've
met my big sweetheart, Tessa? She's been lying low. I'm glad you came,
Joel."

"Brian, wait, let me tell you something first. I *do* seem to be writing
again. I think it's largely due to you."

But if Horkow heard, or cared, he didn't show it. He led Zwilling
into the house and upstairs and there knocked at the closed door of
his daughter's room. "Tess?" He opened the door half an inch, then
ducked behind Zwilling, starting to leave, heading down the stairs.

"Brian—" Zwilling said with alarm.

"No, go on in. She'll come down a little for you maybe. You're
dressed, aren't you, Tess? I'm sure she is. Go in. Please."

Zwilling was left alone. He knocked on the partly opened door before hesitantly pushing it. The colorful room looked empty, though
then Zwilling made out a form in the bed, beneath a purple-and-
white duvet cover. "I'm sorry . . . "

The girl peeked out. "Who are *you*?"

"My name's Joel. I'm a friend of your father's. He wanted us to meet.
Should I come back later?"

"Oh, then I know who you are. *You're* here? From Cincinnati?" She
sat up. The way her upper lip set itself down unevenly to the lower,
giving the impression of amused words held back, was Brian's exactly.
"I thought they maybe all forgot that I was up here."

"Oh, no, no one's forgotten you at all, Tessa."

"Well, they're pretty busy being angry downstairs. My mom's angry that he made her have the shiver, which she says is just a big *scene*. Daddy got Jewish in Cincinnati, she says, and he brought it back from there. From you, I guess. Is that why you're here?"

Getting out of bed, she didn't let him respond. "I read some of one of your books. I didn't know some of the words but I did *pretty* well." She pointed down at herself: "Still in pajamas! I'll get dressed." Zwilling began leaving, but the girl indicated through an open door a space beyond that was nearly as large as the bedroom itself. Inside were shelves and a dressing table: "My closet."

When she emerged dressed, she led Zwilling down the decklike hallway to a set of stairs different than the one he'd come up on, stairs that emptied directly into the kitchen. She had long pretty hair like her mother's and was even thinner, but in no way ravaged-looking. "I have a good place if you want to take a walk."

Outside on the porch, Tessa pointed with her chin: "There's Aug." The tall sports star was getting out of a car. Tessa's mother, outside to greet him, was almost falling toward him with open arms. Zwilling could hear faint sobs before being drawn away by the girl toward a service road bordering some vineyards.

The tall harvested vines gave Zwilling the sensation of going past gallery upon gallery of distorted figures, mute statuary set strictly one behind the other, stretching down past sight. At forehead height some of them had started to brown autumnally at the tips, while a few still bore swags of dusty grapes left behind. The rows taxed Zwilling's peripheral vision and made him a little queasy. It was a help when Tessa slipped her hand into his.

For it also gave him courage. He had judged that now was the time. "One of my children died in an accident too. Your dad ever mention that to you? She also happened to be a twin."

"How old was she?"

"Seven."

"I'm eleven and I'm not a twin."

"No, I know you're not."

"Do you know what it's called, someone who isn't a twin? I found this out recently. It's called a singleton. It sounds like 'simpleton,' doesn't it? Bimmy's going to be *really* lost now."

"You'll all be lost—and then slowly it will get a little better. Then even a little better. But it's hard to see that now. It takes time."

"My dad'll have it roughest because he thinks he—"

Zwilling couldn't allow her to say it. "Everyone will have it rough. Your mother just as much. Your brother. *You.*"

"Different," she said after a silence. "I'll be in *big* trouble. Daddy's going to hate it even more that I'm sick. He'll probably hate *me.*"

Unsure about whether or not to stop, Zwilling kept walking. "Can I tell you something? It's something true, something that happened to me?"

"You can, sure, why not."

"My mother and father were in concentration camps when they were young—"

"Right, that's the book I read some of, so I know. My dad had it around. Were they as young as me now?"

"A little older, in their late-teens. And they were extremely lucky they didn't die there, weren't killed. But the whole experience changed them. They came to America and afterwards had me—I was their only child.

"And this is the part I want to tell you about. Whenever I would get sick, it would drive my parents *very very* crazy. Not even anything serious, just everyday things like colds or the flu or chicken pox, but it would make them go bonkers. Once I broke my leg and two kids had to bring me home from the schoolyard. As soon as those kids left the house, my mother became hysterical. She even started to beat me with the belt of her robe."

"That's soft. It probably didn't hurt too much."

"I know you understand, though, what I'm telling you."

"That she made you suffer because she couldn't stand you suffering. Her child. I figured that."

"Or herself suffer. Or anyone."

"That *is* crazy."

"It is. Because suffering is part of life. Yet as crazy goes, it's one of the more understandable kinds of crazy, don't you think?"

"How did it make *you* feel when she did that?"

"Sorry that I'd broken my leg. Guilty. And that I *hated* her for hitting me." In Zwilling's pocket, his fingers became a blind crab blundering for the loose cigarette, wishing he could remove it and fire it up.

"You know I have CF, right?" the girl said. "This morning while I was in my room I made a decision. Want to hear it?"

"I do, yes. Tell me."

"I'm going to get completely well."

"Well, that's great, but of course it's also old news, you realize. I know it, your parents know it, your doctors, everyone already knows you are. But it's good that you know it too."

"My dad'll just have to get *unused* to me being sick. I don't mean just *better* or staying *okay* for a while. It's that I'm just not dying."

"*Very* good," Zwilling said seriously. "Me, either."

She looked at him with her first real displeasure.

Zwilling went on: "It's not in my plans, either. When something isn't in my plans I don't keep it much in mind. It doesn't take up much room."

"Your mind?" she teased. She suddenly fanned herself. "Now I'm really warm. Are you?" She turned to go back in the direction they'd come.

Tess asked Zwilling to let her walk behind him, to shield her when they got near the house. Later, in the kitchen, before he could lean down and kiss her, the girl ran up the back steps to her room.

Horkow was nowhere to be seen in the living room. Aug Jimmerson's broad back and shoulders blocked the way while the athlete talked to Horkow's parents, yet from a certain angle around him Zwilling could see Selva. She was again where she'd been before—on the floor by the fireplace, her legs tucked sideways beneath her.

When at last their eyes made contact, Selva did not move. She raised the palm of a flattened hand toward him, and the palm couldn't be misinterpreted. The palm said not *Wait* but *Stop*. It said *Do Not*. She once before had told Zwilling she lived in a partial yet not an impoverished world—and she was telling this to him again, right now.

Without words, without even proximity, she was loving him enough to leave him be. She was asking him to try to do the same. They simply both would have to accept such a barely humane freedom.

And then her hand began to tilt, its fingers making a tamping motion of go-away. Go right *now,* she was telling him, go while Horkow wasn't in the room. Zwilling understood, though it was all but unbearable that the best he could give her back was a small unworthy wave as a tribute to that understanding.

At the front door, Zwilling encountered the very famous movie star Phil Dreyer, who was coming into the house. For a moment they blocked each other's way, both of them feinting left and right—"Sorry," "Sorry"—the common idiot's dance of embarrassed laughs, both of them on the wrong time because it was the same time. Finally, it was Phil Dreyer who froze first, letting Zwilling pass.